PRAISE FOR

D1536569

"A. C. Britt crosses bound͏͏ A
suspenseful tale that takes read͏

der

"Non-stop drama-filled action, packed with love, betrayal, passion, sex and truth. A. C. Britt sizzles onto the literary scene!"
—Tony Collins, Author of *Games Women Play*

"*LONDON REIGN* is fire! A. C. Britt brings 'the hotness in the streets' with this incredible story! A must read!"
—Cartel: Castillo, Author of *Ghost Town Hustlers*

"A. C. Britt is bringing a new swagger to the lit game. Ladies, watch out!"
—Kashamba Williams, Essence Best Selling Author

"A. C. Britt's *LONDON REIGN* gets 'tens' across-the-board!"
—Harmonica Sunbeam, Performance Artist

"Hardcore, shocking and suspenseful, A. C. Britt's debut novel, *LONDON REIGN* is superbly written."
—Blue, Author of *Tattooed Tears*

"Captivating and raw, *LONDON REIGN* is an eye-opening tale of sexual identity, social mishap and spiritual redemption."
—Charles D. Ellison, Author of *Tantrum*

"*LONDON REIGN* will have you intrigued from start to finish. The novel is amazing!"
—Self, Author of *Love & Betrayal*

"Like a flaming stick of dynamite, A. C. Britt explodes onto the streets with *LONDON REIGN*! A suspenseful page-turner."
—Reginald Hall, Author of *I'm In Love With A Thug*

GHETTOHEAT® PRODUCTIONS

GHETTOHEAT®
HARDER
CONVICT'S CANDY
AND GOD CREATED WOMAN
SONZ OF DARKNESS
GAMES WOMEN PLAY
TANTRUM
GHOST TOWN HUSTLERS
BOY-TOY
SKATE ON!
PARIS SKY
SOME SEXY, ORGASM 1
SOME SEXY, ORGASM 2

A GHETTOHEAT® PRODUCTION

A.C. BRITT

LONDON REIGN

Published by GHETTOHEAT®, LLC
P.O. BOX 2746, NEW YORK, NY 10027, USA

Library of Congress Control Number: 2007934965

ISBN: 978-0-9742982-3-8

Printed in the USA. First Edition, September 2007

ACKNOWLEDGMENTS

I'd like to thank HICKSON and GHETTOHEAT® for giving me the opportunity to fulfill my dreams as a writer.

My mother, Lynnette Culbreath, for just being mommy—ready to take on whatever adventure I throw your way.

My brother, Brandon, I'm glad that you're released and was found not guilty from the crime you were wrongly accused of. I love you! Stay strong!

Danielle Forde, Jasmine Haynes, Ebony Floyd, Shavon Fulcher, and many more for being my support and encouragement when it seemed like my words would never reach the stands.

Tabitha Gaston, for being the most supportive and encouraging boss I could ever have...thank you!

Naomi and TJ, you made it through some of the hardest times of your life, and you're still here! Don't give up.

To the Housing Department, thanks for being just as excited about this book as I am.

The entire GHETTOHEAT® family...thanks for welcoming me with open arms.

Young people of today, life can be REALLY hard, but if you stay strong, determined, and willing to succeed, to survive, then you will.

Most importantly, I'd like to thank the readers, because without you, *LONDON REIGN* would be just words on paper.

Dedicated to gay, lesbian, bisexual and transgender youth. Who you love and date, does not have to define your whole existence. Strive for the very highest, knowing that there's plenty of support along the way.

LONDON REIGN

ROUTINES

My sister Shantell watches me every morning as I put on a white "wife beater" tank top, two oversized t-shirts, either a oxford or a polo, a sweater, size thirty-four baggy jeans (I wear a size thirty), *Timberland* construction boots, a black flight jacket with orange lining, and a classic *Red Sox* baseball cap that forms to my head just right.

I line up my sideburns every morning, and stop at *Brotha's Keeper* barbershop, getting my fade lined and trimmed when needed.

I'm only sixteen, but I stand at an even six feet, weigh one-hundred-and-forty pounds, and have a size twelve foot. I adjust myself like most dudes do, and make *sure* that my pants are always hanging down low.

"Damn Shantell, why you be *sweating* me every morning?" I ask, as I exit the bathroom and grab my *Gap* one-strap book bag off the bed.

"I don't *understand* you, London," Shantell answers, with the same confused look upon her face she carried every morning.

"You're not suppose to understand me, you're just suppose to love me and let me do my thing," I reply before clearing my throat and cracking Shantell a smile. My voice is fairly deep, most compared to an alto in the music world.

"Seriously, London, you go through this w-h-o-l-e routine. For what, to live up to this *image* you've created? Sometimes I just don't get it. It seems like it just takes too much work," Shantell explains.

"'Sup, ma," I say, as I enter the kitchen several minutes later.

"Nothing, baby! Where are you headed today?" my mother asks as she fixes my father's lunch.

"Hang out with my boys...probably see if Lexi wants to catch that movie *Ali*—and I'm not sure what else after that. Basically chill I guess." I smile at my moms, grab a piece of toast out of the toaster, and head for the front door.

"London," she calls, just as I was about to walk out the door.

"Yeah."

"Please be careful."

My mother always has this look of worry in her eyes…I wish that she didn't worry about me so much, but I guess that's what mothers do best.

"Always, ma. Always," I say, as I walk back into the kitchen and give her a big hug and a kiss.

Moms is mad cool.

She's the type of mother who will put you in your place, but go out of her way to be understanding to the things you do. She's real easy to talk to—never makes you feel like an idiot.

My moms is so beautiful, she's shorter than I am of course, has long black hair that reaches to the middle of her back, and hazel eyes; that are almost scary at times. My mother used to be in all kinds of beauty pageants and stuff, and has won over thirty trophies, and other prizes.

Now, she just kinda stays home and does the "housewife" thing. Moms worked as a teacher at *Martin Luther King's* middle school, but she wanted to open up her own business doing consulting and all that. She's still working on that, but my pops makes enough money to where moms aingt really gotta work.

She comes from a pretty cool family; my mother is the youngest of four girls. My three aunts are usually just as cool as my moms, but none of us really see them that often. Although we live in *"The Bean"*, my mother is actually from *Atlanta, Georgia.*

They moved up here when my moms was fourteen, and my mother's been here ever since. My two oldest aunts have since moved back to *Atlanta,* but the one who's a year older than my moms still lives here.

Like I said, we don't see her, my other aunts or my grandparents that much. It's mainly because of the way my father be acting, but that's a "situation" of its own. My grandparents moved to *Springfield* seven years ago, and they aingt trying to move back into the city.

It's funny because I look at old pictures, and I can tell that moms was pulling *niggas* left-and-right. I mean, I'm grateful that she met my pops, because I wouldn't be here if she hadn't. But hell, I *know* she had *niggas* much better than him trying to get with her.

My moms met my father like two years after she moved up here, and got pregnant with me when she was seventeen; my mother had gotten pregnant with Shantell a few months shy of her nineteenth birthday. I *guess* my pops was her first real love, because of the *way* it's been explained.

Moms was sprung….

They aingt get married until I was five years old, but I guess my father gets a little bit of props for even deciding to marry my moms. She made it work though, my mother finished high school, and got a teaching degree a few years later. She's always been the motivated type, at least when it comes to success.

But lately, it's like moms don't even care about their relationship. She's comfortable, or rather, feels like she has an "obligation" to stay in a *fucked* up situation.

Anyway, Shantell is my fifteen-year-old sister. She looks just like my mother, everything from the eyes, to the hair, to the shape my moms had, before she became a mother. Shantell is mad cool, because she can feel *everything* that I do, and tries to understand why I do it.

Of course Shantell be trying to put me in check and *shit*, but that's because she says I'm a *"straight-up dog"* when it comes to these *hoes* that be 'round here! I tell my sister: *"It aingt like I'm trying to play them or nothing, but if you present yourself wrong, then you get treated wrong."*

Shantell can feel that theory though.

She's just mad because this chick, Lexi is really *digging* me, but all I *really* want to do when it comes to Lexi is hit that! Lexi knows that though, so I don't even know why she even steps to my sister with bullshit.

I mean, I *guess* if I was ready to settle, then Lexi could possibly be the one…but I aingt *trying* to "feel" that right now, so Lexi just needs to stop hoping.

Besides, Lexi's chilling. She still be showing up at my doorstep when I tell her to, and letting me come over and do whatever.

Whenever….

So why should *I* change?

…Lexi's mad sexy though. She's half *Italian*, half *Cape Verdean*. Lexi has short brown hair with blond highlights, and big brown eyes.

12

Her body is banging!

And the sex is off-da-chain.

I will admit, even though I treat Lexi like *shit* most of the time, she's *always* there for me when I need her. Shantell wants me to give Lexi a fair chance, but like I said...I aingt *ready* for all that!

Pops is a different story.

I get my height and temper from him. He's six-feet-four, and weighs two-hundred-and-something pounds. My father is an alcoholic, and mad, mad abusive.

Both physically and mentally.

He comes from a family of alcoholics—his pops was one, his grandfather was one, and his brother is one.

The cycle just continues, I guess...it's *fucked* up.

Moms says that my father has been drinking for as long as she can remember...although he said that he would *"never turn out like his father...or his grandfather...."*

I *guess* it was inevitable.

My pops, Randy James Walters, was twenty-one when he met my mother. I guess the age difference wasn't that bad, but my father still knew a lot more about the world than she did. That *nigga* knew *exactly* what he wanted, and how to get it!

Pops aingt waste no time *fucking* my moms, getting her knocked up—twice! From my understanding, my grandpa was *pissed,* he *knew* my father was no good, but moms wasn't trying to hear it.

It had to be a warped perception of love, because moms ran off with my pops for a while, but once it started becoming noticeable that she was pregnant with me, ole Randy wasn't trying to have no part in it, and my moms showed back up on my grandparents doorstep looking for forgiveness.

No words needed to be exchanged...

Because she knew.

I'd like to say that my moms learned a real quick lesson, but we know that *aingt* the case, because Shantell exist. All my father had to do was sweet talk her right-quick, and moms was right back with him.

She had me, and things were straight, but pops still wasn't trying to settle. He had his "way" with words, and my father was still able to pull mad chicks, and keep my moms.

I *guess* you can say that I get that *shit* from him!

...My way with words.

My ability to pull mad chicks.

It's real funny how I inherited all the negative *shit* from my pops, because there aingt too much good to that *nigga!*

Anyway, before they knew it, moms was pregnant again, and nine months later, Shantell came along. It was rough in the beginning. My father was out doing his own thing, and moms was stuck taking care of us by herself. She'd get a little bit of help from her sisters and my grandparents, but everyone shared the same view then: *"She made you...she gotta take care of you."*

Moms was strong though. She got her shape back, and started entering beauty contests and pageants. Moms started winning, making a little money, getting modeling offers. It was peace, and an eye-opener as well, because pops soon realized that, moms was a dime.

They got hitched.

They still together.

Shit aingt blissful though.

Moms and pops just together to be together.

'Cause we all know that when ole Randy drinks, *everyone* needs to take cover!

My father don't do nothing to Shantell, but he's always taking *shit* out on me most of the time, as well as on my moms sometimes. Whenever pops goes after my mother, that's when I jump in, therefore, I end up getting hit anyway.

But I hold my own though.

I don't just *sit* there and let that *nigga* beat on me, or no *shit* like that. Please, I'll put a gun to his head before I ever let my father just beat my *ass!*

I don't think we've ever really gotten along, except when I was little. I don't even remember when the hitting first started...yet, it's always been understood that, if Randy's been drinking, *shit* will go down!

I guess he used to really beat up on my moms...I can still remember pops coming at me, 'cause I talked mad *shit* to him!

I'm *always* sticking up for moms, and the older I get, the worse it tends to get. I feel like I have to protect her, 'cause moms aingt trying to leave him.

Moms is too content, or insecure or something.

She just *can't* let go.

Don't get me wrong, my father does good stuff, too. Like,

14

keeps this roof over our heads, puts food on the table. Me and Shantell aingt gotta want for nothing—if we want it, pops gets it. But, when he's drunk, *shit* aingt right!

My father used to always take me to baseball and basketball games. He even taught me how to build things like bookcases and cabinets, and other *shit* 'round the house. He says, *"Everyone needs to know one thing they're really good at, 'cause you never know when you might need to use it."*

Me and pops were good.

I felt like he really loved me back then...

But somewhere, we lost that *shit*.

And it *aingt* been right ever since.

I just wish that my father would recognize that he has a problem. It's bad enough that there *aingt* that many Black families out there that have both a mother and a father in the home.

But all is pointless when the family is *fucked* up!

I remember telling my pops once that he should go to rehab, or an *AA* meeting. Needless to say he *beat* my *ass!* My father got arrested, and I landed in the hospital, but before they could even stitch me up completely, his ass was right back at home, sipping on an *Ice House Beer.*

Like I said, a way with words. No charges that stuck, no *DSS* involvement, nothing but a doctor's bill that pops made me work off. It's sad that we fight all the time, it's usually like World War III in this house: when *HELL* breaks loose—watch out!

It's to the point where we can't even be in the same room for more than ten minutes before we're cussing each other out. The police have been called on us so many times that, I can't even count anymore.

My mother has had three windows replaced.

A coffee table fixed.

Two closet doors have been ripped off the hinges.

And my room has had to be re-plastered four times.

It aingt *nothing* to be proud of, but shit happens, you know.

My father has had three felony child abuse charges placed on him, but they were all dropped. Me, on the other hand, has had six aggravated assault charges with three convictions. I spent a year in *DYS,* and like two years on probation.

The officer said that it's because I always threw the first punch, but that aingt true—it's usually equal. But somehow, pops always gets those *damn* self-defense laws to work in his favor, acting like he scared of me and *shit!*

Tell me how that *nigga* is going to be scared of me? I'm *fucking* skinny-as-hell, and he's going to be scared of me?

That's *bullshit!*

Anyway, today I want to get out the house before my father comes downstairs. I'm not even *trying* to hear his mouth. He's just going to say the same *shit* about how he don't like the way I act, and how I dress. That *shit* is old...pops needs to accept me for who I am, 'cause I *aingt* changing for no one! He says shit like, I embarrass him, and that he *never* wants to be in public with me.

I don't give a *fuck* though!

...My father act like hanging out with him is cool.

That aingt doing *shit* for me!

I manage to run out the door, just as pops is coming out the bathroom. We live in a pretty peaceful brownstone, but the neighborhood is anything but peaceful.

* * * * *

"Yo, *nigga,* what up?" my boy Scottie says, as I come 'round the corner.

"Nothing, son; just chilling. What up with you?"

"Same ole, same ole, kid. Trying to make that paper. My seed's mother keeps *hassling* me about how Drake needs this-'n-that. M-a-n, that *bitch* is *fucking* greedy-as-hell, 'cause I gave her a G about two weeks ago. Plus, she works a nine-to-five job—she aingt pressed for money!" Scottie says, as he lights up a *Newport* cigarette.

"Damn, Scottie man," I reply, as I kinda laugh at his situation. "Yo, *nigga,* how long you going to be holding up this corner?"

"For a grip, London, man. So go do your thing, and hit me up when you head back home," Scottie says while giving me daps.

"Yeah, *nigga,* you know I gotta go get my fresh tape and shit."

"All the time, kid."

I walk down this same street all the time, and every day, the same *niggas* and *hoes* either be sweating me, or hating on me. Some cats want to know who I am, while others are just like: *"That's just London."*

16

Take Lexi for instance. I met her about four months ago, and told Lexi what the deal was from-the-jump. That was good for me because, I usually don't put it out there like that so early. I usually just want to *fuck*-them-and-leave-them, and call it a day!

No commitments or any-of-that *shit!*

Everything was peace until her peeps start trying to get Lexi to check me and *shit!* They're like: *"Lexi, you need to check London. Something aingt right about that nigga...."* So she comes trying to regulate on me, but by the time it's all over, were back in Lexi's bed, doing our thing.

It's simple.

I gotta laugh about that *shit* because, it's simple...to me anyway. This whole thing works in my favor. Lexi fronts like the *shit* aingt right, or it don't work...but it does. *Shit,* if she truly had a problem with the way things are, Lexi would say something, or more importantly, she'd stop *fucking* with me.

I'm saying, Lexi's like eighteen, and she's been on her own for mad long. If Lexi didn't like it, she wouldn't let me keep doing it. I don't really understand chicks...how they let their friends brainwash them, making them think that their *nigga* aingt right for them. Half the time, the ones giving the advice aingt even *got* nobody. All of Lexi's friends are trifling anyway, my sister is about the *only* decent person she hangs with.

Lexi aingt going nowhere. Every now-'n-then, she'll come to me with some *bullshit* that her girls put in her ear, but really, Lexi aingt going nowhere.

I guess I could say that I got her wrapped!

Lexi be talking about how she aingt *never* felt this way about no one. I'm always trying to turn our serious conversations into a joke. I usually say some *shit* about my sexual performance... about how Lexi likes the way I go down on her....

Lexi just looks at me and rolls her eyes.

Honestly...I don't want to think about no serious *shit,* I'm too young. I'm just a *nigga* trying to get mine! Shantell has a whole other take on it though. She thinks that I'm lying to myself, and that I really do want more than just sex from Lexi. Shantell thinks that I'm scared about what a commitment would do to my hardcore "AG" image.

I just listen because I can't really say nothing.

Anything is possible...

But that aingt no *shit* I want to think about.

I like it the way it is!

At eleven o'clock, I meet up with my boys, Shawn and Maverick. Shawn is this cool cat from *Dorchester,* and Maverick is this Dominican kid who just moved to *Boston* from *Spanish Harlem.* He's mad funny because, everything he says, has to do with *New York.* This kid has been in *"The Bean"* for six months, but I guess it's a golden rule to always stay true to your block. Maverick just needs to learn that he can't be putting *New York* up against *"The Bean"* all the time.

Maverick's liable to get his *ass* kicked!

Anyway, the three of us do the same *shit* everyday. None of us go to school for various reasons, but Shawn's peoples are the only ones that don't realize that he doesn't go to school. As a result, we always go to Maverick's house; Maverick's mother works all day, so that's another reason why we always go to his crib. We always smoke two L's, then get this drunk named, "Retro" to buy us a case of *Corona.*

The three of us pass by *My Brotha's Keeper* barbershop, and I detour to get my usual line-up and tape. Upon entering the shop, Maverick immediately claims a seat and begins flipping through a three-month-old issue of *Vibe.*

"Damn, London, you don't *need* a haircut!" Shawn says, as if his patience is running thin. *"Nigga,* you do this *shit* everyday, your hair *probably* don't even know to grow anymore."

"Whatever. Shawn, you the one who needs to be sitting in this chair," I say, as I smacked him in his Afro; which is still crinkled from the braids he'd just taken out.

"Please, kid, *no* one is putting a clipper to this head. I'm like Sampson, cutting my hair will drain my energy. How you expect me to *fuck* after that?" he asks jokingly.

"Shut the *fuck* up *nigga.* You aingt getting none no way," I say, as everyone in the barbershop starts laughing.

"Nigga, please! That's why I had Shantell screaming my name last night: 'Oh Shawn'," Shawn replies, trying to sound like a horny female.

"Nigga...your *dick* aingt big enough for Shantell to *fuck.* She said you gotta at least be bigger than your five-year-old brother, before Shantell would ever consider grinding with you." I sit in the chair waiting for a reply, but Shawn just gives me a look that says he'll get me back later. Maverick tries hard to hide his obvious enjoyment in the situation; his body bounces in the failed attempt.

I then pay the usual ten dollars, and the three of us head to Maverick's house, which is only three blocks away. When we walk into the house, Maverick's older sister, Luisa is cooking breakfast: "Why aren't you all in school?" she asks.

"Teacher workday," I answer, as I slightly bite my bottom lip. "What you got cooking for me?"

Luisa rolls her eyes, "Nothing."

"Damn, Luisa, you stay dogging me. What's the deal with that?"

"You *know* the deal, London."

"Do I? I seemed to have forgotten, can you refresh my memory?" I then walk up to Luisa, so close, that I could feel her breath. I have my hands in my pocket, as I look Luisa up-and-down two times: "I'm saying Luisa, you know you're digging me...why you tripping?"

"Tripping? Hell, London, *you're* the one tripping.... Looks like you've fallen flat on your face. Sweetie, I will admit, you are kind of cute, considering...but *you*, don't have *anything* I want!"

Having that being said, Luisa takes her food into her room, and closed the door behind her.

"You gas, *nigga*," Shawn says and laughs, as he breaks open a *Dutch Master.*

"*Nigga,* shut the *fuck* up and roll the blunt." I really don't see why I hang 'round with this kid. Shawn's ignorant-as-hell, and all he talks about is wanting to *fuck* my sister. I mean, I know I can be the same way at times, but that's my little sister he be talking about. Yet, within the hour, the three of us killed two blunts and one case of *Corona.*

Now, I'm feeling good, and think it would be a cool time to connect with Lexi. We meet up 'round one o'clock, and she gives me the best head I've had in a long time.

"London," Lexi whispers.

"What?"

"Why is it that you *only* call me when you're high and horny?"

"That's not the only time I call you," I answer, barely looking in Lexi's direction.

"Okay...so when you're trying to prove yourself as well," Lexi says in a sarcastic tone. I glance at her while smiling, noticing that Lexi has an attitude. *She stays with the in-depth conversations.*

"Well, Lexi...why is it that you *always* let me come over?" I ask, even though I already know the answer.

"Because I'm stupid, and because I love your complicated ass," Lexi replies with tears forming in her eyes.

"First of all, you aingt stupid, but overall, Lexi, that *aingt* my fault," I retort, trying to pretend that I don't care. "You know as well as I do that, no matter how bad I treat you, you're going to be ready to give me head, any time I ask," I say before I laugh.

"Well, maybe I should stop! You're a fucking asshole sometimes!" Lexi shot back with tension.

"Maybe you should...but you won't." I give her a kiss, and begin putting my clothes back on. Lexi continues to lay down while shaking her head in disbelief.

I do treat Lexi like *shit.*

But I treat *everyone* like *shit.*

When they get tired of it, they leave.

But Lexi won't go...

And I aingt trying to push her away, for whatever reason.

"WHAT?" I ask.

"Nothing"

"Lexi, you just be *pushing* me too hard. You asking me for shit I can't do. You know that when we first got together, I *told* you how I wanted it. You said you understood."

"I do...it's just that, what I *don't* understand is how you could really *fuck* somebody almost everyday for the last four months, and feel absolutely nothing for that person. That's what I'm saying, London.... It's okay though...I *don't* even care."

Lexi then put her clothes back on and went into the bathroom to take a shower. I had to leave, it was already three o'clock, and Shantell wanted me to meet her at school. Shantell briefly mentioned something about some kid named, Ryan who was pushing up on her and *shit*—of course Shantell needed me to take care of it.

"Yo, I'm out, Lexi," I yell, as I walk out the door. She doesn't respond, but I don't have nothing to worry about. Lexi needs to try and "check" me from time-to-time, to feel alright about this *shit.* I *guess* I need to act like I don't care, in order for me to feel alright as well.

I make my way to Shantell's school—she always needs

me to take care of shit for her. Ever since we were kids, Shantell would come running to me for help, because some *nigga* was fucking with her on the playground. I didn't mind then, and I still don't.

It's one of those things that has become expected—you know, understood. If there's a problem: go get London.

It'll be taken cared of.

I'll say what I gotta say, or do what I gotta do, then everything would be cool. Sometimes, I just wish Shantell would fight her own battles though, she's too dependent on me. I don't mind protecting my sister, but I just need to know that she's capable of taking care of herself.

Shantell don't always realize how much heat I take because of the shit she gets into. But she's my sister...it's my job.

I'd die for Shantell if I had to.

BEAT-DOWNS
chapter 2

I stand outside of the main entrance to *John D. O'Bryant High School.* I watch as all the students file out in mobs, rushing to catch the bus heading to *Ruggles Station.* I use to go to this school, but I got kicked out. Then I enrolled into *Madison,* right next door, but I got kicked out of there, too.

I'm not even suppose to be on the grounds, but I aingt about to let some *nigga* disrespect my sister and *shit!* It's not like I'm bad or nothing, it's just that I got a bad temper, and I use to get into a lot of fights. It's like when I get to a certain point of rage, I just lose all insight of what's going on.

The administrators were tired of me fighting and destroying *shit.* They began to classify my physical aggression as a weapon....

Fucked up, right?

They'd told me if I got into another fight, then I would be expelled under the *No Tolerance Law.*

I aingt last one day.

My father worked something out, and I was able to enroll into *Madison* a month later. I fought a teacher at that school, and got expelled from the entire *Boston Public School System.* That was six months ago, and I aingt bother to do anything else since.

I'm glad today is Friday, because this chick named, Nina, usually comes to the city on Saturdays to see her grandmother. Nina is this fly honey that live out in *Bridgewater.* She started staying with her grandmother on the weekends after her grandfather died.

Nina's real sweet...A little *too* sweet for my kind.

I want this chick real bad, but it's been a little harder getting Nina than I expected. The closest I've gotten was a kiss, but she became very scared. Nina's one of those innocent girls, the ones who mess with *niggas* that go to church and ask their parents permission to date their daughter.

Nina said she can't bring nobody like me home, because her pops would flip! She's a virgin, so Nina really aingt trying to fuck...but I'm working on that.

She's cute, straight-up *Portuguese*—nothing else.

Pretty green eyes…

Full luscious lips…

Big breasts for days!

Nina's only like fifteen, so I guess that aingt bad. Anyway, she's suppose to come into the city, and if Nina does, I'm going to work my charm.

Shantell and her girls were the last people to come out the building. I'm standing on the wall giggling to myself, because I can hear her friends talking about how fly I am and *shit!* They had some new chick with them, she's kinda cute, not really my type.

But cutie is definitely *"fuckable"*.

The girl sparked a little interest in me because, the rest of Shantell's friends are kinda at the bottom of the barrel. I don't even know why my sister kicks it with them like that. They make Shantell look bad. She's the prettiest one of all, by a long shot. Ha, perhaps that's why Shantell hangs with them.

No competition.

"Shantell," the new chick states, "check out that dude over there. He's so off-da-hook—how do I look?" the girl asks while trying to fix her hair. Shantell and Ariel just laughs a little.

"Camille, I hate to burst your bubble, but that aingt no one but London," Ariel says. Camille's mouth literally drops to the ground.

"That's London?" Camille responds, shaking her head in disbelief.

"Don't make any sense, right?" Ariel asks.

"Not at all," Camille answers. I leave my chill spot and walk over to where the girls are standing: "'Sup, kiddies?"

"Kids? The last time I *checked,* London, you were *only* a year older than us. But why is it that we'll *graduate* before you, by like, three years?" Ariel retorts with much attitude.

"Suck my *dick!*" I spit.

"Grow one first, London," Ariel replies. Camille now starts to laugh.

"What the *fuck* are you laughing at?" I ask violently. Camille looks at me, confused.

"London, chill. They aingt the enemy," Shantell indicates. "London, this is Camille. Camille, this is London," Shantell introduces us.

"Peace," I say.

"Yeah," Camille responds, still sounding confused.

"Don't mind me, that's just how I am," I reassure her, but Camille then gives me a look like she isn't feeling me.

"London, walk us to the station. Ryan usually hangs around there until he sees us walk by, then he *aggravates* us the whole way home practically," Shantell says.

"Yo, what this *nigga* look like anyway?"

"He's shorter than you, London, but you both weigh about the same. Ryan's a little *punk,* but he got a lot of mouth!"

We then walk to *Dudley Station*, because the girls wanted to get something to eat. I tell Shantell that if she and her friends take the bus to *Ruggles Station*, then they probably wouldn't even be going through this right now. But you can't tell Shantell nothing though, she thinks she's hard and shit, but Shantell's a little prissy when it comes down to it.

Shantell's has a big mouth, but, every time she gets into a situation, Shantell comes running to me. She now wants me to walk with one of the other girls, because Shantell figures that Ryan wouldn't try to mess with her, if he saw me walking with Shantell.

Halfway to the station, this dude who had to be at least nineteen or twenty-years-old, came out of nowhere grabbing on Shantell's arm.

"'Sup, Shantell? You can't give a *nigga* no love?" Ryan says aggressively.

"Get out my face, Ryan," Shantell blurts. She tries to walk around Ryan, but he keeps jumping in Shantell's path.

"Shantell, all I want is a hug, maybe a kiss...why you *acting* like this?" Ryan asks, still blocking Shantell's way.

"Get the *fuck* out my face, Ryan!"

"*Bitch* what? Who you trying to show out for? These hoes? This *punk*-nigga?"

"Hold up, hold up," I say, pushing Camille and Ariel behind me. "*Nigga,* you aingt *hear* what she said? Get the *fuck* out her face!"

"What? *Nigga,* do you *know* who I am?" Ryan asks, almost appalled that I stepped to him. "Who the *fuck* is this *punk*-nigga? With your *bitch*-sounding *ass.* Move, *fool,* before you get a *cap* bust—"

Before Ryan could even finish his sentence, I knock him in his right eye. So hard, that Ryan loses his balance, and falls to the ground. I then jump on top of Ryan, and start jabbing him in his face. Ryan tries to push me off, and kicks me in my stomach.

When I fall to the ground, Ryan then tries to kick me in my head, but I move out the way and catch his foot, causing Ryan to fall back down. We were both punching each other any place we could.

Ryan then has me pinned up against this brick building, trying to punch me in the eye. I kick him one good time in the nuts, before some people on the street come and break us up. It takes like four people to hold us back.

"*Nigga,* I will *kill* you if you *ever* step foot on this side of town again!" Ryan shouts, obviously embarrassed because he looks a lot worse than I do.

"*Fuck* you, *nigga!* Stay away from my sister!"

"*Nigga,* if your *bitch*-ass sister wouldn't present herself like a *fucking* hoe, then I wouldn't treat her like one! She want to try and play me and *shit!* Want to be all friendly and flirting, but then when I step to her, she want to run and get you? *Fuck* you and *fuck* her!"

"I don't care, *nigga.* However the situation went down, my sister aingt trying to deal with you now, so stay the *fuck* away from her!" My eyes are now red, because when I get real angry, I always cry a little.

"*NIGGA,* I WILL *KILL* YOU!" Ryan yells, as Shantell and her friends tries to pull me away.

"Yeah right, kid. You look like a *fool* for even putting that threat out there. *Nigga,* if anything happens to me or my sister, or her friends, you'll be the first person they come after."

Shantell and her girls continue to push me in the direction of the station. I snatch my body away from their grip, and walk like two feet ahead of them. I think about everything that just went down, before I stop dead in my tracks, causing Ariel to bump into me.

I then turn 'round, and I must have a real evil look on my face, because all three of the girls jump when I turn 'round.

"Stay away from him!" I yell. "You *can't* keep having me fight all these crazy *muthafuckas,* Shantell. You trying to get me *killed* or something? It's bad enough that daddy tries to *beat* my ass, all the *damn* time! *Shit,* Shantell, this nonsense is driving me crazy! Chill with it, aiiight? Don't even come this way anymore, or I'll *beat* your *ass!*"

The three of them then looks at each other, not really certain if they should respond, or even breathe for that matter. This *shit* is intense! The way Ryan threatens to kill me, the look he had in his eye—that *shit* shook me a little, but not enough for it to matter.

You know…I got into a lot of fights, but I aingt *never* had no *nigga*, threaten my life, even if it was just words. This *nigga*, Ryan though…there's something about him. He aingt no average *nigga*. You can tell Ryan's *ass* has a lot to prove, and a lot of people to prove it to.

This *shit* is real fucked up!

"London," Shantell begins. There's no need to respond verbally, the look on my face says it all, and as a result, the rest of the travel home is silent.

I hate fighting.

Both of Shantell's friends live on our block. It's kinda one of those things where first impressions are lasting, because Camille just gives a nod and goes on her way. Ariel walks with me and Shantell for another five minutes before detouring up her dead-end street. I kinda wonder what's going through Camille's mind…what Shantell and Ariel have told her about me, and how Camille feels about it. In a way, I really don't give a *fuck,* but the constant look of confusion upon her face, makes me wonder.

"Thanks," Shantell now mumbles, as we walk up the stairs to the house. "I wasn't trying to get you caught up. I wasn't even trying to get you to fight Ryan, I just—"

"Just knew I *would* end up fighting Ryan, which is fine. You're use to me protecting you, but *shit,* Shantell, half the *shit* you get into, you create.

"Shantell, you like the attention from that *nigga.* You like the fact that some *fucking* asshole, yelled *shit* at you as you walked by. If you didn't truly like it, then you would've stopped walking by Ryan's *ass* a long time ago.

"It was all good, until you *fucked* up and started flirting back—you got scared once he started taking your *ass* seriously. That's the *shit* you didn't like, then—"

"London, that's not *even* the case," Shantell says, interrupting me.

"Then, like I was saying, when Ryan's *ass* really pushed up on you, you come running behind me."

"Hell, London, if that's how you feel then, you didn't

26

have to fight for me; it aingt that *fucking* serious, London."

"Shantell, you're missing the *fucking* point. Seriously, listen to what the *fuck* I'm saying."

"Speak then."

"Shut-the-*fuck*-up then!" I retort. Shantell gives me this look of aggravation, and sarcastically sat down on our couch. She looks up at me and pretends to patiently wait for me to finish. "As I was saying, you put yourself in these *fucked* up situations, and I'm constantly bailing your ass out. Understand me when I say that I would do anything to protect you, but just be cautious. Shantell, stay away from that nigga" I demand.

Shantell smiles at me and stands up. The top of her head comes just above my breastbone. "I love you, London, and seriously, thank you." Shantell then smiles, reaches up and kisses me on my cheek. I kiss her back on her forehead, and go into the kitchen to get something to eat. My moms looks up from the meal she's preparing and smiles.

"You're home early," My moms says.

"Yep."

"Come here...who you been fighting today?" she asks, as my mother examines the small cut I have over my left eye.

"No one, just this *nigga* that was messing with Shantell; that's it."

My moms shakes her head and continues to cook dinner. I reach over her shoulder and grab a piece of fried chicken that my moms just took out of the scorching hot grease.

"London, did you wash your hands?"

"U-m-m-m."

"I didn't think so—get out of here," my moms replies. I now grab a paper towel to place my chicken in, and reach in the freezer for an eye pack. My black eye is beginning to form, and I don't want it to swell too bad. "London, you need to *stop* all that *damn* fighting, enough goes on around here. You don't *need* to be out in the street doing it, too."

"I was protecting Shantell, ma."

"I don't give-a-*damn*. Shantell needs to learn how to protect herself. I tried my hardest to teach you all that there are other ways to handle situations without using your fists." My mother holds up her fists to reiterate her point: "You would *think* you'd get tired of stitches and black eyes, London."

I have no comment.

My moms has this way of lecturing you, and making you feel like *shit* by the end of it. I just smile, because I honestly can't promise that I won't fight no more.

That's like saying I'm not going to fuck Lexi no more…

It's just not realistic.

I grab the ice and chicken, and run up to my room. Within the hour, I go back out on the street and chill with Scottie, as he holds down the corner….

*　*　*　*　*

Three weeks passes since the fight with Ryan. Shantell mentions something about seeing him downtown. She says Ryan was talking about how I better watch my back, because he's going to kick my *ass,* and all that other *shit!*

I'm not pressed though.

I'm saying, this *nigga* is all talk anyway, at least that's what I was told. Many cats said that Ryan wouldn't have even fought me if there wasn't an audience.

They say he's a *punk!*

And that Ryan always gets beat up.

Shit, the way they make it sound, Shantell didn't even need me to handle him. But she aingt about to fight no chick, let alone a *nigga.*

The tension 'round here is starting to rise again. My father is drinking a lot lately, and of course, I'm always the one to suffer from it. If he's not lashing out at me, then pops is all in my mom's face about all kinds of *bullshit!* But mainly the fact that *shit* 'round the house *aingt* how my father wants it to be, and how *I* don't "act" the way he wants me to "act".

FUCK THAT!

Pops may have made me, but he aingt got *no* control over me! …*Nigga* aingt worth it.

The past few nights have been filled with arguing, and crying, and all kinds of *shit* that neither Shantell nor me, wanted to be 'round. I decide to get a room out in the burbs, and choose to take Shantell with me.

"Where the *fuck* do you think your going?" my father asks angrily.

"Out of here, away from your *crazy* ass!" I say. "Yo, I'm not trying to stay here in this house while you're on vacation—*nigga,* please!" I then begin to walk away, and he grabs me by my collar and pushes me into the door.

"Randy no!" my mother shouts. "Please don't start that right now. Just let them go wherever they're going. Please, Randy," she begs.

"WOMAN, SHUT UP! ...You two aingt going *nowhere*, now, get up stairs!" he says while smacking me upside my head.

"Daddy stop!" Shantell cries. She freaks out when pops and I get into it. Shantell always assumes that one of us will end up dead or something. She backs herself into the corner by the stairs and slides down the wall, screaming and begging my father to stop. Moms just stands there, like a deer caught in the headlights.

Pops then snatches my bag out my hand, and throws it to the other side of the room. This causes the lamp to fall first, followed by the vase on the mantel as well.

"GET YOUR *ASS* UP THOSE *DAMN* STAIRS NOW, LONDON! I'M *NOT* PLAYING WITH YOU! GO!" he yells.

"This is why I aingt trying to be here while you're home—this right here is the reason. I aingt going nowhere but out that *damn* door! Now, you move!" I snap, before I push my father in his chest, hoping to move him out my way. But he doesn't move. Pops then violently grabs me by the throat, and forcefully pins me against the wall.

"Daddy stop! Let her go, daddy, let her go!" Shantell pleads, before picking up my grandfather's walking stick, and hitting my father in the back of his head. The stick breaks, but causes a gash to open in my pop's head. Out of reflex, my father backhand-slaps my sister while still gripping my throat. Shantell then falls to the floor, bleeding from the hard hit my pops laid on her.

When pops realizes what he did to my sister, he throws me into the wall, and goes straight to Shantell to see if she's okay. My father tries to help her up, but Shantell pushes him away, runs upstairs to her room, and slams the door shut.

"Why do you care if you hurt her? You don't give a *damn* if you hurt me! I'm your daughter, just like she is, but you don't give a *fuck* about me! *Fuck* you, man!" I yell while trying to fight back my tears.

"Oh, so *n-o-w* you want to recognize that you're my daughter! You *aingt* my daughter! You don't *look* like my daughter, you sure-as-hell don't *act* like my daughter—you run around looking and acting like a grown man! I've told you time-and-time again, if you going to *act* like a man, then I'm going to treat you like a man. You're a *fucking* embarrassment, London!"

"*FUCK* YOU!" I say while dodging a punch my pops tries to lay on me.

"You're right...I *don't* give a *damn* about you! ...When you started acting and thinking that you were a man, *that's* when I stopped caring about you. As far as I'm concerned, London, you don't even exist." My father then stands here for a minute, picks up his bottle of *Jack Daniels,* and looks at my mother: "Lorraine, clean up this *mess!*" He then walks out the door for a short while, and when my pops arrives back, both Shantell and I are gone.

When pops returns, the house is spotless—you would've never known that anything had gone on. Moms sits in a lounge chair that's positioned in a corner by the wall, leading to the kitchen.

She says nothing to my father when he enters.

The intense smell of alcohol that lingers from my pop's body, and his slurred speech indicates that, my father is at the drunken point that he enjoys the most. Moms wipes the tears from her cheeks, and sips on her own special glass of "juice".

"Lorraine...you-you don't understand...London needs to learn.... *She* needs to know that this shit happens for a reason. You understand that she needs to learn, right? ...Right, Lorraine?"

"Yes, Randy, I understand," my moms says at a whisper. Her own thoughts travels through her brain. This is a continuous cycle that desperately needs to be broken.

But moms doesn't have it in her to do so.

She tries to sit back and think about the first time our family began falling apart. There's been so much tension for so long that, moms can't even put a time frame on it.

It's just a lot of stupid stress...

Stress that's derived from Randy's drinking.

Moms wants to believe that I'm the source of the drama in the house, the fact that I'm gay, and live life as a boy most of the time, pisses Randy off.

But that's far from the reasons.

Pops can give every excuse in the book, but when it all comes down to it, it's the alcohol.

30

My father now walks back-and-forth from the kitchen to the living room. Moms listens to him stumble around, searching for miscellaneous objects.

Perhaps he's hungry.

Maybe pops will request that my moms cook him something

It's a typical action…one that's become routine.

"Lorraine…you baby her *way* too much. You need to show London tough love…that's the *only* way she'll learn" he states from the kitchen.

"Tough love? …Yeah," moms whispers dryly. She readjusts herself in the chair, and begins wiping her face again. Pops strolls in with a sandwich and glass of "juice". Moms is almost impressed. She expected my father to demand that she cater to him.

"Lorraine…why you sitting there all quiet and *shit!* Come on over here, and give *daddy* some loving," pops states. His large body then plops hard on the couch: "Lorraine—"

"Not right now, Randy," moms interjects with little to no emotion. She just stares into space…

Deep in thought…

My pops then finishes his sandwich, and passes out before moms can even reconsider his offer.

"Are you okay?" Shantell asks, as we walk down the street to Scottie's place. He always lets us stay there when *shit* gets rough at home. It's mad crazy because my mother just lets my pops beat on me.

She don't say *shit* or do *shit*!

But when my father's gone, moms be coming to me, trying to make sure I'm straight—trying to reassure me that everything will be aiiight. But it *aingt*, because my pops still lives there, and the same *shit* keeps happening.

Half of her problem is that, my mother doesn't believe in divorce and all that...but everybody knows my father's crazy!

My grandparents don't even come over no more.

Matter fact, no one comes, because we never know when my pops going to start acting like a fool!

"London, are you okay?" Shantell repeats.

"What? ...Yeah...just thinking. Are you okay? Let me see your face," I say before Shantell stops so I could get a good look at the bruise that my father left on her. "I can't *believe* he hit you! I want to *fucking* go back there and just blow his *fucking* brains out or something!"

The anger in my voice is something Shantell is far too familiar with.

"London, that *aingt* going to solve it. It's the type of situation where we just gotta wait until were old enough to move the *fuck* out—that's it! It *aingt* like ma is going to have him put in jail—that aingt happening. There aingt *nothing* that's going to help that situation, London."

We walk up the stairs and ring the bell to Scottie's apartment. He lives in the projects, a block away from us.

"Peace, shorties," Scottie says as he opens the door. "Damn, kid...what the *fuck* happened this time?" Scottie asks, before taking the bag out of Shantell's hand, and stepping out the way so we can come inside. "Yo, that *nigga* hit you, too, Shantell? *Fuck* that, we gotta do something," Scottie then states while holding Shantell's face, as he gets a closer look at her bruise. "Yo, get me some ice," he demands to the half-dressed girl, standing in his living room. "What happened, man?"

"Well, my pops got mad over some stupid *shit* as always. He's all pissed because Shantell and me wanted to spend the weekend out. We aingt want to be there because he's off all weekend, and we *knew* some *shit* like this would happen—"

"So he just started flipping out on us. Our pops was already arguing with our mother about some other *shit*," Shantell interrupts.

"Yeah, so when my pops sees us coming down the stairs with bags and *shit,* he just starts wailing on me; trying to make us go back up stairs and *shit!"* I explain to Scottie. "He hit Shantell because she hit him with granddaddy's cane. My father aingt mean to hit her, I can tell. Because he forgot all about me, and ran over to Shantell to see if she's okay.

"He told me straight-up that, he don't give-a-*damn* about me.... Said as long as I continue to act like a dude, that I don't exist. So I told him to *fuck* off!"

I now place the *Ziploc* bag filled with ice that the girl hands me on my bruises. Shantell also places ice on her face.

"I can't take much more of this, Shantell. I can't even feel it," I say. "This whole situation with pops—it's not cool." Shantell just looks at me; she hates when I talk about leaving. Shantell hates it because she knows that she won't be able to come with me. Shantell doesn't want me to leave her at the house, but if she left, Shantell can catch truancy charges.

"London, I *don't* want to talk about this. Scottie, where can I sleep? I *just* want to go to sleep." Shantell picks up her bag and heads to the room that Scottie points toward.

"Damn, n*igga.* You gotta handle this. You can't keep letting that man beat on you and *shit.* You're his daughter, and he be *beating* on you like your a man. Yeah, you look and act like a dude, but you *aingt* one! And your pops knows that!

"That's *fucked* up because, no matter how hard you are, or how strong you are, he's still stronger than you, because he's a man. London, dawg, you have to *handle* this, kid," Scottie insists.

"How you figure I do that, man? How do I handle this? No matter *how* many times my pops gets arrested, he *never* goes to jail. So how the *fuck* do you expect me to handle this? All I can do is keep fighting and standing up to him, because ma *aingt* going to put him out! So what?" I look at Scottie for answers, but he

33

doesn't have any.

I know what Scottie's suggesting...

And believe me, I've been considering it...

But, I aingt *never* taken no man's life!

And I aingt about to start.

Scottie stands in the middle of the kitchen, sipping on a *Corona* and smoking a blunt. He has this look on his face that shows that, regardless of what I say, Scottie wants to "handle" this.

"Scottie...it aingt worth it, dawg. Aingt no point in even *thinking* it. Trust, there have been *plenty* of days that I wanted to show my father that he's *fucking* with the wrong person...but kid, that *nigga* is a piece of *shit!* The *nigga* would probably haunt me in my *fucking* sleep, and beat my *ass* all over again. *Fuck* him! That's all I got to say."

"Whatever, kid. Do whatever works, but don't keep *coming* to me, because there aingt going to be *too* many times that I can patch you up, and tuck you in at night. London, I'm a thug, and you my *nigga.* Thugs do for their *niggas,* and, well...I'm just saying...there aingt going to be *too* many more times."

* * * * *

We stay at Scottie's house for like four days, and when we go back home, my dad has returned to work. Shantell's still having anxiety over the whole situation, so I decide to take her to the mall, and buy Shantell some stuff.

I feel bad because, I do act like a dude a lot, and I know there are times that Shantell wishes that I would act like the big sister that I am.

It's hard though.

I've been acting and looking like this since I was thirteen, but my parents said it didn't get this severe until a year-and-a-half ago. They said once I started fading my hair, it took over my whole persona. I let it "consume me", they said.

I just say: *"I finally found myself."*

Yo, it's mad weird because my parents don't ever mention the fact that I'm gay or whatever. They just *tripping* off the fact that I act so much like a dude.

I don't know...

I just don't know.

Shantell and I ride out to the *South Shore Plaza Mall* in

Braintree, and while there, I buy her some clothes out of *Gap* and *Express.* Shantell wants to get a couple of outfits, just in case she decides to go on a date.

"London, let me tell you," Shantell begins as we walk through the mall.

"What, Shantell?"

"You know that kid, Pauly? The one who lives off of *Warren,* but always be on our block?"

"Yeah, that Italian kid, right?"

"Yeah, that's the one. He's is straight trying to get with me, like, for real, London."

"For real-for real?"

"For real-for real. He brought a dozen roses to my school, London, borrowed his father's limo, and picked me and the girls up the other day," Shantell says excitedly.

"His dad has a limo?" I give her the one-eyebrow arched look.

"His dad drives a limo, but he drove Pauly to my school to pick us up. Pauly's trying mad hard, London. He be writing me poetry, dedicating songs to me and *shit*. It's overwhelming. I aingt *never* had no dude show that much interest in me—they all just usually want to *fuck,*" Shantells says, almost self-consciously.

I look at her, and I can tell that she really needs me to play the big sister role right now: "Do you like him? I mean, can you see yourself with him?"

"I don't know...I aingt never thought about Pauly like that, but I guess he's cute. He's not fully Italian, Pauly's mixed with Dominican," Shantell says and smiles.

My sister has a thing for Dominican boys—it's funny.

"Shantell, I think that if you like him, then you should at least give him a chance. I mean, after all, Pauly is going through all that just to be with you. *Shit,* give the man a chance. If it don't work, then you would've at least gotten a good meal out of it," I joked.

"You're so damn silly, London. Give him a chance, like you gave Lexi a chance? You know, that girl is so in love with you. Even *after* she found out that you were a girl."

"What? Lexi knew from the beginning. She just wanted an easy way to try dyking. But I feel you, that *shit* with Lexi is strange. I know how much she's feeling me, and I admit, I'm feeling her, too. But I'm a man, you know. I gotta do what a man gotta do."

"That's just it, London. You're not a man...so why don't you give Lexi a chance?" Shantell says while giving me this look.

A look that tells me to at least think about it.

Lexi calls me today—she wants to know if I still want to go catch a movie. I been supposing to take her to the movies, but *shit* happens, and *shit* don't get done. I figure that I should take my own advice and give Lexi a chance.

I mean, being a dog isn't *really* doing *shit* for me...

And Lexi want to love me and *shit*...so why not let her?

It's not like I'm not capable of loving her...

Or anyone else...but, I *just* don't want to be in love.

If I *do* fall in love, I don't know if I want it to be with Lexi. She's fine-as-hell...but I don't know if Lexi's *really* "wifey" material. Besides, I aingt trying to stay here too long.

So I don't *really* want to get attached.

Shantell's a little nervous about going out with this kid, Pauly, so she asks Lexi and me to double with her. Pauly's cool with it, he don't really care, just as long as he can spend time with Shantell.

I have to admit, they look real cute together.

Pauly is this short kid, but he's taller than Shantell. He has blue eyes and brown hair. Pauly's has a fade, wears a goatee, and has long sideburns. Pauly's wearing a *Rocawear* sweater, some *Sean John* baggy jeans, burgundy *Timberlands*, and like three silver chains.

The kid is cute, but the *nigga* just tries so hard to win over Shantell. I watch as Pauly opens every door for her; even arrives with flowers.

Shantell has on a real simple outfit, one that she got from *Gap:* a pair of dark denim boot-cut jeans, and an orange turtleneck sweater. Shantell also has on some brown leather *BCBG* boots with a crazy high heel, and some real sophisticated looking glasses by *Prada.*

Lexi, damn! She's off-the-fucking-hook!

Lexi has on some leopard print pants that stuck to her skin like glue, and a brown turtle neck sweater. I guess this is the night for those type of sweaters. Lexi also has on some brown *Steve Madden* pumps that matches her outfit exactly.

Lexi smells like *Victoria's Secret's* "Endless Love", and as soon as she sees me, Lexi gives me a real intense kiss. I kiss her back, but I kinda pulled away because, the kiss did something to me that it never did before. I guess it's because Lexi and me don't really tongue-kiss that much. We just do our thing, and be out!

The kiss was nice.

"You smell amazing," I say in a very soft, sweet voice. Lexi gives me this bashful smile, and playfully pinches me on my side. She fixes my shirt and straightens out my eyebrows. Lexi always begs me to let her arch them, but I aingt feeling that *shit!*

"We ready?" Pauly asks. We all agree together and head towards the car. The whole evening is cool. The four of us go out to eat before heading to the movies. Pauly is a perfect gentlemen with Shantell, and I think that she's really feeling him. At the end of the night, Pauly drops Lexi and me off at Lexi's house before he takes Shantell home.

"They look real cute, don't they?" Lexi states as we walk into her apartment. She places her purse on the couch and takes off her shoes.

"Yeah. That *nigga* is cool. Pauly seems like he's really feeling Shantell. He just better not hurt her."

"London, you're so *damn* overprotective sometimes. Shantell can handle her *shit*. You aingt gotta worry about her all the time, you know. Did you have a good time?"

"Yeah, I did actually…it was kinda fun going on a real date with you."

"You see, I *am* a real person, not just some piece of *ass!*"

"What? You were never just some piece of ass—"

"London, please. I'm not stupid, I know how you feel. We've had enough conversations, and I've heard enough to know that most of the time, I am just a piece of *ass* to you. I don't even know why I deal with—" Lexi stops herself abruptly. "Perhaps because you're young, and it's somewhat expected. But at the same time, I do want you to realize that there's more to me than sex."

"I know that, it's just that you be trying to be on some commitment *shit,* and I'm not really trying to feel that right now. I'm only sixteen."

"London, I'm aware of that, but you *aingt* the average sixteen-year-old. If you were, then I would've never messed with you in the first place. You've seen more, and been through more than a lot of people. That's the *shit* we bonded on—the connection me and Lexi made when we first met.

"Sweetie, trust me...I would love to be more than your fuck partner, London, but I aingt in no way, trying to convince you to be in no commitment with me."

Lexi and me talk a lot tonight, about a lot of *shit* that puts more *shit* in perspective. For the first time, I begin to get to know Lexi. Hell, we're not even having sex!

We kiss a lot...

Talk some more...

Kiss some more...

But no sex.

It's cool. It's nice.

I do kinda want to see where this will go if I let it.

But the idea of me loving someone, scares me....

I spent the whole weekend at Lexi's. When I return home, Shantell practically attacks me at the door with her Pauly update: "London! Let me tell you, Pauly is *so* sweet! Oh-my-God, London, the other night when we went to the movies, he didn't even kiss me. I wanted him to, but Pauly didn't, so that was kinda cool. We spent the rest of the weekend together. Pauly and I drove down to *Cape Cod*. It was mad cold, but it was still nice.

"I'm surprise mommy let me go, but she said that she likes Pauly, that he seems like a decent guy. Anyway—"

"Breathe, Shantell," I interrupt. Shantell smiles.

"London...last night when Pauly walked me home, he held my hand and put his arm around me. When we got to the door, Pauly asked if he could kiss me. That was *so* sweet. London, Pauly asked me for a kiss! I've *never* had a guy be that polite," Shantell says before closing her eyes in a young schoolgirl fashion.

"Well, did you kiss him?"

"Of course, London, of course. It...that boy...damn!"

"Damn, Shantell. That boy got you speechless like that? That's serious. I'm happy for you, sis—for real-for real," I give Shantell a hug, and start unpacking my bags.

"S-o-o-o, what up with you and Lexi this weekend?" Shantell asks with curious eyes.

"What you mean?"

"Don't play dumb, London! What happened with you two all this weekend? You *never* spent a whole weekend with Lexi. *Niggas* on the block thought you were on lock or something. Shawn and Maverick came by like six times. I told them to call you over Lexi's place, but Shawn and Maverick thought I was kidding when I said that you were with her."

"Yeah, them *niggas* found me earlier. Shawn and Maverick were mad shocked when they saw me with Lexi. It was peace, I have to admit. Lexi went out her way to make me happy and all that. She even bought that coat out of *Gap* that I wanted; Lexi got it as an early birthday present.

"Lexi aingt sure if she's going to be here for my birthday,

because she has to go to *New Hampshire* for a function that her caseworker is having. So Lexi gave me my gift early."

I pull the coat out of the bag and show it to Shantell. It's the navy-blue wool one that has the weird looking cylinder-shaped buttons and a hood. I've been talking about that coat forever, but I knew Lexi would get it.

As I put the last of my stuff away, the phone rings.

"London, it's Lexi!" Shantell says in a teasing way. I shoot her the bird with my finger and snatch the phone out of Shantell's hand.

"Peace," I say.

"I don't mean to bother you, London, knowing you just left, but I just wanted to call and say thank you."

"Thank you? What are you saying 'thank you' for?"

"For spending the weekend with me. I don't know about you, London, but I had a *really* good time. It's the happiest I've been in a real long time; I just wanted you to know that.... I-I aingt trying-trying to," Lexi begins to stutter, "sweat you or nothing. I just wanted you to know that."

Silence....

There's something *r-e-a-l* sweet about Lexi.

Something that I *never* noticed before.

"Lexi...I had a good time, too. You shouldn't be thanking me, *I* should be the one thanking you."

I feel my eyes starting to water.

That *aingt* like me!

"Look, Lexi, I'm about to go, but I promise I'll talk to you later."

"I-I love you, London. More than you'll ever know."

CLICK.

Before I can respond, Lexi hangs up the phone. I want to tell her that I'm really feeling her as well.

But Lexi hangs up.

"H-m-m-m," Shantell says with a smile on her face.

"What?" I ask.

"What was *that* all about? Seems kinda intense. What *exactly* happened this weekend, London?"

"Nothing really. Lexi and I just chilled, tried to get to know each other better.... This is complex, she trying to make a

40

nigga fall in love—I don't know how I feel about that! I'm saying...do you *really* think Lexi and I would make it as a couple? I don't know...I mean, I guess I can try. But it's kinda hard on the image."

"London, that's half your problem. You *always* so *damn* worried about your image! You fight with daddy because of your image, you hang out in the street because of your image—*fuck* your image, London! Out of *a-l-l* the chicks you've fooled, *fucked*, and forgotten, Lexi's the *ONLY* one who *still* puts up with your *shit!*

"Lexi's the one who would do *anything* for you. Shit, London, she's the one who's allowing herself to fall in love with you."

Shantell looks at me with much concern, hoping that I will understand where she's coming from.

I do.

And truthfully, I want to give this whole *damn* situation a chance.

* * * * *

"London, it's for you!" Shantell yells, after answering a minute worth of hard knocking on the door. It's 8 PM, and I go to the door to find Shawn and Maverick, standing there looking simple.

"London, man, where the *hell* you been, kid?" Shawn loudly asks, trying to sound pissed.

"What's the deal, playas," I answer.

"Naw, *fuck* that, London! Don't try to act like you been around everyday. How you just going to forget about your dawgs?" Maverick asks.

"See, why you tripping? I aingt even forget about y'all. It's just that I've been a little busy. You know, handling *shit,*" I say slyly.

"Yeah, *nigga,* handle it! I'm saying, you going to invite us in, or are we just going to stand around chit-chatting like some *bitches?*" Shawn facetiously asks.

"Ha-ha-ha, get in here and watch your *damn* mouth—my mother's home."

Shawn and Maverick enters my house, and goes straight to my room. Shantell stands at the top of the stairs shaking her head. She immediately then throws a towel at us.

41

Shantell knows exactly what we're about to do.

Three blunts later, Shawn, Maverick and myself are beyond *fucked* up, and decide to get into a little trouble. We decide to do our usual: drive to one of the overpasses off *I-93,* and drop *mad* water balloons on the cars below.

Fucked up, I know!

It's not long before the cops start to come, so we dip from there and get food from *McDonald's* on *Massachusetts Avenue.*

Three hours later, Shawn and Maverick go their separate ways, and I make my way to Lexi's house.

"I wasn't expecting to see you tonight," Lexi says. "To what do I owe this surprise?"

"I can't just want to see you?" I walk into her apartment and close the door behind me.

"When have you *ever* just wanted to see me? You usually have a motive."

"Yeah, and you usually comply. But I aingt about to get into this argument again. I just wanted to see you, for real."

"Have a seat; stay awhile," Lexi says as she pats the empty spot on the couch. I walk over to where she is. It could be the weed talking, and especially all the beer I drank, but Lexi looks really beautiful tonight. Her outfit is simple: some jogging pants and a T-shirt. To anyone else, Lexi would've looked like a bum. S*hit,* to me on any other night, she would've looked like a bum. But, tonight, is a little different.

"So, I've been thinking," I say, breaking the five-minute silence, "I guess I can try this relationship thing. I mean...I aingt really got nothing to lose…. And you're fly—"

"Thanks," Lexi interrupts.

"Seriously, I'll be a *fool* to let a chick like you pass by me. Like Shantell said, you've put up with more *shit* than anyone else would. You done gave up mad friends because of my *shit,* I guess I've been taking the whole thing for granted. You gotta understand though...a relationship aingt *really* been in my three-year plan. But it's whatever, if you want to try this, then I'm game."

Lexi just kinda sits here for a minute...

I guess she's contemplating her decision or something. "Well?" I say.

"Well what? London, you *know* how I feel. All I've ever

wanted was a relationship with you. I got to be a damn *fool* to even be *considering* this *shit*. But your little *ass* got me sprung.

"Honestly, I should say no. I should come to my senses and end this *shit* right now—but I aingt. All I want to do right now is run around this house, jumping for joy. But I'm trying to keep my cool. I'm trying not to look like you got me wrapped around your little finger," Lexi says and smiles.

"But I do! So *fuck* all the fronting and give me a kiss."

Lexi straddles me and kisses me softly.

I can feel every bit of love she has for me in the kiss.

I have *no* idea what I'm getting' myself into...

Fuck it!

* * * * *

Months continue to pass, and things between Lexi and I are getting really good. My birthday was cool, even though I aingt really get everything I wanted, it was still cool. I like the coat Lexi got me, and Shantell bought me some black "Chukka" *Timberlands*. My moms just gave me money. And, well, my pops...he's just my pops.

Pauly and Shantell's relationship is moving nicely, too. I can't tell if they're having sex yet, but I know it will be happening soon. My sister *aingt* been a virgin in a long time.

Hell, I done *even* had sex with a dude....

One night, about a year ago, me and Scottie got real drunk and...well, aingt no need to go into details.

It's like nine o'clock at night, and I climb through the fire escape window that leads to Shantell's room. I do this when I don't feel like dealing with either one of my parents. I slip in-and-out without them even knowing that I'm home.

I creep into the bathroom, but before I could close the door, I hear mad screaming coming from my parents' room: "LONDON IS *NOT* A BOY!" my father yells at the top of his longs. "LORRAINE, I DON'T UNDERSTAND WHY YOU ALLOW HER TO WALK AROUND TALKING, ACTING, DRESSING, AND LOOKING LIKE SOME *NIGGA* OFF THE STREETS!"

"Randy, she's *our* child! *Our* daughter! No! N-O-O-O! RANDY!" my mother screams, before my father slaps her hard across the face.

"YOU JUST LET *LONDON* ACT LIKE THAT!

LONDON DON'T *LISTEN* TO ME, AND YOU DON'T DO *NOTHING* TO HELP THE SITUATION! YOU JUST CONTINUE TO CONDONE IT!" my pops shouts violently.

"Randy, no, I *don't* agree with it, but she's *our* daughter, *our* first born. The one you, *you,* Randy, took everywhere with you. The one *you* sent out to play baseball, and basketball, and peewee football. The one *you* took to all the games and pool halls, and all that other *shit!* Are you that *damn* surprised that London acts the way she does? If anything, *you* made London this way!"

I stand at the door, listening to the argument.

"Randy, you don't think that it hurts me to see you and London fight, and *scream* at each other? You two use to be so close, Randy, so close," my mother says and cries.

"Woman, I did not *make* our *child* a *dyke!* I did not *make* London *dress* the way she *dresses,* or *act* the way she *acts!* London did that on her own. London woke up one morning wanting to be a man, and you let her do it! All I know is how to be a man.

"It's *your* responsibility to raise our girls up to be mature women! YOU *FUCKED* UP, NOT ME! London's *your* daughter, because she *aingt* my daughter! *Your* daughter is a *fuck* up, and I want London out of *my* house, NOW!"

"Randy, are you crazy? Are you—"

"WHAT?"

...I hear a loud thump, and I burst into the room, because I know that my pops is smacking my mother around: "Leave her alone, daddy! Leave her alone! Hit me, *nigga!* It's me who you have a problem with, so hit me!" I stand right in front of the fist my father has drawn back, and wait for him to plant one on me. Yet, my father just stands there.

"London, you are *no* longer worth my energy. You *don't* exist to me.... London, you are a disgrace, a failure. You *don't* go to school, you *don't* have a job, you don't know how to do *nothing* but be a mannish-looking *dyke.* You're not worth it, you're no longer worth my hits. I *refuse* to let you stress me out anymore, London."

My pops now looks at my mother with seriousness in his eyes: "I'm going to stay with a friend.... I want London *out* my house. When she's gone, I'll return, but until then, you'll have to figure out how to pay all the *damn* bills, and all that other *shit* I take care of.

"I want her *out!* Do you hear that London Janae Walters? You are no longer welcome through that front door. You-you better be gone.... London, if you want to be a bad-ass, and you want your mother and sister to suffer, then stick around. But y'all know, I run this *shit!* That money your mother gave you for your birthday, *that* came out *my* wallet!"

"Then take the *shit* back then!" I yell, as I reach into my pocket and throw all the money I had at him.

"Hmmmph! You better let your mother keep that, because *she's* going to need it. If you're as smart as you try to be, you will leave—go!"

My father walks out the bedroom, down the stairs, and out the front door. I turn and look at the blood dripping from my mother's eye and lip. I try to help her up, but my moms snatches her arm away from me.

"What, ma? Why you mad at me?" I ask.

"I can't *take* this anymore! He aingt *never* use to beat me, London. Or *any* of you for that matter. I can't *take* this!"

Moms has a look of sorrow that scares the *shit* out of me!

"What? You kicking me out? You picking that *nigga* over your own flesh and blood? Your first born, ma? You just kicking me out like that?" I begin to cry.

"London, you are *not* a child anymore. Everything that you've done, you *chose* to do, London. You don't need to be here.... You don't hardly be here *anyway,* London."

"Ma, I'm only seventeen, and you're going to *kick* me out? I don't get that, ma." My crying causes my voice to sound pleading and feminine: "How the *fuck*...forget it, forget it. Ma, you want me to leave, I'm out! But you're going to be the one to regret it."

I walk out my parents' bedroom.

Slam the door to my bedroom as I enter.

Grab the suitcase out of my closet.

Pack all the clothes that fits in it.

I then take the money I have hidden in the trunk from some hustling I use to do, and snatch a sheet of paper out of my desk to write Shantell a note. She's out on a date with Pauly, so Shantell has no idea that any of this is going down:

Dear Shantell,

You know that ma picked that nigga over me? You know that she finally let him talk her into kicking me out? That's fucked up, right? Ma said that pops aingt start beating on her until I made him do it. What kind of shit is that? Anyway, I don't know where I'm going, or how I'm getting there...but I'm out!

Little sister, you are my strength, and I need you to be strong. I know you made me promise that I would never leave you, but Shantell, I aingt got no choice. As soon as I get somewhere, I will let you know. But take care, Shantell, and tell Lexi that I love her, and that as soon as I get settled somewhere, I'll come and get both of y'all. I'm a soldier, and I'm up in here crying.... I love you always, Shantell. Hang in there.

London

I fold the letter up, put it in an envelope, and place it on Shantell's pillow. All *Amtrak* trains leave at like midnight, so I grab my stuff and run straight to Scottie's. I explain the whole scenario to him, and ask Scottie if I can borrow a little cash to get wherever I'm going. He says yes, and hands me an envelope that contains three thousand dollars.

Scottie must of just finished a big deal, because he *never* keeps that much cash in his house.

Easy target for a drug bust.

"London, I want you to be careful," Scottie says, trying to keep himself from crying. "I'm serious, London. You're my *nigga,* my heart. If you were straight, I'd propose to you right now. For real though, please call a *nigga* when you get wherever, man."

Scottie gives me a hug, and wipes the lonely tear from his eye. I catch the bus, then the train to *South Station.* I get on the first train leaving to *Detroit, Michigan,* which is at 12:30 AM.

I try to keep myself from crying, but I break down before we even pull out the gate. It's going to be a ten-hour trip, so I decide that the best thing to do is go to sleep.

*   *   *   *   *

"Hey ma!" Shantell yells, as she runs into the house and up the stairs.

"Shantell...come here," Lorraine says, as she tries to hide the fact that she's been crying.

"Wait, ma. Let me change my clothes." Shantell runs into her room and throws off the smoky, sweaty clothes she has on. Just as Shantell sits on her bed, she notices the letter that says *To Shantell*.

"N-O-O-O-O-O-O!" Shantell screams, which causes Lorraine to start crying again. Shantell runs back downstairs to the room that her mother's in. By the time Shantell gets there, her father returns, because Lorraine called him to tell him that London's gone.

"How could you? How could you?" Shantell yells.

"Shantell, calm down," Randy says in a soothing voice.

"Calm down? Calm down? *FUCK* YOU, DADDY! This is all your fault! It's *your* fault that my sister's gone! How could you do this?" Shantell cries. "London's all I have, all I have, and *you* two don't even *realize* that. Y'all took London away from me."

Shantell puts her hands over her face and begins crying harder. Randy begins to speak to her.

"Shantell, sweetie—"

Lorraine interjects, "It had to be done, it's better for London, sweetie. She isn't happy here." Lorraine and Randy now both tries to reach out to Shantell.

"GET OFF ME!" Shantell yells, "OFF! You two think y'all can play these *mind* games on me? Y'all think y'all can look me in my eyes and *tell* me that it's okay that my big sister is gone? Who knows where London is. She's gone! You expect me to-to just sit here and be like, it's cool? WELL IT'S NOT!

"It's not cool, that *you*," Shantell points to her mother, "let *him*," Shantell now points to her father, "talk you into putting your *own* child out! Your *own* child, ma. How do I know that *I'm* not going do something, and *he* starts beating on me, and eventually, talks you into putting me out?

"I can't *believe* you, *SHIT!* If London aingt here, then *I* don't want to be here either!" Shantells yells and stares into her parents' faces with conviction.

"Are you done?" Randy asks.

"I don't want to hear nothing you say, nothing. I don't *have* a father. And, ma, for you to choose your husband over your child, that makes me not want you as my mother either," Shantell says, before she runs upstairs and packs a small bag.

She then crawls out the fire escape window, and calls Pauly from a nearby payphone. He arrives immediately after Shantell hangs up the phone.

"You okay?" Pauly asks, as he opens the car door for her and gives Shantell a kiss.

"Naw, my parents put London out. I don't know where she is. Can we stop by Scottie's, and then Lexi's?" Shantell asks with a quivering voice.

"Of course."

Pauly then put the car in drive, and heads halfway down the block to Scottie's. Scottie reveals that London went to the train station, but he doesn't know where she's going.

When they arrive at Lexi's, Lexi can tell that as soon as she opens the door, that something is wrong. The tears in Shantell's eyes causes Lexi to start crying immediately. At first, Lexi thinks that London has been killed or something, but she's slightly relieved when she hears that London just bounced.

The reality of it all hasn't hit Lexi, until Shantell gives her the message that London loves her. Both Lexi and Shantell sits here crying, trying to figure out how they're going to find London. They realize that there isn't anything they can do until London calls.

Pauly and Shantell crash at Lexi's for the night, but for the next couple of weeks, Shantell makes Pauly's house her home.

It's been three weeks since all that *shit* went down. I haven't called anybody yet, even though I know I need to.

I'm just not feeling it.

I have *so* many emotions, I *don't* know how to deal, I—

...I just want to give up.

I walk down *E. Jefferson Avenue* in *Detroit* in my new coat and black *Timberlands*. *"London be careful,"* play over-and-over in my head.

Like a broken record.

Everyone said it: my moms, Shantell, Lexi—everyone. As much as I hate how things are going down, I'm kinda glad though. I need a break from everything, and everyone.

I decide that I'm not going to call anyone. I know I need to let them know that I'm okay, but, I *don't* want to talk to no one!

I want to new start...new people, new circumstances.

My first few days in *Detroit* were anything but peace. It's nothing like *Boston*, and having to start over is no joke. I stayed at the *Comfort Inn Hotel* for the first week, but that was burning a hole in the money that Scottie gave me. I already used a great deal of it, because all my stuff got stolen in some little *ass* town on the way up here!

Some *crazy* people on the train!

I was kinda shook, but I aingt let them know that. Anyway, I had to buy new clothes, a bag, and all that other stuff. I didn't feel like lugging all that *shit* around, so I bought a storage locker to hold my stuff in, until I find a permanent place to rest my head.

That's *another* reason why I don't want to call no one.

I don't want them to know that I'm struggling like this. Fortunately, it's not cold, so that make things kinda aiiight. I spent a couple of nights in a shelter, but I wasn't *feeling* that either— they wanted to know *too* much. They had a w-h-o-l-e bunch of questions for me, once they realized that I was girl. After three nights, I'd had enough, and moved on.

While eating breakfast in *Dunking Donuts* on *East 8 Mile*

Road, I come across an ad in a newspaper, indicating that there's a room available in a local boarding house. I'm hoping that the room is still there, because this paper is kinda old.

I stop by my locker and grab a change of clothes. I sneak into the *Y*, like I do many mornings to take a shower and all that. I put on a brand-new "wife beater."

I never have to wear a bra, because I aingt got no na-na's.

I'm smaller than an A-cup, so you can see how it's easy for me to pull off this man thing. I put on a polo shirt and a pair of khakis. I stuff my *Calvin Klein* boxers with a pair of socks, because women tend to look for a bulge when they see a man in khakis.

Even though I'm not a man, I still look like one.

If I'm going to play the game, then I need to play it right.

I follow the instructions on the ad to the location. It's a three-story brick building titled *"The Lawrence House"*. I open the front door, and knock on the apartment with the director's sign on it. A short, stocky Asian woman answers the door.

"Yes, how may I help you, sir?" she asks, straining to look up to me. She speaks clear English, which seems interesting to me; an Asian who doesn't have an accent.

"U-m-m-m, I saw in this paper that you have a room," I say. I look at her with hope in my eyes.

"What's your name, son?"

"London. London Walters."

"Age?"

"Nineteen," I lied.

"You aingt in no trouble, are you?" the woman asks, definitely pondering her decision.

"Naw. No...No trouble at all. Just moved here—haven't found a place yet."

"Really? wait right here."

The Asian woman closes her door, and comes back five minutes later. She hands me a monthly lease, and tells me to: "Sign at the bottom." The woman then lays down a few rules, and tells me that the room will cost two hundred dollars a month.

That's cool.

I have enough to get me through the first few months.

But I need to find a job quick!

She now hands me a key that reads "Room 23". I walk up three flights of stairs to the room that matches the key, and open the door. The room isn't *nothing* special, but it's a place to rest my head. It contains a bed, a mini refrigerator and a closet. Each floor has two bathrooms, which has three showers and two toilets.

I'm not too *keen* on that...but it's whatever!

I sit on my bed, and end up falling asleep for like an hour. I now open the door, and peek out into the hallway...It's w-a-y too quiet...but perhaps that's good.

I'm not really trying to make any friends.

I just want to regroup.

The sun has gone down, and I go back to the storage place to get my stuff. It seems like everyone came out at night because, that's when I met three of my neighbors: this dude named Dennis, and two girls named Latoya and Tracy.

They all live on the second floor, and tell me that the building is pretty cool. The three say a lot of college kids live here because they didn't want to curfew. Come to find out, Ms. Wong throws the building a block party once a month.

Perhaps this isn't such a bad situation after all.

I go on with the lie that I'm nineteen, and continue to let people think I'm a guy. It's easier, I mean, I have every intention on changing everything about me. I haven't *acted* like a chick in so long, I don't even remember how.

Latoya is aiiight looking. She's an average chick, but *extremely* ghetto! Latoya has a blondish-brown weave, light-brown eyes, and breasts for days. She's wearing tight black pants that makes her look like she has a yeast infection, and a ribbed sweater. Latoya's hair is cut in some type of asymmetric style that I could've sworn played out a long time ago.

Whatever! She keeps smiling at me as Dennis keeps talking.

Latoya has pierced just about everything on her face: her eyebrow, lip, nose, labret, tongue. I wouldn't be surprised if Latoya gets struck by lighting one day while walking down the street.

I can tell right here that she's going to be hard to deal with.

I might just have to tell Latoya the real deal...

Before there's any chance of getting anything started.

Tracy is more attractive: light skinned, long black hair, sexy ass lips, and the perfect shape. She's no Lexi now, but Tracy is fly.

It's obvious though that she and Dennis have something going on. He has his arm resting on Tracy's lower back, as to let me know that she's "his property".

That's peace.

But I know that I can pull *both* of these chicks if I want to.

I now walk down the street to see if there's any restaurants along the way. I realize that I haven't eaten in like forever and I needed something. The only thing around is a local sub shop.

I order a turkey and cheese on wheat bread, an orange soda and some chips. By the time I make it back to the boarding house, Dennis and the girls are gone.

* * * * *

"Shantell, have you heard from London yet?" Lexi asks in a very concerned fashion while ironing her pants.

"Naw, I was hoping you did. It's been over two months, Lexi."

"I know. I'm scared...London told Scottie that she'd call to let him know that she was okay. But, London hasn't even called him!" Lexi's nose is beginning to turn red, indicating that she's upset. "Shantell, I don't know *what* to do. I can hardly function without that girl. I gave up so much to be down with London, and just when she's starting to appreciate me, this *shit* happens!"

"I know. I haven't been home since my parents put London out. I told them that, *'I will not stay here without London.'* They fight too much, I can't deal with that. I feel like my parents are going to put me in a nut house. That *shit* aingt cool."

"Naw, it's not, Shantell. It's not.... You and Pauly seem to be doing well," Lexi says, trying to change the subject so that neither one of them will get too emotional. "Shantell, so what's up with you and Pauly? I know you two are fucking,"

"Yeah, well...I gotta tell you something," Shantell ends quietly. Lexi can tell that it's something juicy.

"What, Shantell? Don't keep me in suspense," Lexi replies and stands up, as if it will help her hear what Shantell has to say better.

"Lexi, I think I may be pregnant," Shantell says with an uneasy look in her eyes.

"Are you *serious,* Shantell? ...Pregnant?" Lexi says before grabbing Shantell. She hugs Shantell long and hard, then immediately lets go. "Damn, sweetie, what are you going to do?

Does Pauly know?"

"Yeah, he knows. I just told him—I mean, I'm not sure. I took a home pregnancy test and it came out positive, but I want to go to the clinic to make sure.... Lexi, will you go with me?"

"Of course, sweetie. Of course," Lexi replies as she hugs Shantell again. Lexi now feels Shantell's body shaking— Shantell's nerves are on edge from the thought that she may be pregnant.

"Listen, Shantell, everything is going to be alright. Whatever happens, I'm right here...and London will be right by your side, too," Lexi assures Shantell.

"You think? I feel that she's going to be disappointed," Shantell answers with uncertainty.

"I disagree. I think that London is going to be concerned, but you're her little sister. London's not going to be so upset that she won't be there for you—that I know."

"I hope so...with everything that's happening right now, being pregnant is the *last* thing I need!" Shantell says before she finished ironing her shirt. Shantell then changes her clothes so she'll be ready when Pauly comes to take her to the clinic.

Soon after, Shantell's becomes queasy and begins to experience having a "bubble gut". The reality that she really might be pregnant is starting to set in.

In a few hours, Shantell will have an answer.

* * * * *

Pauly, Shantell and Lexi walks into the busy free clinic: the best place to go when you don't have any health insurance, the worse place to go if you're on a time schedule.

Shantell signs the log, and notices that she's the fifteenth person on the list; meaning two hours of waiting. Pauly sits down and helps Shantell fill out the forms that the clerk hands her. Lexi sits in the chair to the left of Shantell, and begins flipping through an old *Motherhood* magazine.

Young, rowdy kids are screaming all over the place, and the local neighborhood chicks that frequent the free clinic are running around, chasing after these same screaming kids whom belong to them.

"Pauly, our baby is *not* going to act like that," Shantell retorts, looking stressed out from all the chaos around her.

"I know, baby. He's going to be in check."

53

"I do hope it's a boy. We have enough girls in my family."

"True. Well, in my family, we have all boys, so I will probably make a boy. My brothers both have sons, so it's like a trend or something," Pauly answers before kissing Shantell on the cheek. Shantell name is now being called, and Pauly holds her hand as they walk into the examination room.

"Hey Shantell," Lexi calls out, "everything is going to be alright," she encourages. Once Shantell and Pauly are in the examination room, Lexi decides to go into the *Hip Zepi* clothing store, located next door to the clinic.

The pregnancy test doesn't take long, and Shantell is able to find out right then that she's indeed pregnant. Pauly and Shantell are both filled with mixed emotions. Shantell is scared because she's only sixteen, Pauly just turned eighteen, and recently got a new job working at the paper factory.

It is what it is.

Pauly plans to work long hours, but it's going to be worth it in the long run. He and Shantell briefly talk about getting married, once Shantell graduates from high school. There's even talk about her going to college.

It's almost *too* sappy.

* * * * *

"Hey London, where you going?" Latoya asks flirtatiously.

"U-m-m-m, I'm going to check out this gig. Some mechanic is hiring assistants or something to do little odds-and-ends work, so I'm going see what's up," I respond without slowing down much.

"Cool. Well, how about you stop by on your way back?" Latoya says, as she waves and winks her eye. I just kinda laugh at her and keep on going.

"Naw, Latoya. I don't think that will be a good idea." I then walk down the street to the *Fix It 'n Go* shop, but as I'm walking, I notice a barbershop, and decide to get a fresh cut.

"'Sup, playa? Sit right here," a tall, light-skinned barber says. "How you want it?" he then asks.

"Number two blade all over."

"Kid, I haven't seen you around here before. You new?" the barber asks, trying to make light conversation.

"Yeah, just came into town not to long ago," I answer in a quiet response. "I moved here from *Boston* about two months ago."

"Damn, kid, what brought you here?"

"*Shit*...a whole lot of *shit*. Just had to get away."

"Where you headed after this?"

"I'm about to check out this job, that's all."

After getting my haircut, I pay the barber and begin to walk out the building.

"Kid, what's your name?" the barber asks.

"Why you need to know my name?" I ask, now confused.

"Just like to know the names of the people I cut."

"London."

MOMS CONCERNED
chapter 6

Today, Shantell walks out of the building of *John D. O'Bryant's High School,* to find her mother standing at the door. She has the look of a worried soul, and pleading eyes of a mother who wants nothing more but to make sure that her kids are okay.

"What are you doing here?" Shantell asks. "Go ahead, y'all, I'll catch up," Shantell then instructs to Ariel and Camille, as the two nod their heads and walk toward the bus stop. "What are you doing here?" Shantell asks again.

"Are you okay?" her mother asks.

"I'm straight, no complaints; not really anyway," Shantell answers as she looks into her mother's eyes, which are now beginning to weld up with tears.

"Shantell, please come home. You are too *young* to be out here on your own. It would make me feel a lot better if I knew that you were okay."

"But I am okay. I'm fine, ma, I'm not out on the streets. Besides, I can take care of myself. I'm aiiight."

"Shantell stop. You're starting to sound like London. You need to come home. You are *too* young to be out here by yourself."

"Ma, I'm not by myself, I'm with Pauly...and I'm fine. I told you that I'm not coming home. As long as London is gone— I'm gone," Shantell replies, as she begins to walk off; now turning 'round in her tracks. "Ma, what I *don't* understand is how you can just put London out like that. How could you let Randy make you *kick* her out? Your first born child? It's like no one ever cares about her.

"You two treat me and London completely different and that aingt fair. You let him *beat* her day-after-day. You just *sat* there, you just watched. You expected me and London to take your crying as sympathy, when all we ever wanted was for you to put Randy out. Did you do that? Naw. Instead, you stood by your man, and let you own *child*, walk out the door.

"Ma, are you that insecure? Are you that incapable of taking care yourself, that you need to stay with a *man* who would raise a hand to you and his child? That's *fucked* up—real *fucked* up. I can't *live* in a house like that. I can't remain in an environment where every other word is *fuck* this, or *bitch* that. I can't function in a house that has to be refurnished every *two* months, because my *father* wants to go on a rampage and tear everything up. I can't," Shantell retorts, as she stands there waiting for her mother to respond.

"Until you are married and have kids, you will *never* understand. Shantell, I did not *want* to put my daughter out, I did what I felt needed to be done, in order to protect London. It was *killing* me inside to see London and your father constantly fighting with each other. I just knew that one day, I would wake up, and one of them would be lying on the floor dead, or severely, severely hurt. I didn't want *any* of that to happen.

"Shantell, this whole thing has been *replaying* itself, over-and-over again in my mind. Do I feel like I did the right thing? Of course not. Of course I regret telling London she had to leave. But it needed to be done. London is a *very* strong girl. I mean, mentally, London hasn't needed me to be a mother to her in a very long time."

"See, that's where you're wrong, London *always* needs you. There have been *so* many times that London wanted to talk to you about different things, but she was too scared to. There were so many times that London just wanted to sit you down, and make you understand her, because London felt like it would've made things easier. How can you say that she didn't need you?"

"Shantell, what I'm saying is that, London is a survivor. You and I both know that she's probably a lot happier wherever she is. Shantell, I didn't come up here to get into an argument with you. I didn't come up here to explain nor justify that night. You need to come home.... No, I'm not going to force you, because learning from London, the only thing that will happen is, you'll just end up running away or something; but you need to come home," Lorraine replied, as she stands there with tears rolling down her face.

"I don't think I can do that. I don't feel comfortable. I haven't felt comfortable in a really long time, and now that London isn't here, I just can't feel it. Ma, I gotta go...but you know what time I get out of school. Maybe I'll call sometime," Shantell says before she hugs her mom and walks away.

"Shantell, I love you...be careful."

Lorraine said the words that she'd often said to her daughter, London. Lorraine never thought that she'd have to express that type concern for both of her children. She couldn't believe that things were happening this way. Lorraine never imagined losing her children before they were legally grown.

Figuratively speaking that is.

"WHERE YOU BEEN?" is the first thing Lorraine hears when she walks into the house. Randy is sitting on the couch drinkin, and watching a western: "I *asked* you a *question,* where the *hell* you been?"

"Randy, don't curse at me. I'm *not* in the mood. If you must know, I went to go see how Shantell is doing. It's been several months since both of them have been gone, and you aingt going to check up on them. I needed to know where my girls were, how they're doing," Lorraine says as she reaches into the refrigerator and grabs herself a beer; followed by fixing herself a glass of wine.

"Well?" Randy states a few minutes later.

"Well what?"

"How are they?"

"Shantell is fine, I guess...she's staying with that boy, Pauly. I think Shantell might be pregnant."

"Why you think that?" Randy asks, finally looking in Lorraine's direction.

"Her stomach seemed a little more poked out than usual. Shantell use to have a flat stomach, and well, it's not anymore."

"Did you ask her?"

"No. I could barely get Shantell to tell me where she was staying. Do you really think she would reveal to me that she was pregnant? My main concern was trying to get Shantell to move back in here, but she doesn't want to come anywhere *near* this house. Randy, she is deathly afraid of you. You have succeeded in driving *both* of our kids away."

"Lorraine, this was a good night. We are *not* going to get into this. So don't *fucking* start with me. Shantell is sniffing her own *ass* right now. Shantell will come to her senses, and she will be home—especially if she's pregnant. Don't *fucking* blame me because Shantell left.

"I told you to put *London* out. Not because I don't love

58

her, because I do, but I cannot live in this house with London, acting the way she does," Randy states as he sits there, completely convinced that it's London who's the problem.

"I can't *believe* you, Randy! You found *every* reason in the book to *beat* on the child. You've broken so many bones in London's body, but yet, that *never* seem to stop you from fighting with her. The *only* reason why I made London leave is because I knew you wouldn't. I should've just let you go when you put up that ultimatum."

Totally pissed off this time, Lorraine gets up and goes back into the kitchen. She can't believe that Randy is talking such *bullshit*. Everyday, for the past several months, Lorraine has cried herself to sleep. If she wasn't worried about her kids, then Lorraine was fighting with Randy, and if she wasn't fighting with Randy, Lorraine was wishing that she'd kicked him out instead.

The sad part about it is...Lorraine is weak. Randy is the *only* man she's ever loved, and Lorraine doesn't know how to survive without him.

Randy has provided so much for her. He's even given Lorraine two beautiful children, but, in reality, Randy has caused her so much anguish. Lorraine has known what's needed to be done, but will she truly be able to kick out the only man she's ever loved?

The whole thing is *too* much for Lorraine to process...

She decides to go to bed.

*   *   *   *   *

"Hey Lexi!" Shantell greets Lexi as she walks into Lexi's apartment. "You won't believe who had the *nerve* to show up at my school," Shantell says with disbelief.

"Who?"

"My moms. She's really on some come-back-home type *shit!* Like I'm trying to be in that house without London. I told her that it makes me uncomfortable to even *think* about being there. My moms even tried to give me some excuse or reason, as to why she chose my dad over London. Said it was for London's own good, because she was afraid that something real bad was going to happen. Whatever! There is no *fucking* excuse to explain why she would kick London out! Simple as that!"

"I miss London, Shantell. I miss her *so* much. I don't know what I'm going to do. It's like things were finally starting to look up between us. Do you think I expected too much? Do you think I created this whole fantasy, but all along, me and London was never meant to be? All I know is that before London came along, I was all about *niggas*. I thought being with a chick was the nastiest thing around.

"The first couple of times me and London went out, I really aingt know that she was a girl. Well, I did in a way, but wasn't really sure. I mean, you know what your sister looks like, and most of the time, me and London were high, so my logic wasn't that great anyway.

"One day, it was me, Shawn, Maverick, Scottie, and some other cats at Scottie's house, and we were all drinking and *shit*. My girl, Lisa was trying to kick it to Scottie, so they were in his room doing whatever. Shawn and Maverick were in the front playing video games, and me and London were in the bathroom talking.

"We started kissing, and *shit* was getting real intense. Usually, London is in control of our make-out sessions, but she was so *fucked* up that night that, I had to dominate the situation. All I know is that, I was horny, and I wanted to feel a nice hard *dick!*"

"Oh my God, Lexi! Do I *really* need to hear this?" Shantell asks emotionally, breaking the flow of the conversation.

"Shantell, just listen. Anyway...I had to dominate the situation. Me and London started kissing and touching. First, I pulled her shirt off. I mean, I noticed that London had nubs, but that *shit* aingt register. But when I went to give London head...obviously that's when I realized that London was a girl.

"I got real pissed off at first, but I was horny, so I let London do her thing. Now, here I am all *fucked* up over this chick, and she aingt even around to love me. I mean, I guess I knew, it's psychological. ...I knew, but didn't want to believe it.

"We kept it from my friends for a real long time, but during one of the many times that me and London were arguing, it all came out that London was a chick. My people wasn't *trying* to hear that, so I told them that I didn't know, and that London tricked me. They wanted to fight her, but once they realized that I was fully aware, they all dropped me like a bad habit. It was a decision *I* made, and it's one that I have to live with. Now, I'm in love with your sister, and I was finally getting London to realize that she should be in love with me. ...She ain't here though."

MERCEDES...NOT THE BENZ!
chapter 7

I show up at this raggedy-ass car place, and look at the address about four times to make sure that it's the right place. I'm suppose to ask for a guy named Jaguar. His daughter, Mercedes, greets me: "Yeah, what can I do for you?" says the five-foot-five-inch woman, who stands before me in a dirty jumpsuit and baseball cap.

"I'm looking for some dude named Jaguar. I'm here about the casual labor work," I answer as I look her up-and-down.

"Well, that's my father, and he's not *here* right now. But leave your name and info, and he'll get back to you," Mercedes answers with a bit of an attitude.

It's kinda sexy.

"Yo, do you know when he'll be back? I kinda need this job."

"Yo? You'll be lucky if my father even *looks* twice at you. Come in here talking about 'yo'. *Nigga* please!" she retorts, and walks back to the opened car hood where Mercedes, the young lady is working in.

"Why I gotta be all that? You know, a *nigga* and *shit.* You don't even know me, and you calling me out my name and *shit.*"

I look at her, waiting for a response, but Mercedes just rolls her eyes at me.

"You been inhaling too many fumes I see. You probably *aingt* going to tell your dad that I asked about the job," I spit as I head towards the opened garage door.

"Probably not. Even if I do, *I* make the final decision, because my father looks to me to make all the important judgments."

"You? Forget it-forget it!" I storm out the garage and head back to the boarding house.

* * * * *

I need a job, but *shit* isn't popping quick enough, so I start looking for work on the other side of the law.

I hear Dennis and them talking about some nigga named

Saul, and how he be pushing. They say that Saul is always looking for someone to make drops for him and *shit,* so I decide to find this *nigga* and see what he's all about. I don't really want to get back into hustling, but I have to make that paper.

I'm almost out of the money that Scottie gave me, and rent is due real soon. I find this *nigga,* Saul in *Buffalo Homes.* He's some big-time banger and dealer, and once I meet him, I'm not sure if I want to be down, but I'm here so, might as well see what Saul's talking about.

As soon as I walk down the alley, Saul and his boys jump to their defense, and put their hands on their pieces.

"Who the *fuck* are you?" one of Saul's dudes demands.

"London. Dennis sent me, he said that some dude named Saul is looking for some help," I answer; still a little apprehensive, but I'm already here.

"Bring your pretty-boy ass over here," another dude says. He pats me down, searching for a piece.

"I aingt got nothing," I say. "I'm just trying to make a little money."

"*Nigga,* you need to be carrying something, walking through this neighborhood. I'm Saul. What kinda money you trying to make?" he asks with a blunt in his hand.

"Small-time *shit.* I got *shit* I gotta take care of, and I aingt found no real gig yet."

"So you expect me to be the unemployment office? Get the *fuck* out my face, *nigga.*"

They all laugh at Saul's comment. I begin to walk away, but before I get completely out the alley, Saul calls me back.

"London. That's your name?"

"Yeah."

"That's kinda a *sissy* name, don't you think?"

"I guess, I don't know," I reply, as Saul hands me a bag, then a wad of cash. I'm not really sure what's in it, but from the weight, it definitely isn't weed.

"Take this to the *Bricktown Station*, and give it to the attendant. He'll give you another bag—bring that back to me. You do all this by midnight, and you keep the money. That's a thousand dollars, cash—deliver my *shit!* Trust me, anything comes up missing, and that's your *ass.* If Dennis knows you, then I know where to find you."

Later, I make the drop and bring Saul back his bag. He

gives me this funny look before he speaks: "We don't deal in small-time *shit*. Get your *ass* a job. You'll never make it doing this."

Perhaps Saul is right. It was different holding up the corner with Scottie. He made sure nothing happened to me, and if something went down, Scottie was always there to take the blame.

I tuck the money in the inside pocket of my coat, and make my way back to the boarding house. When I get home, I have a note on my door from Latoya, asking me to come down to her room.

I throw it in the trash and go to bed.

* * * * *

SHIT!

Another month passes by, and I *still* haven't found a real gig. I decide to go back to the mechanic shop to see if they still needed any help. I know that *bitch*-ass, Mercedes didn't tell her father that I came by, so it's up to me to follow-up.

I walk back into the garage, and the girl, Mercedes is there in her same uniform, this time, she's talking to some other girls. They all stop and look at me when I walk in.

"You're back? You didn't catch the hint?" Mercedes says to me sarcastically.

"Naw, I guess I didn't. Is your father here?" I say and look at her, as Mercedes ponders whether or not to tell me the truth.

"Yeah. Papa! ...That kid I told you about is here to see you." She now points to the short, gray-haired man, working on a 1965 *Porche*. I walk over to him, as I hear the girls talking about me.

"Mercedes, you have to admit, he's kinda cute," one girl says.

"What? No he's *not*. Dude's aggravating, that's what he is," Mercedes spits as she looks in my direction. Just like everyone else, the girls think I'm a guy.

"So, kid, what's your name?" Jaguar asks.

"London Walters," I answer as I shake his hand.

"Don't mind Mercedes. She's a tough person to impress, but a sweetheart. My baby girl. I have four girls—them all over there are my daughters. They range from age nineteen to thirty-four. Mercedes is nineteen. How old are you, London?"

"U-m-m-m, almost nineteen." *Yeah, in like two years.*

63

"Mister Jaguar, I don't know nothing much about cars, but I really need a job. I'm running out of money, and I'm new in town."

"Where you from, kid?" Jaguar asks, sticking his head back under the hood.

"Boston," I reply while trying to see what he's doing.

"When can you start?"

"Today if you want."

The excitement causes my voice to crack a little.

"You said you're almost nineteen, kid?"

"Almost." I look at Jaguar, having a worried expression upon my face. I take a deep breath.

"MERCEDES! ...Show London around. Get him a uniform, and start teaching him the logistics of things."

Mercedes shoots both of us a look of disgust, before telling her sisters that she'll talk to them later.

"Bye, papa," the other three daughters say in unison.

"Bye-bye, sweeties."

Mercedes now turns to me: "I don't know why my father *hired* you. You don't know *nothing* about cars. I am so *not* in the mood to be teaching some busta-ass *nigga*." Mercedes then mumbles many other things, but I can't understand what she's saying. This is the second time we've been in each other's presence, and the negativity is still the same!

"Why you acting like that? I aingt done nothing to you. I barely said a few words to you." I reply, looking at Mercedes with concern, trying to understand where she's coming from.

This is crazy...

I'm really starting to miss everyone at home.

But I can't go back there; not right now.

*   *   *   *   *

The first few weeks at work are horrible.

Mercedes and me *stay* at each other's throats!

Every time I turn around, she has something negative to say to me, and about me. There were so many times where I wanted to cuss this little *bitch* out, but I couldn't risk my job just to get back at her.

"London!" Saiel calls. Saiel is the daughter who's a year older than Mercedes.

"What?" I ask from under a Ford. I'm suppose to be doing an oil change, but it turns out to be an oil spill. "AH, *SHIT!*" I shout, as I quickly roll myself from under the car.

Everyone in the room is laughing.

I look at everybody with a mad embarrassed look on my face, and go to the bathroom to get this oil off my face.

"Maybe next time you won't try to be so cute!" Mercedes exclaims.

"I wasn't trying."

"Sit down!" Mercedes then demands. I sit on the toilet seat and wait patiently, as she uses some stuffed called *Goo Gone* to remove the oil off my face. When Mercedes is done, she washes her hands and face, and walks out the bathroom. "I'm going to lunch, papa."

I just sit in the bathroom...

Watching Mercedes...

As she sashays away....

It's two o'clock when Mercedes returns from her lunch break. I'm in the corner, munching on a sandwich I bought with me, and writing a well-overdue letter to Shantell and Lexi.

"Lunch is over, *stupid!*" Mercedes snaps. I just look at her and stuff the last piece of my sandwich in my mouth. As I begin to fold up the sheet of paper, Mercedes comes out of nowhere and snatches the letter out of my hand.

"Yo, give that back! What is with you? Damn, girl!" I yell.

"Let's see, what does London have hiding in here," Mercedes says slyly, before reading the letter I wrote. *"Dear Shantell and Lexi,"* she reads aloud, as I try to grab the letter from her hand again. *"I'm sorry that I've taken so long to let you all know that I am okay. I'm in Detroit and well, it's aiiight. Shit is mad different around here, but anything beats being at home with moms and pops. Shantell, are you still with Pauly? Probably so. Lexi, what's up, sweetie? I know you're mad at me probably, but I'm sure Shantell explained the situation to you,"* Mercedes pauses, looking at her sisters as they just laugh.

"Mercedes, give me my *damn* letter, girl!"

"I know you wanted to try to make things work, but I just couldn't stay around there no more. It's hard, Lexi. Everything that went wrong, I got blamed for. It got to the point where I was ready to slice that nigga or something.... I'm aiiight though. The

65

bruises went away, and well, that's all that matters in the long run. How's Scottie? Tell him I gotta job and I'm going to pay him back. Lexi, take care of my sister, please. Check on her from time-to-time. I gotta go. Peace and love. London," Mercedes finishes reading my letter. She then just looks at me and hands me the paper.

I aingt got *nothing* else to say to Mercedes!

I finish up my assignment and go home.

At nine o'clock, I hear a knock at my door. I'm a little apprehensive about opening it, because cats 'round here know that I don't be wanting to be bothered; so I'm real curious as to why *muthafuckas* is knocking.

I go to the door with much attitude!

I figure if I show in my voice that I don't want company, that they will go away. I shouldn't even answer the door: "WHO IS IT?"

"*Nigga,* open the door!" Mercedes yells in her ghetto voice.

"What the *fuck* you doing here?" I ask behind the closed door.

"Just open the *damn* door, London! *Shit!*"

I can hear Mercedes talking to someone else, so I know she's not alone. I open the door, and Mercedes and her sister, Saiel are standing on the other side...with these big-*ass*, goofy smiles on their faces. Before I can say "come in", they're already sitting on my bed, flipping channels on my TV.

"What do you want, Mercedes?"

"I just want to apologize—see if your feelings are still hurt," she says tauntingly.

"My feelings was never hurt. I just think that you were being a fucking *bitch* for snatching my *shit* out my hand, that's all." I then roll my eyes at Mercedes, and go sit in my chair.

"Well, my bad, London. It's just that you're so *damn* uptight—I be trying to loosen you up and *shit!* Get you to smile...flirt...something."

"Why you want me to flirt with you?" I ask in a non-flattering way.

"I aingt *say* I want you to flirt with me, London. But, at least if you did, I would know that you had a nice side to you,"

66

Mercedes sneers, before she picks up the picture of Shantell and Lexi and asks, "Who are these chicks?"

I just take the picture out of her hand and put it back in its place.

"See, London, *that's* what I'm talking about! You're so *damn* secretive and *shit!* Like you got mad *shit* to hide! All I did was *ask* you a question, and you can't even answer it! You're a fucking *asshole!*" Mercedes says with a disgusted look on her face. Saiel just sits on the bed, shaking her head.

"The one on the left is my sister, Shantell. And the other one is Lexi, this chick I was kicking it with back home."

"Now, see, that wasn't so hard, right?" Mercedes asks.

"Whatever."

I walk to the mini fridge and pull out a *Corona.* I was about to roll a blunt when the two knocked on my door, so instead, I'll just settle for a beer.

"London...what kind of girls do you like?" Saiel asks. It kinda shocks me because, she hasn't said anything all night.

"What? ...Why?"

"Just curious," Saiel replies.

"Ones who will let me *fuck* them, and then leave me the *hell* alone!" I respond in a nasty tone.

"So that's what Lexi did? I don't believe that. Because you wouldn't have a picture posted up with her in it. Stop trying to be so *hard* for a minute and just answer the question. Maybe you'll see that there's a reason behind it," Saiel snaps.

"Why don't you get to the point? I don't have a particular type of chick that I mess with. I've been with over thirty women, ranging from age fifteen to thirty-five. All races...all levels of intelligence. Most of them I just wanted to *fuck....* Actually, all of them I just wanted to fuck.

"Lexi was the closest thing to a relationship that I've ever been in.... But as you can see, I'm here, and she's not. I'm a *fucking* dog—always have been, so, whatever's your point is, you can erase it. Because I can't feel it."

I then guzzle down my beer, and go get another one to guzzle, too.

"London, you drink a lot, don't you?" Mercedes asks inquisitively, almost sounding concerned.

"Why?"

"Why you always jump to the defense? Lighten up,

London. Saiel asked you that question because *I* wanted to know what kind of girls you like. I would actually consider dating you, if you wasn't such an *asshole.*"

"That's suppose to be a compliment? Should I say 'thank you?' And what makes you *think* that I *want to* mess with you? ...You going to let me fuck you? Because that's all I want. Don't flatter yourself, Mercedes. Besides, you don't want to *fuck* with me anyway." I then give Mercedes a wicked look that makes her think twice about her approach.

"Mercedes, let's go," Saiel interjects. "London, we're sorry for just showing up over here. It won't happen again," Saiel then says, as she pats me on my back, and walks out the door. Mercedes walks pass me, then stops and backs up. She looks me in my eyes, then kisses me on the cheek.

"You intrigue me, London Walters. I don't know why...but you do," Mercedes confesses, and walks out the door.

Fuck! Fuck! Fuck!

This *shit* can't be happening!

I can't let that girl mess with my head like that!

I drink four more beers, and pass out for the night.

*   *   *   *   *

This morning, I walk into work an hour late. Thankfully, Jaguar wasn't there, but I have to listen to Mercedes talk about how she's going to front on me and *shit!*

"What the *fuck* you want to do that for? Jaguar aingt gotta know I'm late," I snap, suffering from a hangover.

"Why not? I aingt got nothing else better to do," Mercedes says and smiles, and goes back to work on the car that she was named after. I start working on a *Chevy* that needs an alignment and a CD player installed.

By mid afternoon, the place is jumping, and *niggas* is in-and-out, trying to holla at Mercedes. This one kid named Raymond comes in, and I guess this is her man or something because Mercedes is all over him.

Yet *I'm* the one who intrigues her...

Fuck that!

I close the door to the truck I'm working on, and go to the cooler to get some water. Three more of Raymond's friends come in, and they begin acting real ignorant and talking loud.

They're now trying to get under my skin by asking me

who am I at a distance, but I'm not even paying no attention to them. This pisses this one kid named Marcus off, because he comes right in my face to make sure I hear what he's saying.

"*Nigga,* I asked, no, *fuck* that, I said, who the *fuck* are you? When I ask, you answer, *nigga!*" Marcus yells and laughs.

"Whatever, man. Get the *fuck* out my face, son. You don't *fucking* know me," I shoot back, and go back to the car I'm working on.

"*Nigga* what?"

Before I can repeat myself, Marcus sucker-punches me in the jaw. His weak-ass punch doesn't hurt that much, but it does pisses me off. Before I know it, we're fighting all over the auto shop.

"HEY-HEY-HEY! CHILL! YO, CHILL!" Mercedes yells. Everything is being knocked off the wall, and *shit* is flying everywhere. Me and Marcus are so caught up in the fight that, neither one of us notices Jaguar walking in and grabbing the fire extinguisher.

Jaguar then pulls the pin and sprays us until we stop fighting: "Knock it off, Marcus! I told you never to step foot in this shop again. Mercedes, you know that. London, go home," Jaguar then demands.

"But, Jaguar, he hit me. I was just defending myself. I—"

"LONDON, HOME, NOW—GO!" Jaguar shouts and points to the door. I grab my things and head for the streets.

"Daddy, wait! London!" Mercedes begs. "Daddy, London didn't do nothing. Marcus started the whole thing. I telling the truth, daddy. London was just doing his job, and Marcus started messing with him. London was just protecting himself, daddy."

Mercedes then looks at me with much sincerity in her eyes. Jaguar stands there for a while, accepts Mercedes' explanation, and lets me get back to work.

"Get yourself cleaned up, London. Change your jumpsuit," Jaguar instructs, before he walks back into his office and makes some phone calls.

I run into the bathroom and change my jumpsuit. Just as I finish zipping it up, Mercedes comes in with a first aid kit.

"You okay?" she asks in a soft, caring voice.

"Yeah, I'm straight," I answer, while stuffing tissue in my nose to stop the bleeding.

"Sit down. Let me look at it," Mercedes insists. She sits

me down and takes the tissue out my nose. "You have to apply pressure to it, London," Mercedes says while pinching my nose.

"Ah! Damn, girl! I know, but that *shit* hurts." I jerk back to force Mercedes to loosen her grip. "I have had enough busted noses to know how to take care of it," I then say softly.

"You've been in a lot of fights?"

"Something like that," I answer bashfully. Mercedes then cleans the blood off my face and hands, and puts a few *Band-Aids* on where I'm cut.

"Mercedes, why are you doing this?"

"Because, that's my nature. Let me see your lip." Mercedes then pulls my face closer to her, causing me to stand up. "E-w-w-w, it's all big and busted. Does it hurt, London?"

"A little bit—not really." Mercedes now rubs her finger over my bottom lip gently, and looks me in my eyes.

"You beat the *shit* out of Marcus. He needed it. Marcus thinks he's so *damn* hard all the time."

Mercedes continues to stroke my lip, then she gently kisses it. She grabs my side, and the pressure causes me to scream in agony.

"What? London, your ribs hurt? Let me see." Mercedes now lifts up my shirt, and I quickly pull away.

"Yeah, but I'm okay. I done had plenty of broken ribs, too."

"London, you need to go to the doctor."

"No. They aingt going to do nothing but wrap them up real tight, and like I said, I had them broke enough to where I know how to do that myself. I'll be okay."

I then look into Mercedes' eyes. She kisses me again, walks out the bathroom, and goes back to work.

This *shit* is getting hard.

I can't do her like this…

I just can't.

MORE ROUTINES
chapter 8

Although I aingt know what the *hell* I was doing at first, I'm now becoming a damn good mechanic. It's gotten to the point to where I'm developing a clientele. Cats really request me to work on their cars. Saying that other cats referred them to me—that they hear I do a good job.

Jaguar said that if I keep up the good work, he would look into having me placed in a bigger shop. I don't know how I feel about that. I kinda like the intimacy of this shop, and being able to look at Mercedes everyday...isn't half bad.

Tonight after work, before I'm able to lock up all the doors, Saul shows up out of nowhere: "Yo, kid, what's up? I need you to make a run for me." Saul's standing in the garage door, dressed in all black, smoking a blunt openly: "I need you to take something downtown—it's worth three grand. So hurry up and do this."

Saul now hands me a block of something that feels like a pound of sugar.

"You got two hours—not even," Saul instructs, as he begins to walk out the auto shop.

"Yo, Saul, I can't do this right now. I got something else I need to do, I'm sorry, man." I start to hand Saul back the package, and he laughs.

"Oh, London...you must've gotten confused somewhere. I wasn't *asking* you to this," Saul says, pulling out a glock and pointing it to my head, "I *telling* you. I'm just paying to ease the anxiety. Now *take* this *shit* to the *McDonald's* downtown!

"Sit the package on the ashtray barrel, then stand across the street. Wait ten minutes, a black *Impala* will drive up. A dude will get out the car and take the package. He'll leave another package, bring that back to me, and I'll give you your three grand," Saul directs, saying the last sentence in a singsong manner.

"Saul...I can't do no more runs after this, I can't get caught up in no *shit*," I reply and look at him sincerely, hoping that Saul will understand.

He doesn't.

"*Nigga,* you approached *me,* you weak-ass *bitch!* You came crawling to me begging for money like you some *damn* junkie. Now, I'm going to use *you* for a little while. London…you going to make runs for me when I *tell* you to, and if you don't, well…that's your *ass.* Now *take* my *shit!* Be back by twelve. If you aingt back at twelve, you better pray your *ass* gets arrested."

Saul then finishes his blunt and walks out the shop. I realize that there isn't anyway out of this, so I grab Saul's package, and run to the spot as fast as I can.

*　*　*　*　*

The guy Saul described showed up.

I'm now back at the alleyway with time to spare.

Saul hands me the three grand.

And I run home.

I started not to even take it, but if I'm about to take a risk and help this *nigga,* Saul out…

…I might as well get *paid* for it!

I run upstairs and put the cash into the lock box that I keep in my closet. I can't deposit all this money in the bank—they will know that something is up.

I *have* to figure out a way to get out of this situation with Saul. I made the mistake of making drops for him, and now Saul *thinks* he owns me!

Where's Scottie when you need him?

I change my clothes and jump into the shower. When I return to my room, I find Mercedes sitting on the floor outside my door.

"Hey," Mercedes says, extending her hand in order for me to pull her up. "I was in the neighborhood, so I thought I'd stop by. Can I come in?"

"I guess."

Mercedes now follows me into my room, and watches as I put all my toiletries away.

"So you were just in the neighborhood, huh?"

"Yeah. I left something at the shop, and decided to see what you were up to. You know you're happy to see me, London."

"I'm glad your confidence is so great."

"You ought to know that by now. You should be use to me messing with you like that. You *fucking* challenge me. You make me work for *shit.*"

"And what *exactly* is it that you're working for?"

"You, of course."

"Me? You don't want me. I aingt going to do nothing but break your heart. Then you're going to be hating on me and *shit,* and have my *ass* jumped. *T-h-e-n,* you're going to have your daddy fire me, and I'll be *fucked* up without a job. I aingt *trying* to have that *shit!* Trust, Mercedes, you don't want to mess with this."

I reach for my ritual *Corona* and lay on the middle of my bed. Mercedes sits in the chair and stares at me for a long time....

"What you thinking about?" I ask.

The silence becomes unbearable.

"Well, I was wondering what it would be like to kiss you."

"You've kissed me before."

"Yeah, I kissed you. But you didn't initiate it. I want to know what it would be like if you initiated it—I know you can be aggressive...you talk about being with women as old as thirty—I can see how some of that can be true.

"You know you *want* me...I don't know why you fronting. You stay talking about this chick, Lexi, but yet you aingt talked to her since you got here. I know you aingt called Lexi, and you've only written her one letter, if you even mailed it. All I'm saying is that, you need to kiss me. You need to be a man and kiss me."

"Mercedes, you do realize that if we do something right now, I still wouldn't be initiating it. It would be happening because you've suggested it."

Mercedes now sits across from me with thoughts written all over her face. The truth is: I want to pin Mercedes down to my bed, and just turn her *ass* out like no tomorrow. I want to do far more than just kiss Mercedes.

But I can't!

I'm still trying to change my ways...

I mean, I'm not ready to tell anybody that I'm a girl...

But, I'm *really* not trying to fool no more chicks...

Really!

Anyway, Mercedes sits in the chair for like another six minutes, then she sits on the bed next to me.

"London, stop *fucking* around and kiss me!" Mercedes now pulls me up, and stares into my eyes.

"Mercedes...you have *no* idea what you're getting yourself into. Ultimately, you're going to end up hating me."

"We'll talk about that when the time comes—stop talking and kiss me!"

Mercedes' soft, luscious lips are just inches away from my mine, and I know I really need to stop this situation...

But whatever!

We kiss like we want to rip each other's clothes off. And trust, it takes everything for me not to do so.

And I don't!

Reasons being: I'm a chick. Mercedes isn't gay or bisexual, or nothing even remotely close. Also, Mercedes is a virgin, believe it or not!

Sure, I can pull out "Joey the ding-dong"...

But I'm not!

I'm not about to fool Mercedes' *ass* into thinking she lost her *shit* to some sexy-*ass* man, one that works in her *daddy's* shop.

BUT *DAMN* THIS GIRL CAN KISS!

The way Mercedes slowly moves her tongue around...

I can't even think!

She stays the night, because I'm not going to let her go home this late.

We kiss all night...

And Mercedes lets me do a few "minor" things...

But I keep it real basic.

I don't even go down on her, and *trust*, I want to!

...We talk when we're not kissing...

...Kiss when we're not talking...

If things were different, I would give Mercedes a chance.

This is something I really gotta think about.

*　*　*　*　*

This morning, me and Mercedes leave out for work. On my way there, I run into Dennis, and decide to see if he can do something about the Saul situation.

"Mercedes, I'll see you at work. I gotta handle something."

"Cool," she says and proceeds to walk.

"Yo, Dennis. How tight are you with Saul?"

"Not too tight. Why? You want me to put in another good word for?"

"Naw, just the opposite. I want you to get Saul to stop sending me on runs. I aingt trying to get caught up. I just needed to do so that one time, and I thought he understood that. But now he just pops up. I don't like that *shit*. That *aingt* my world."

I look at Dennis, hoping he will know what to say or do.

"London, you just going to have to deal with it. When Saul is tired of you, he'll drop you. Aingt no *real* way in getting away from Saul. ...Hang in there, maybe he'll get tired of you soon," Dennis answers and walks away. I then continue on in my direction.

I haven't gotten a haircut in a grip. Can you believe it? My shit is now a mini 'fro, and I'm not really feeling it. So I stop into the barbershop, and have my barber cut me the usual way. It feels so good to get a haircut. I haven't gotten one in I don't know how long.

When I walk into the shop, Mercedes and Saiel both just stop and look at me.

Neither one of them say a word.

I wonder if Saiel knows about me and Mercedes' night...

The two work as some weird duo!

Mercedes is the evil one who plots and *shit*.

And Saiel: the manipulating voice of reason.

There's no telling what Mercedes told her!

Shantell and Lexi walk into *Beth Israel Hospital* for Shantell's eighth-month pregnancy check-up. Pauly is working thirteen-hour shifts, so Lexi plays "substitute", whenever he can't make it.

It's been months since London or Shantell have been home. Shantell ran into her mother a couple of times, but hasn't been back to her parents' house, since the day she left with Pauly.

The last time Shantell saw her mother, she told Shantell that Randy was still staying with her, but things were extremely stressful, now that neither one of the girls were there.

Lorraine wants so badly to be apart of Shantell's life, and to experience her pregnancy, but Shantell has made it clear that, as long as her father was still living there, that Lorraine would never be a part of her unborn child's life.

It's also been four months since Shantell and Lexi had received the letter from London. London didn't put a return address on the envelope, so Shantell and Lexi were unable to write her back.

The two have decided to go search for London, once Shantell has the baby and school is out. Lexi is heartbroken, but she knew not to get her hopes up, when it came to London.

Lexi has been messing with this guy named, Corey for four months, but her heart is still with London. She didn't realize how bad London had turned her out until now, but she isn't trying to mess with no other chicks except London.

Shantell's examination goes well. The baby boy she's carrying is doing great, and the doctor says that the baby is fully developed, and any week can be the moment. Shantell's a little scared though—she's gone to all the classes, watched all the movies, but, Shantell's still not ready to give birth.

Pauly has saved up enough money, so now that Shantell is eight months pregnant, he's going to take a leave of absence from his job, to be with her. Pauly isn't going to miss the birth of his son.

The two of them are still trying to decide on a name, but

Shantell recently remembered having a conversation that she and London once had about naming Shantell's child, if she'd ever gotten pregnant. London had said that if Shantell ever had a kid, she personally wanted to name the child Raven.

London didn't want to be the only one with an unusual name. Shantell thinks that the name Raven is kinda girlish, but she's definitely considering it: Raven Isaiah Rodriguez, or Raven Paulino Rodriguez. Either way it goes, the baby will have one of Pauly's names—Isaiah being Pauly's middle name.

*   *   *   *   *

Scottie is having a party tonight, so Pauly, Lexi and Shantell heads to the old neighborhood to check things out.

"Shantell, what's up, sweetie. Look at you, all pregnant and *shit,* you looking like you about to pop!" Scottie says, as he gently hugs Shantell, then Lexi.

"Hey Scottie, how's life?" Lexi asks.

"Chilling. Always making that paper! I got a new seed on the way, too. I hope it's a girl, since I already got a boy and *shit.*"

Scottie takes the *Jack Daniels* to the head, and goes into the bedroom, where he, his girlfriend, Nature, and a few others are smoking, and doing whatever.

Nature's now in the kitchen cooking up some food. She smiles when she sees Shantell, because Nature has been wanting to talk to Shantell about being pregnant.

Shantell soon looks around the room, and notices her old friends, Ariel and Camille. The three start screaming when they see each other. Since all that drama had gone down at her parents' house, Shantell hasn't really been in touch with her two friends.

"Oh my God! I am so, so happy to see you!" Shan says. "I'm sorry that I haven't been around, please don't hate me," she then pleads and hugs Ariel and Camille.

"Well, I was *hating* on you for a grip," Ariel begins, "but once I found out what was up, I had to give much love to you. You just better get right now. I want to see this baby and *shit!* I can't believe you're pregnant, Shantell—you of all people; but I'm so happy for you though!" Ariel exclaims.

"Yeah, Shantell, when are you due?" Camille asks.

"*Shit,* any *fucking* day. This little *nigga* could pop out right now if he wanted to," Shantell jokes.

"*Shit,* don't say that. We can't be drawing *no* attention to this place," Scottie stated from around a smoky corner. The girls all laugh and decide to go outside to play catch up.

"So what are you going to name him?" Ariel asks.

"Raven. London likes that name," Shantell answers sadly.

"Shantell, How is London?" Camille joins in.

"*Shit,* I don't know...me and Lexi got a letter from her four months ago, but London didn't put a return address on it or nothing. All I know is that she's in *Detroit* somewhere, and London seemed okay at the time."

Camille and Ariel both hug their friend, sensing that the ordeal Shantell is experiencing, has her on the verge of crying. Soon after, Shantell discovers that the party Scottie is throwing, is actually a surprise baby shower for her. The sadness Shantell's feeling quickly turns into excitement and gratefulness.

Shantell receives everything that she can possibly need for the baby—including the unborn child getting enough baby clothes to last him until next year. The baby shower soon ends, allowing the "real" party to begin.

Tonight is a real cool evening.

* * * * *

Ever since that fight I had with Marcus, me and Mercedes have gotten real close. She's always in my room at all times of the night, and we made out a few more times.

I *never* let Mercedes do anything to me though.

Because as far as she "knows", I'm London the "boy".

Not the girl.

I don't want to deceive Mercedes like this, but *damn*...she's so sweet! And Mercedes still don't strike me as the type to even *think* about messing with a chick.

We've been messing 'round for like three months now. Mercedes wants to *fuck* real bad...but I tell her that I don't want to take it there. I told Mercedes: *"I'll be glad to eat you out whenever you want me to, but I'm just not ready to go all the way."*

Besides, there's still a lot that Mercedes don't know about me. She knows nothing of my home life, or even that I'm about to turn eighteen, not twenty.

Yet, Mercedes don't have a reason to question, whether I'm a boy or not anyway, because the strap-on that I wear contains a censor...causing "Big Joey" to rise; whenever I get really horny. So as far as Mercedes "knows", I get hard...

Just like the rest.

*　*　*　*　*

Everything is great! Beautiful! She is *so* beautiful!

Jaguar restores a 1957 *Chevy,* and gives it to me as a birthday present.

"I can't take this, Jaguar."

"But I insist. London, I haven't seen my baby girl this happy in a *long* time. Mercedes wanted to do something special for you, and I suggested this," Jaguar says while handing me the keys.

"This is too much!" I reply. I have to admit, I'm really happy, too! I mean, I'm still missing Lexi, but I don't think we will really work.

I know she's probably *fucking* other dudes anyway. Lexi probably doesn't even feel like she's cheating, since I'm really a girl, technically, and she's *fucking* a dude.

I open the door to the car and sit inside. Jaguar has done an *excellent* job at restoring this car. It's beautiful!

"Take me for a ride!" Mercedes orders. She jumps into the car, and I back it out the garage. We drive all over *Detroit,* and before the night is over, me and Mercedes are back at the boarding house making out.

She's trying so hard to get me to *fuck* her.

But I come up with every reason why we shouldn't.

Mercedes kisses me on my neck and chest, and my hormones want us to be skin-to-skin. It helps that I don't really have any breasts, because the little that I have, just looks like underdeveloped pecs.

She now licks 'round my nipples and *shit,* but doesn't think twice as they get hard.

It actually turns Mercedes on a little more.

I'm losing control, but I quickly regain it before it goes too far.

"London, you have more willpower than I have ever seen. You've seen my *entire* body...and I've *only* seen you from the chest up. What? ...Do you think you have a little *dick* or something? Because, from what I can tell...you don't," Mercedes states, pointing to the fake, hard imposter.

"It aingt that...it's just that I want us to wait. Every girl I've been with, has been just a *fuck.* I don't want it to be that way

79

with you. I'm actually changing my ways for the first time in my life. It feels good. I mean, there are still a lot of things you don't know about me. But I promise, I will tell you when the time is right."

"You've been saying that, but you haven't said *anything* yet. Whatever it is, I'm still going to be feeling you," Mercedes says, as she tries to assure me.

"I wouldn't count on that...I know once I reveal *all* my secrets, I will be the last thing on your mind. Let's just enjoy this time. For once, I'm truly happy. It's kinda fucked up because, things aingt completely right."

"What are you *talking* about London? What is it, baby?" Mercedes holds my face with her left hand. She kisses me gently, and starts gathering her things: "I have to go, but I will see you at work."

Mercedes leaves the room, and closes the door behind her.

*   *   *   *   *

"PUSH! ...PUSH! ...*P-U-S-H!*" the nurse instructs. Shantell's water breaks an hour ago, and little Raven is now curiously coming headfirst. He doesn't waste any time entering the world—the doctor pulls out a scared, screaming baby boy. The nurse wipes Raven off, wraps him in a towel, and places Raven onto Shantell's chest.

"He's beautiful," Shantell whispers in between tears. The nurses then take Raven back to fully clean him up and weigh him.

"Seven pounds, nine ounces," the doctor says. "What's his name?"

"Raven, Raven Isaiah Rodriguez," Shantell answers while taking Raven back into her arms momentarily. She then hands him over to Pauly, and resumes pushing; now releasing the placenta. Pauly holds his baby boy in his arms, and gently kisses Raven.

Raven tries to open his tiny eyes, but the strain from just being born doesn't allow him. Raven has a head full of hair and gray eyes. He's really light, but the top of his ears is darker, letting us know that Raven will get a bit more color to him.

As the doctors take Raven and move him to the infant room, Pauly goes out into the hallway to tell Scottie, Lexi, Ariel and Camille that Raven has been born.

"He's so tiny—oh my goodness! Raven's beautiful! He tries to open his eyes, but can't really do so. And keeps yawning

80

and everything!" Pauly explains with excitement all over his face.

"How's Shantell?" Lexi asks.

"Great. She did really well. Shantell didn't even cry until after Raven was born. I think she's just happy, you know."

"Yeah. Can she have company?" they all ask in unison, followed by laughing simultaneously, realizing that they all asked at the same time.

"Yeah, but they're taking her to another room now. So once Shantell gets settled, y'all can see her. We can go look at the baby though," Pauly says, and starts walking toward the viewing window.

Raven is right in front behind the glass. Pauly goes inside the infant room, put on scrubs, and picks up his son to show Raven to his adoring fans.

"He-is-so-c-u-t-e," Camille coos.

"That little *nigga's* going to be a heartthrob," Ariel playfully states. Pauly then puts Raven back in the bed, and the group then heads to Shantell's new room. She's dozing off, but wake's up immediately when Pauly and her friends walk in.

"Shantell, Raven is beautiful, just beautiful!" Camille raves.

"Isn't he?" Shantell replies and smiles at the crew, as they then talk about Shantell's experience delivering the baby. Fifteen minutes later, the nurse wheels Raven in for Shantell to feed him.

The nurse then teaches Shantell the best technique to breastfeeding. She explains that there's an art to it, and if not done right, the baby won't be fed properly. Shantell catches on quickly while nursing Raven, who gently tugs onto her with his hungry mouth, eager to get is mother's milk.

"Damn! Pauly, you can't play with those for a while. You gotta wait 'til they dry up. Breast milk is mad nasty, kid!" Scottie jokes.

"You would know," Shantell slyly interjects.

"Hey, I can't help it if my son's mother was a freak. She wanted to do it as soon as she was released from the hospital, but they say you're suppose to wait a month; you know, so that *shit* can heal," Scottie explains before sipping on his soda.

Shantell continues to feed her son, *I wish London was here to enjoy this moment.*

*   *   *   *   *

As Shantell puts Raven's clothes on, and packs up her things to go home, her mother walks through the hospital room. Pauly had just left the scene a few minutes before, to get the doctor to sign the release forms.

"Hey sweetie," Lorraine says. Her mother's voice startles Shantell, causing her to jump and turn around.

"Ma, what are you doing here?"

"Pauly called the other day to tell us that the baby had been born. I just wanted to see him before you all went home."

Tears immediately fill Lorraine's eyes, as she sits in the chair, next to the bed. Shantell sits on the bed, and thinks to herself for a moment, contemplating on whether or not she should let Lorraine hold her newborn child.

The look in Shantell's mother's eyes is genuine, but desperate. Shantell then decides to let down her guard: "You can hold him," Shantell says, pointing towards Raven as he lays inside the crib. Lorraine walks over to her grandson and picks him up. She cradles Raven, rocking him back-and-forth, which causes Raven's eyes to open.

"Oh, he has beautiful eyes," Lorraine says softly.

"Yeah. They're gray, like yours. Me and Pauly assumed that he got them from you, because no one in Pauly's family has gray eyes. We hope the color stays."

"Yeah, hopefully they will. What's the baby's name?"

"Raven. London likes that name."

"I know. I remember you two talking about it a long time ago. Shantell, have you heard from London?"

"Not in a while; and then it was only once. She's in *Detroit* somewhere. London didn't give an address or a phone number, but when the baby gets a little older, we're going to look for her," Shantell replies, as she takes the baby back from Lorraine and heads toward the room door.

"Honey, if you ever need anything—"

"I know...I know," Shantell answers back, before she meets Pauly in the hall. Shantell, Pauly and Raven then exits out of the hospital.

Shantell wants Raven to know his grandparents, but she still has a few apprehensions. Shantell is very adamant about them not seeing the baby until her father is out the house, and seeking help.

Shantell does feel good about seeing her mother though;

it's been a while since Shantell has last seen her.

Unfortunately, Shantell hasn't seen her father since the day she'd left her parents' house.

CONTINUANCES
chapter 10

Lorraine walks into her house, and as usual, Randy is sitting on the couch, drunk, and half passed out. She quietly puts her keys in the dish on the living room table, and attempts to wake him up. At first, Randy doesn't budge, but after a few taps by Lorraine, he decides to look in her direction.

"What?" Randy says flatly.

"I saw Shantell and the baby—he's beautiful. His name is Raven, and he's an exact mixture of Pauly and Shantell. She even let me hold Raven, which shocked me a little."

"That's nice," Randy replies dryly, and gets up to get another beer. When he returns, Lorraine looks at Randy oddly.

"What? Lorraine, what do you *expect* me to say? I'm happy? *Hell* no I'm not happy! Shantell just had a baby and she's *barely* seventeen! You want me to jump for joy? Run down to the hospital and shower Shantell with gifts? *Fuck* that! Shantell wants to be grown, so *let* her!"

"You are such an *asshole, Randy.* Such a complete *asshole.* I can't *believe* that I have put up with your *bullshit* for as long as I have. You're a waste of my time," Lorraine says angrily, as she walks away in bitter disgust.

"I'm a waste of your time? *Bitch,* I've *only* been with you for as long as I have, because of the girls. Your tired *ass* aingt *ever* go out and get no *damn* job. Your *ass* aingt *ever* discipline them *damn* children. It's because of *you* that London and Shantell turned out the way that they have."

"*My* fault? Are you really going to sit up here and pretend that our children's personalities and actions are because of me? Randy, *fuck* you!"

"*Fuck* you!"

"Well, Randy, let's go with your theory for a little while. You say you were here *solely* because of the girls—well, they're not *here* anymore. So why are you *still* here? Why are you *still* climbing in bed with me every night trying to get you some? You're nothing but a *womanizer* with one thing on your mind. London gets *that* from you!"

Lorraine then attempts to walk past Randy, but he snatches her back by her upper arm.

"*Bitch*...watch yourself. You trying to get all bold and *shit?* You bound to get *fucked* up!" Randy threatens.

"Really? ...You know what? ...You can *do* what you *want* to do! You can *beat* my *ass* until you pass out from exhaustion—I don't care anymore! But I *promise* you this, you lay *another* hand on me, and I will *kill* you myself!" Lorraine spits defiantly.

The look in Lorraine's eyes shows how serious she is.

Randy loosens his grip.

Sits back on the couch.

Keeps quiet....

"Randy...I think it's *time* that you went on your way. When I come back, your *ass* better be gone," Lorraine sneers, as she picks up her keys and heads out the door.

Lorraine finds everything possible to keep herself busy while being out. Six hours later, she returns home, and Randy is gone. Lorraine isn't really sure if he's gone for good, but, when she falls asleep and wakes in the morning, there's still isn't any sign of Randy.

This is what I wanted, Lorraine thinks to herself in between yawns. *Now it's time to get my family back in order.* The first thing she does is call her mother, whom Lorraine hasn't talked to in over five years.

They talk for hours over the phone, and try to plan a weekend visit. Lorraine explains the years of abuse endured, and how both London and Shantell are no longer living in the house. Lorraine also expresses to her mother that she has no idea where London is, but that Shantell is doing well.

She then tells her mother that Shantell had a baby boy, and how they all will meet real soon.

*   *   *   *   *

"London, London, London," Saul begins, "*Nigga,* you are r-e-a-l-l-y trying to get on my bad side."

"What are you talking about?" London asks, as she follows Saul into the back alley where he always hangs out at.

85

"Why you asking shady *niggas* like Dennis about me? Telling this *nigga* to speak to me on your behalf. It doesn't work that easy…. I told you before—I own you. And when I'm ready, I'll hang you out to dry. *Nigga,* you seem to forget that, *you* came to *me!* I didn't come finding your sissy *ass*, you came to *me!* So that means you need me!"

"Saul, that was a one-time situation, I thought you understood that," London replies, as she looks into Saul's eyes, with hopes of him being compassionate.

"Its *not* my job to feel sympathetic, *nigga.* I don't know why you trying to play these games."

"Saul, man, please. Just let me chill. I don't *want to* be down with this *shit* no more. I'm cool…I don't need all the extra *shit* no more. I'm saying, if you want your money back, I got most of it; and I can get the rest if you want. Just let me chill.

"Saul, I'm trying to stay out of trouble. I don't need any cops on my *ass* asking me questions and *shit,* questions I don't know how to answer. And you be sending me to do deals with *niggas* twice my size—that aingt cool, man."

"London, stop sounding like a *punk!* You can handle your *shit,* you're a tough man," Saul retorts, as he begins to roll up a blunt. He then hands London a corona. London takes a deep breath, pauses, and makes one of the hardest decision of her life.

"Saul…I aingt a dude…I'm a chick. I look like a dude, but, Saul, I aingt. So I'm asking you kindly to chill, please."

Saul stops rolling his blunt and laughs in London's face.

"*Nigga,* what? What kind of *shit* you trying to pull on me?" Saul then asks with a slight bit of anger.

"I'm not trying to pull nothing on you. It's complicated, trust me. But-on-the-real, Saul, I'm asking you nicely to please just let me be," London pleads, standing there hoping that Saul will give her a break. Saul now has an evil expression upon his face, which makes London feels that her pleading is hopeless.

"You know what, kid? You aingt even *worth* my time. Get the *hell* out of my face! Don't come to me no more about no *bullshit!*" Saul then walks away, leaving London standing in the alley alone. She feels fortunate to have gotten out of this bad situation with Saul, yet, London vows to herself to never make any more mistakes like this again.

*   *   *   *   *

"I'll get it!" Pauly says in response to the ringing doorbell. Shantell is nursing Raven, and is preparing to change his diaper. "Who is it?" Pauly asks.

"It's Lorraine...may I come in?"

Pauly unlocks the door to his townhouse and let Lorraine in. "Hey," Pauly says, uncertain if he should've warned Shantell of Lorraine.

"I apologize for just showing up, but I need to talk to Shantell. I have some news for her that I think that she'll be happy to hear. Is she home?"

"Yeah, she's in the other room." Pauly now shows Lorraine to the room that Shantell is in. The immediate silence gives him the cue to leave.

"...What's up, ma?" Shantell greets Lorraine.

"I just wanted you to know that Randy is no longer living at the house. We had our last argument.... You were right, sweetie, my priorities are off, but I want to be your mother again. I want to help you and Pauly raise the baby. I want you to be able to come to the house without feeling apprehensive. Shantell, baby, I'm sorry for everything that you had to endure."

Silence....

"...I talked to your grandmother the other day," Lorraine announces.

"Really? How was that?"

"It was great actually. She was more than excited to hear from me, I'm going to visit her. We would both love for you, Raven, and Pauly to come as well...think about it at least," Lorraine says and smiles. "Shantell, your hair is growing; it looks great," Lorraine states, moving a stray piece of hair out of the corner of Shantell's mouth.

"...I don't know what to say. I never thought that you would actually stop dealing with daddy. I mean, I guess I understand the whole love thing.... I totally love Pauly, and I'm sure I will do every and anything to keep our relationship going. But I swear, if he *ever* raised a hand to Raven—we're through!" Shantell retorts, standing while holding Raven. Lorraine then throws away the soiled diaper.

"Still nothing from London?"

"Naw, ma. Honestly...I don't think we're going to hear from her anymore...not any time soon. Whatever London's dealing with out there, has got her consumed. I hope she calls or something. I mean, the weird thing is, London hasn't even called Scottie. He's pissed, but Scottie's trying to be cool about it. You know how he feels about her."

"Yeah. When we see each other, Scottie just apologizes; as if he's the one who caused London to leave. Anyway, I don't want to think about that right now, I've been crying ever since you and London have left.... May I hold Raven? Please?" Lorraine randomly asks. Shantell hands Raven to her mother.

"He's only three weeks old, but Raven's already starting to get spoiled."

"How's he sleeping?"

"He wakes up every five hours, it's cool though. I love looking in Raven's eyes, so when he is awake, I try to play with him as much as possible," Shantell answers while smiling.

"How's Pauly doing with the baby?"

"Ma, he is great. Pauly gets up more than I do. Some nights, he won't let me get up at all. Pauly's off on the weekends, so he usually takes care of the baby then."

"He seems like a good guy...just don't make the mistakes your mother here has made.... Shantell, I have to go. I have some things to take care of around the house. Please call me later in the week. I really want you all to come with me to your grandmother's house."

Lorraine then kisses, Shantell, followed by kissing the baby and Pauly as well. Before she leaves, Shantell assures her mother that she will be in touch.

WHEN IT RAINS IT POURS
chapter 11

It's been a year-and-seven-months since I've set foot in *Boston*. I have no idea what is going on back at home, so I decide to take a little trip. I request a week off from work, and head for the train station.

I'm not sure what I'm in store for, but I need to see my sister. And I need to pay Scottie back. Things with Mercedes and me are great.

Shit, we even had sex.

I pulled it off like this: I had Mercedes put on a blindfold, and I gently tied her hands to the bedpost.

That way, Mercedes couldn't see nor touch me.

I just wanted to do my thing to her. The moment was great, and Mercedes was *a-l-l* for the role-play.

I made her cum three times....

It was straight, although now, I'm feeling bad about the whole thing. I need a break, so I decide to head back to *"The Bean"*.

I arrive at *South Station* 'round nine in the morning. It's kinda windy out, so I put on my *Carhardt* hoodie, and make my way to the "orange" line. I didn't want to drive my car, because I don't want *niggas* in the hood sweating me and *shit!*

I walk onto the sidewalk that makes up *Roxbury*, and feel a real, interesting vibe.

"Hold up, I *know* that's not my *nigga* London? What the *fuck*, man?" Shawn says, as he runs up to me and gives me a big hug.

"'Sup?" I ask with a crackly voice.

"Where the *hell* did you blow in from?"

"*Detroit,* man. I've been in *Detroit,*" I answer, as we walk towards the barbershop I used to go to.

"*Nigga,* you know your sister had a baby right?"

"*WHAT?* A baby? By *who?*" I ask; real shocked.

"Pauly, man, who else?"

"They're still together? Damn!"

"*Hell* yeah, kid. They about to get married and *shit.* The

89

kid is mad cute, he has gray eyes and *shit,*" Shawn says with much excitement.

"Damn, what else is going on 'round here?"

"Well, Maverick's on lock—got caught with rocks; charged with possession with the intent to sell. Lexi's still *fine* as ever, but she kicking it with some *nigga*. Lexi talk about you all the time. You turned that *hoe* out, man! Lexi be trying to pretend she all straight, but Lexi's really just a *dyke*.

"This *nigga* she messing with be on some stupid *shit*, too. He be getting mad 'cause Lexi spends so much time with Shantell, and he knows the deal with you and her. Be trying to control her and *shit*." Shawn then takes a breath. "…Scottie's a big-timer. He got another kid on the way, too. Oh, your nephew's name is Raven. That's fly, right?"

"Raven? For real?" I ask, being very pleased.

"Yeah, I think it's spelled R.A.—"

"V.E.N.," I finish.

"Exactly. Other than that, not much is happening. Your pops is still an *asshole*. He got arrested not to long ago—a *'D.U.I.'* charge I think. Oh yeah, Shantell aingt been staying there since you left. She been kicking it with Pauly ever, since man. They happy though—real happy," Shawn explains to London before they part ways.

London heads for Pauly's crib.

* * * * *

Pauly is in the middle of changing Raven's diaper when there's a knock at the door.

"Who is it?" Shantell asks from the other side. Pauly and Lexi looks at each other, both not expecting company.

"Is my bridge still standing?" London asks. Lexi and Shantell looks at each other and immediately opens the door.

"LONDON!" Shantell screams with much excitement. "Oh my God, London! O-h-h-h!" Shantell holds London tightly in her arms.

"What's up?" London asks, hugging Shantell back. "'Sup, Lexi? You still looking good and *shit*." London says to Lexi before walking over to her; London now gives Lexi a long hug.

"Yeah. You look good too, London; real good," Lexi states, as she wipes the tears from her eyes and sits back down; Lexi now feeling a little faint. Pauly finishes changing Raven's diaper before giving daps to London.

London immediately goes toward her nephew, who now lays in the bassinet in the living room. She awkwardly picks Raven up. London has very little experience with holding newborns—she struggles for a minute while trying to position Raven correctly; securing the back of his head.

"I can't believe you had a *fucking* kid, yo," London says to Shantell, keeping her eyes fixed on Raven.

"Are you mad?" Shantell asks with concern.

"Not mad...but—"

"Disappointed?"

"Yeah...a little," London now looks at Shantell, concerned. London then sits on the couch and cradles Raven in her arms. His eyes flutter—the left eye opens, the right remains closed. Soon, Raven begins to cry and turn red, signaling London to pass him back to Shantell.

"He's really cute though, Shantell. I'm happy that you're safe and healthy, but I don't want you to lose focus, you know?"

"I'm not going to loose focus, but I understand your concern." Shantell then leans over and kisses London on her cheek. Shantells happy that her sister is finally home.

London, Shantell and Lexi then catch up and talk for hours. At first, Shantell and Lexi expressed how pissed they were at London for not keeping in touch, but eventually, the two forgave her, and quickly updated London on all the news.

After spending most of the night with Shantell, Lexi, Pauly and Raven, London decides that now's a good time to pop up on Scottie. Having the three thousand dollars that Scottie had given her, London now wanted to pay him back.

Scottie was like a brother to London. He'd always made sure that London was alright. Scottie taught her everything she knows about acting like a dude, and playing the game.

He thinks it's funny how London is able to pull mad chicks—most of them not knowing that London's a girl. Some are pissed off when they find out the truth about her, but honestly, many of the girls don't seem to care.

London walks to Scottie's apartment and knocks on the door.

"WHO THE *FUCK* IS IT?" Scottie yells in an angry,

aggravated tone.

"*Nigga,* it's London!" she answers in her manly voice.

"London? Yeah right. The only London I know, dipped a long time ago, and aingt ever been heard from again."

"Well, it's me, Scottie, now *open* the door, *nigga.* I'm surprised you're not outside holding up the corner.

Scottie immediately opens the door, and his evil frown quickly turns into a smile, when he sees his friend, London, standing before his eyes.

"*Nigga,* give me a hug! I am *so* happy to see you! Are you okay, London? Do you need something," Scottie asks worriedly.

"No, Scottie. I'm chilling. I just popped in town for a quick visit. I had to get my mind right before I came back," London says, as she sits on the love seat in front of the big, forty-five-inch *Sony* television screen.

"You seen Shantell yet?"

"Yeah, I saw her and that beautiful baby boy of hers—I still can't believe it."

"I know, kid. But Shantell's doing well for herself. Pauly is really taking care of her—they're getting married and all."

"I heard," London responds, amazed.

Scottie and London continue to sit and talk into the wee hours of the morning. Later in the day, London and the whole crew gets together and hangs out. Everything is peace, but no one has any idea that Ryan's gotten word that London is back in town.

Ryan found out a few months ago that London is really a girl, and doesn't like the fact that he got his *ass* kicked by a chick. Now that Ryan has heard that London has surfaced, he's out for revenge.

Ryan knows where Scottie hangs out, and believes that London will more than likely be with him. He started to do something to Shantell, but once Ryan found out that she had a baby, he changed his mind.

Ryan wasn't trying to make the kid no orphan.

* * * * *

Back in *Detroit,* Mercedes is bragging to her sisters about how great the sex is with London. She's truly falling in love with "him", and wants to do something really special for London.

Tonight, Mercedes goes over to the *Lawrence House,* and convinces the landlord to let her into London's room. Mercedes has all kinds of decorations and gifts for "him", wanting to surprise London when "he" comes home.

"I can't *believe* you're going through all this," Saiel says before she starts blowing up balloons.

"I know. I can't believe I'm *feeling* this *nigga* this hard. I think I'm just whipped!" Mercedes replies.

"From what? You and London *only* did it once."

"But London can eat the *fuck* out of some *pussy* though! That *nigga* stay having me climbing the wall. You know...I have never been in here when London wasn't home. I wonder what he got *going* on around here that he doesn't want me to see," Mercedes says, as she begins to go through London's things.

"Mercedes! Don't go through the man's *shit!* You might *find* something you *don't* want to see—and then what?" Saiel spits.

"...This *nigga*, London keeps talking about how there's *shit* I don't know about him anyway, so I *might* as well play detective. He's taking *too* damn long to tell me." Mercedes then picks up a pile of papers out of a file cabinet and starts flipping through them. "Pay stubs...bills...bills...more bills," Mercedes says to herself.

"Mercedes, you *really* need to stop."

"Perhaps you're right, Saiel," Mercedes answers, as she puts London's papers back and opens the closet door. Saiel then looks in the closet.

"Mercedes, why you leave so many *tampons* over here? That's weird."

"...Yeah, it is...because those *aingt* mine." Mercedes pulls the box of tampons out the closet, and looks in it to see how many are missing. "I don't even *use* this kind, must belong to some other *bitch.*" Mercedes then put the tampons back where she found them, yet, Saiel now picks up a stack of medical papers that had fallen when Mercedes opened the closet.

Saiel reads the contents of the paper, and her mouth practically *drops* to the floor. Mercedes notices her sister's reaction, so she immediately walks over to Saiel.

"What, Saiel? ...What is that? What does it say?"

"U-m-m-m...doctors' papers."

"What? London aingt got no *disease,* do he? Because I don't even know if London used a condom," Mercedes confesses. Saiel looks at Mercedes again and shakes her head.

"Naw...no disease...and whether London used a condom or not, doesn't matter," Saiel answers worriedly, having a traumatized look upon her face. "Mercedes...I think you better sit down."

"Why? What that *shit* say?" Mercedes asks anxiously.

"London aingt...Mercedes, this nigga...damn! Mercedes. W-O-W! London *aingt* no dude!" Saiel says emotionally; completely shocked.

"WHAT?" Mercedes asks with much confusion.

"London...Mercedes, London is a girl!"

Mercedes can tell by the look in her sister's eyes that Saiel isn't kidding. Mercedes immediately snatches the papers out of Saiel's hand, and reads everything from the name of the patient, to the diagnosis of a urinary tract infection.

"A girl? ...But I *fucking*...I *fucked* him! Her...it! We had *sex,* Saiel, how the *fuck* is London a girl?" Mercedes now being hurt, quickly turns into anger: "THAT'S WHY THAT *MUTHAFUCKA* NEVER WANTED ME TO TOUCH DOWN THERE! AND WHY HE...I MEAN SHE, *WHATEVER,* DIDN'T REALLY WANT TO HAVE SEX WITH ME!

"I am so *fucking* stupid! He made me...*FUCK!* She made me wear a blindfold. Said she wanted to try something new.... I don't understand Saiel, I've seen London's chest, and she *aingt* got no breasts. I mean, there are nubs, but I aingt think nothing of it," Mercedes explains as she begins to cry.

"Mercedes...sweetie, she had us *all* fooled! London don't *look* like no girl! She doesn't *sound* like no girl, and London *sure-as-hell*, doesn't *act* like no girl! We had no reason to think otherwise. Sweetie, just leave this *shit* alone and let's go!" Saiel instructs, taking the papers out of her sister's hands while ushering Mercedes to the door.

"WAIT!" Mercedes shouts. She turns 'round and starts ransacking London's room—pulling all her clothes out the closet, throwing London's books and papers all over the place.

Mercedes knows in the long run that destroying London's room will only make the situation worse.

But it makes Mercedes feel damn good!

Mercedes and Saiel returns home, and Mercedes tells her father the whole story about how London has been lying to them

94

the entire time.

"Daddy, London aingt even twenty-years-old—she just turned eighteen! London tricked me, daddy, she *used* me. Daddy...I even let London take my virginity," Mercedes regretfully confesses, before burying her face in her father's chest.

Mercedes then cries for the rest of the night.

She now wants to do everything hurtful to London, in the name of revenge. But little does Mercedes knows that, what London is about to go through back home in Boston, will be sweet satisfaction....

*　*　*　*　*

POP-POP-POP!

The sound of three gunshots fill the busy air of *Roxbury*.

POP-POP-POP-POP!

Four more shots are fired.

Everyone scatters for shelter.

Lexi screams London's name from behind a parked car.

On the ground lays both Scottie and Ryan.

"S-C-O-T-T-I-E!" London cries. "NO, NO, NO, SCOTTIE! ...Come on, man...you *can't* die on me. I *NEED* YOU, SCOTTIE! ...I *need* you, man." London holds Scottie's lifeless body in her arms.

Scottie has two gun shot wounds to the chest, and one to the stomach. Before Scottie died, he killed Ryan: one shot in the head, and Ryan's gone....

"Scottie, I am *so* sorry, man. I aingt mean to for this to happen. Scottie, please...please, Scottie," London continues to cry and holds Scottie, until the paramedics and police comes. Lexi tries to console London, but she doesn't let her.

"NO! GET THE *FUCK* AWAY FROM ME! I DON'T *WANT TO* BE BOTHERED!" London yells angrily.

"But, London...baby?" Lexi begs.

"NO, LEXI! WHAT THE *FUCK,* MAN? ...HE'S *DEAD!* MY *NIGGA,* SCOTTIE IS *DEAD!* IT'S *ALL* MY FAULT! I SHOULD'VE *NEVER* COME BACK...I SHOULD'VE STAYED, MAYBE HE WOULD STILL BE ALIVE!"

London, still on her knees, continues to cry her eyes out. Lexi attempts to console her again, but London pushes her away, and runs swiftly up the street.

*   *   *   *   *

Scottie's funeral is three days later.
London gives the eulogy.
Over two hundred people here are sadly crying.
Folks are passing out left-and-right.
Scottie is now buried....
London can't take all the emotions.
She catches a train out tonight.
This time, London makes sure to give Shantell and Lexi all of her information. London then cries the whole way back to *Detroit.*
Before heading home, London stops at the store to pick up a case of *Corona* and a few *Dutch Masters* cigars. She has every intent on either drinking or smoking her sorrows away.
London isn't fully successful.
She just gets drunk in the streets.

*   *   *   *   *

I walk up the stairs, then down the hall to my room. Just as I'm about to unlock the door, I notice that it's slightly open. I peek inside to make sure that no one is in there. I turn on the light, and notice the mess everywhere.
"WHAT THE *FUCK,* MAN!" I say out loud.
My room is completely *fucked* up!
This shit don't make no sense...
There's balloons and other decorations and shit in here that don't belong to me. I sit on my bed, and open a bottle of beer.
I haven't had a haircut in a while 'cause Mercedes wants me to grow my hair out, so I start twisting the short Afro, as I ponder the chaos in here....
I don't really understand what happened.
I look 'round to see if the stuff I have in hiding is still secured...it is. I'm *so* hurt by Scottie's death that, I don't want to think about this *shit* right now!
I drink the rest of the case of beer, and smoke three blunts by myself.
Needless to say I pass out.

At four in the morning, I wake up to a loud knock on the door. *What the fuck, man?* Still completely drunk, I stumble to the door. I'm seeing like three of everything, but against my better judgment, I open the door.

"What?" I ask flatly. Saiel stands on the other side of my door. "What are you doing here? Where's Mercedes?" I ask before stumbling back to my bed; I fall hard on it.

"U-m-m-m, trust me, Mercedes is the *last* person you should be thinking about right now," Saiel states and sits down on the bed next to me.

"What do you *mean* by that?"

"London, how much have you been drinking?" Saiel then asks, answering my question with a question.

"I don't know, why?"

"You reek, and well, the stumbling doesn't help. You *really* need to stop drinking. You're going to be wrinkled before your time."

"I'm surprise you care, Saiel—why are you here? It's *fucking* four in the morning, I'm *fucked* up, and all I really want to do is go to sleep. But I'm trying to figure out why you're here."

"I have my reason."

"…I'm waiting."

I'm not sure what *game* Saiel is playing, but I don't really have the energy to fight with her. Saiel now sits and looks 'round the room.

"It's a mess, Saiel, I know. I don't know what happened though. I came home and my *shit* was all over the *fucking* place. I want to say I got robbed, but I don't think I'm missing anything. I really don't give a *fuck* though; I got other *shit* to think about. Mad crazy *shit* is going on at home. I—"

"You went home?" Saiel interrupts.

"…Yeah, I needed to get away. Shit was getting too intense here. I needed to have a revelation or something. I mean, I needed to get away from Mercedes for a while. She's trying to be all into me. I don't know how I *feel* about that. I mean, don't get me wrong, I'm feeling your sister, but—"

"But what? Personally, I don't think that you and Mercedes are right for each other. I think that you two should just chill out."

"Why you say that?"

"Because...I just don't think that you two are good together."

"Well, half the time, I don't think we're good either, but I think my situation with Mercedes will be cool, once I explain a few things."

Saiel now sits quietly, staring in my face for a long while. Before I can even register the events, she leans in and kisses me.

"Yo! What the *fuck?* What's the deal with that?" I ask, pulling away from Saiel.

"London, just go with it," Saiel whispers seductively. She starts kissing on my neck and nibbles on my ear. With the combination of the beer and weed, it doesn't take much for me to get aroused.

"Saiel...what are you doing? How are you going to *fucking* play your sister like that? I know I'm drunk and high and *shit,* but I aingt going out like that."

"London, my sister don't want *shit* to do with you right about now. You want to talk about playing her? *Bitch,* you're the one who *fucking* played her!" Saiel now rises from the bed and begins to unbutton her blouse.

"What are you *talking* about?" I ask, somewhat confused. Saiel then moves in closer to me, and begins to take off my shirt. "Saiel?"

"All you had to do was tell her, London," Saiel whispers, as she starts unbuttoning my pants.

"You really need to chill," I say, pushing Saiel's hands away. "I'm dating your sister, what kind of *shit* is this? Straight *grimy,* yo."

"Grimy? You're grimy. You're the one who fucking led my sister on." Saiel continues to unbutton my pants. I try to readjust myself, hoping that she will get the point.

Saiel doesn't.

I'm *fucking* confused.

I truly have no idea as to what she's talking about.

"London, did you *really* think that Mercedes wouldn't find out? Did you think that she would go through you all's relationship without even touching or seeing your shit?" Saiel asks facetiously, referring to me not having a penis. She then leans forward, and begins running her tongue down the center of my stomach.

"Saiel?" I breathe.

"Mercedes *hates* you right now. She wants to rip your *tongue* out of your mouth and feed it to you," Saiel laughs. "Right this very moment, Mercedes is sitting in her room, plotting." Saiel then lifts my "wife beater" over my head and straddles.

"Why's she so mad?" I ask naively, completely in heat.

"Because you tricked her." Saiel begins caressing my chest and kissing me deeply...for whatever reason.

I go with the flow...

I think the beer and weed is in complete control, and even though I know where this is leading, I don't care. Saiel now rocks softly on top of me. At a time when a *dick* should be hard, "mines" wasn't. I don't have "Joey" on, and I don't even bother trying to explain anything.

"So what's your point?" I ask.

"You're an *asshole.* Sexy-as-*hell,* but an *asshole.*" Saiel takes off my pants completely, and removes the *Hanes* boxers I'm wearing. She just sits here, looking over my body.

At this point, I don't care about nothing.

Everything that matters is *fucked* up right now.

There isn't *shit* else to do but chill in the moment!

"Mercedes did this to my room?" I ask in between intimacy.

"Yeah. We wanted to surprise you. Mercedes and I thought you needed a nice, little surprise. But, we discovered some *shit* about you that neither one of us were prepared for.

"Personally...I find this bit of information, rather intriguing.... But Mercedes, she didn't take it that well—so here we are. I felt bad...I wanted to clean it up before you got back, but I couldn't get in the building. What you did is real *fucked* up, London."

"Like what's going on right now?"

"...I know what I'm doing right now is *fucked* up...but I don't care. I've wanted to *fuck* you since that day you came in my father's shop, but you were all in Mercedes' *shit.* The fact that you're a chick, makes it even more interesting."

Saiel continues to kiss on me....

Even though I want this shit real bad, I can't do this to Mercedes. Perhaps she does hate me. *Shit,* I was wrong. This game always backfires, but yet, I continue to play it.

"Saiel, you gotta go. I don't care what your motive is, but you gotta go."

"You're kidding, right?"

"No, I'm not! Put your *shit* on and get out!" I demand.

"Aren't you the one who said you date girls who will let you *fuck?* Your loss! My sister isn't going to get down with your *dyke*-ass! You ought to be happy that one of us wants you!"

Saiel now gathers her belongings and heads toward the door. "London...if I were you...I'd stay away from my family."

She then walks out the door, and I try to process the moment. I don't know what the *fuck* is going on here. All I know is that, I'M COMPLETELY *FUCKED* UP, AND ALL I WANT TO DO IS GO TO SLEEP!

So I do.

DECISIONS
chapter 12

I walk into the car shop three days later, still suffering from the severe hangover I had. Mercedes and her sisters are standing by the water cooler talking, but they get extremely quiet when I arrive. Up until this point, I had no recollection of the night with me and Saiel, but once I see her standing in the room, I remember immediately.

I go to get my jumpsuit, but before I can, Jaguar approaches me: "London, we need to talk," he says in a very fatherly, but demanding voice.

"Jaguar, I know I was suppose to be back to work a few days ago, but my best friend got killed while I was in *Boston.* I just couldn't deal for a while—I'm sorry, Jaguar," I explain and apologize, hoping that will clear everything up.

"That's *not* what I want to talk to you about, London. *Look,* I don't want to make this a long, drawn out thing, but, I have to let you go," Jaguar states, handing me my paycheck.

"But why? Jaguar, I'm for real, my boy, Scottie got killed and—"

"It's *not* about that, London. It's the fact that you have been *lying* to all of us since you got here," Jaguar retorts while pointing to his daughters and himself. "You could have gotten me shut down, London, do you realize that?"

"What are you talking about, Jaguar? What did I lie about that could've done all that?"

"First of all, your age!" Jaguar spits angrily. "When I hired you, you said that you were almost nineteen, but come to find out, you'd just turned seventeen. I am *not* supposed to put anyone under eighteen around the type of equipment we work with!"

"Jaguar…I really needed this job, I was about to be living on the streets. I'm sorry I lied about that, I'm sorry, Jaguar. I still need this job, please don't fire me," I beg.

Jaguar just walks away.

Mercedes now walks up to me with disgust ridden all over her face: "You are such a *fucking* asshole, London! Everything

101

that comes out your mouth is a lie!"

"What the *fuck* are you talking about?" I ask, knowing exactly what Mercedes meant. I figure if I play dumb, shit will go smoother. I need this job really bad!

"You lie so much, you don't even recognize your *own* lies, London. It's pitiful. How could you *do* this to me, London?"

"Do what, Mercedes? What did I do?"

"*DAMN* YOU, LONDON! ...PERHAPS THE FACT THAT *YOU* HAD ALL OF US THINKING THAT YOU WERE A DUDE WHEN YOU'RE REALLY NOT! WHAT KIND OF *SHIT* IS THAT? I AINGT NO *FUCKING* DYKE, LONDON! HOW DARE YOU! YOU'RE SUCH A FUCK UP!" Mercedes screams, and pushes me in my chest. Her sisters stand at a close distance, observing the situation. Saiel has a smirk on her face that I finds questionable, as if she's enjoying this confrontation.

"Mercedes!" I plead.

"HOW COULD YOU, LONDON? I LET YOU DO THINGS TO ME THAT *NO* MAN HAS EVER DONE! I WAS FALLING HARD ENOUGH TO LET YOU TAKE MY VIRGINITY! DO YOU *REALIZE* HOW HARD THAT WAS? DO YOU?"

Mercedes strikes me hard in my chest again.

"Mercedes don't hit me, please."

"WHY THE *FUCK* NOT, LONDON? YOU AINGT NO *NIGGA*, SO I CAN HIT YOU IF I WANT! YOU PLAYED ME FOR A *FOOL*, LONDON! YOU *USED* ME! IT'S NOT MY *FAULT* IF YOU CAN'T GET NO GIRL TO LIKE YOU! YOU DON'T HAVE TO TRY AND *TRICK* them INTO DOING SO."

"Stop *hitting* me, Mercedes," I say, trying to move out her way, but Mercedes keeps on yelling and swinging. I quickly walk into a back room at the shop, Mercedes and her three sisters follow.

The two older sisters then stand near the doorway with their arms folded—they seem equally pissed. I just hope they don't try to put their two cents into this situation. Mercedes still continues to hit me.

"Stop!" I demand. "*Damn*, Mercedes! Stop *fucking* hitting me! Stop, stop, *STOP!*" I yell, as I push her as hard as I can, causing Mercedes to fall and scrape her arm. Mercedes two older sisters immediately run to her aid, now shooting me dirty looks. Saiel runs in my direction and tries to block me, as if I'm going to hit Mercedes. I get away from Saiel.

"*FUCK,* MERCEDES! WHY YOU GOTTA HIT ME? WHY YOU GOTTA COME AT ME LIKE THAT?" I cry and slide down the wall. "I'm *sorry* I lied to you—I was going to tell you, I swear!"

"WHEN? When were you going to tell *me,* your girlfriend, that you're a girl? What, when you're down on your knees about to propose? *FUCK* THAT! I *aingt* no *dyke,* London!"

"Mercedes, please, listen to me. I was going to tell you, but the more-and-more I tried, the harder it got. It aingt *never* been this hard for me! I aingt never cared before. I would just *fuck* a girl, then tell her later that she's just been turned out. But I was feeling you *hard,* Mercedes...I'm still feeling you.

"Mercedes, I wanted to tell you so bad, because I could see how much you were digging me. I kept telling you that you didn't want to *fuck* with me, that there was a lot of *shit* that you didn't know. But you kept trying, and then you kissed me."

"That's *bullshit*, London! There was plenty of time to tell me," Mercedes yells with tears in her eyes.

"I didn't want it to go here, Mercedes. I didn't want you to find out like this. I am *so* sorry; I really am…. I wasn't trying to turn you out or nothing, but the more time we spent together, the harder it got, Mercedes—you made me happy.

"You made me smile…you said it yourself, Mercedes, that I was so uptight. But you taught me what it was like to have fun, to enjoy just being alive. Then you told me you loved me...and I *really* believed you. I felt safe with you...but every night you left my place, I sat there asking myself, how I was going to tell you," I confess before pausing to take a breath, and to wipe my eyes.

"…Mercedes…you asked me why I came here, why I moved all the way from *Boston* so randomly—this is why, right here!" I point to myself, "The way I *look,* the way I *act,* both has gotten me in *so* much trouble; not by outside people, but by my family! I told you the scars on my body were from all the fights I've been in, in a way that's true, but *every* last one of those scars were put on my body by my father! He beat the *shit* out of me all the time, because of how I look. All the time, Mercedes," I whisper softly.

"You asked if I drank a lot, I do, 'cause it's the only way I can get rid of the pain. I'm here because my *own* mother chose my father over me. He made her *put* me out, 'cause my pops said that beating my *ass* wasn't doing nothing anymore. My pops don't even *claim* me! So, my moms put me out, she put me out, and that's why I'm here. Mercedes, that's...why...I'm...here.

"The *only* front I put on was letting you think that I was a guy, based on the way I looked. But I've looked this way for a long time. Mercedes, I didn't intentionally set out to hurt you. I'm sorry, and no, I don't expect you to understand or forgive me, but, know that you made me happy; you said you loved me, and truly meant it." I then cough a little and take another breath from going on a tangent.

"London, Lexi loves you...go back to her," Mercedes says in a cold, uncaring tone.

"Perhaps...but I don't love her—Lexi's from the old me, not like this," I blurt out while pointing back-and-forth to myself and Mercedes. I then look at the tears forming in Mercedes' eyes...

Before walking out the door to go home.
My w-h-o-l-e world is now crumbling!
I don't know what to do about it...
So I drink...
...And drink...
...And drink...
For twelve hours straight!
I then throw up.
And drink again...
I'm self-medicating...
But slowly committing suicide....

*   *   *   *   *

I sit on the stoop of the boarding house, drinking.
Turning into a little sad alcoholic.
I'm depressed.
I don't see no point in living...
But I'm *not* about to take my life.
Not directly anyway.

I have no job, but have mad money saved; plus the money that Scottie refused to take back from me. Scottie's girlfriend, Nature, cleaned out his apartment, and counted up all the money he'd stashed around.

Scottie didn't have no family—Nature was the closest thing. She's now having his kid, and has her name on the lease at

Scottie's place, so the landlord can't evict Nature.

Nature recently gave me six thousand dollars, and told me that she was sure that Scottie would have wanted me to have it. I blow a chunk of it on bullshit, but decide to save the rest, 'cause there aingt no *telling* when I will get another job!

Earlier today, Saiel had the *n-e-r-v-e* to try that seduction *shit* again. I had to *check* her real quick! Saiel got the point! Told her this shit is stupid, and that her silly, impulsive-*ass* move was worthless! Now, I'm alone—left here to *fucking* fall apart! *I refuse.*

"Long time no see," Saul says, breaking my thought process.

"Yeah. Well I've been a little busy, Saul."

"Haven't we all. Yo, I know we had that talk and whatever, but I really need you to make a run for me."

"Saul, m-a-n, I can't do that *shit*—you *know* that."

"Yeah, kid, but, you were the best runner I had; the one I trust the most. I guess it's true what they say, London.

"What?"

"If you want something done right, let a woman do it," Saul replies and smiles. I just look at Saul blankly.

"I can't feel that, Saul—sorry."

"London, it's straight; it's an easy gig. All you have to do is run up to the high school, six blocks up. There will be a chick named Courtney waiting. You see, I got your back."

"I don't need it."

"Anyway...all you have to do, is hand her this block. That's it; simple."

"Well if it's so simple, Saul...why can't you do it?"

"'Cause, the king vulture never lands first." Saul now holds his hand out, and in it, rests a solid block of heroin. "Ten thousand dollars, London. Think about what you could do with that...think about it, London."

...I sit here strongly contemplating the situation.

It does sound simple...

What could go wrong?

I've done runs for Saul time-and-time again.

It's all-good, right?

"...I can't—sorry."

I stand up and go back into the house.

The last thing I need right now, is a case.

* * * * *

It's been months since I've seen or heard from Mercedes. People 'round here know I use to push for Saul, and although I cut that loose, I still have a bad name 'round town.

It doesn't surprise me.

Latoya finds out that I'm a chick, but still wants to kick it, so finally, I give her a chance. I'm quickly back to living the same life I left in *Boston.*

I don't care.

I have nothing to succeed for.

Shantell doesn't need me.

Lexi gave up on me.

And my parents don't give a *damn* about me.

I let my hair grow out, and many say that it makes me look more feminine. I start letting Latoya braid it, and she convinces me to let her arch my eyebrows. For the first time, I'm getting' attention from both chicks and niggas.

It's weird.

I'm not feeling dudes, but it's still weird.

Today, I run into Saiel at a cookout. She says that Mercedes is doing great without me, and that she's kicking it with some *nigga* named Junior.

"You're gaining weight," Saiel says, as she points to my breasts that are finally starting to grow.

"Yeah, it's all the beer and weed." I answer. "Tell Mercedes I asked about her, please."

"I don't think that will be a good Idea. London, just let it go; you *fucked* up. You could've had a really good friend. And now you have nothing." Saiel then gives me a hug, "Shit, you could've had me, but you *fucked* that up, too."

* * * * *

Pauly and Shantell wants to be closer to me.

They feel like I need them for a change.

So they pack up and move to *Detroit.*

I'm mad happy to see them!

Raven has gotten so big, and he still has his gray eyes. He's trying to walk, but it's not happening just yet.

"I like the hair, London," Shantell admits when I pick them up from the train station. I gave Jaguar back his car, but bought myself a *Neon.* While at the car, Pauly takes charge of putting the luggage and Raven's stroller in the trunk.

"Do you? It takes some getting used to, but I think I'm feeling it."

"It's cute. You got mad pretty hair; it's about time you let someone see it," Shantell replies.

"What's going on in *'The Bean'*?"

"Not a *damn* thing, London—nothing! Daddy's still locked up, and ma actually filed for divorce. I guess she's happy. Ma wants you to call her. It *has* been about two-and-a-half years," Shantell says sarcastically.

"Yeah...maybe I will; I don't know though," I answer.

We drive to my loft apartment, and I show them where they will be sleeping. Pauly and Shantell promises that they'll be out and into their own place soon, but I tell the two that I like having them with me.

* * * * *

More months pass by, and before we know it, it's time to celebrate Raven's first birthday. We have a nice little party for him, which consists of more adults than kids; it's nice though.

Shantell soon makes me go into an *AA* program, 'cause she says that she doesn't want to see me turn out like daddy.

I'm trying *r-e-a-l* hard to get my life in order.

I *WANT* to be happy.

It feels good to be happy.

I have my sister, my Raven...I'm lacking a love life, but, things happen for a reason. Pauly even got me a job at the plant he's working at.

Finally, I call my mom for the first time in almost two-and-a-half years: "Hey," I greet her.

"LONDON!" she replies with surprise, "My gosh, you are the *last* person I was expecting to hear from! How are you?"

"Okay, I guess. I've been worse, so I should be grateful."

"Yeah," my moms answers. We talk for hours, and for the first time, I remember what I was missing. For so long, I pretended that I can take care of myself: *"Shit, I'm London! I don't need nobody!"*

But we all know that's a bunch of *bullshit!*

If Shantell and Pauly didn't come out here when they did, I would be either dead, or on lock.

I ended up making that run for Saul that night, and it was the *worst* mistake ever! The *fucking* cops raided that *shit* and

107

charged me with possession. I sat in jail for two months before the cops allowed me to make a deal.

It's kinda *fucked* up but, Saul flipped the *shit,* and the one who ended up taking the fall was Dennis. Come to find out, Dennis was stealing from Saul all that time, and Saul wanted to just blast that *nigga!* But instead, Saul pinned all the drug charges on Dennis. I don't know how Saul did it...but it cleared me.

Jail *aingt* no shit!

Yo, there are chicks *harder* than me in there, and flipping more chicks than me, too. This one *bitch* tried to *pimp* me! That's when I knew I had to get the *fuck* out of there.

I sat in jail for so long, 'cause they wouldn't let me use my own money to get out. I couldn't get in touch with Saul, 'cause he's one of those *niggas* you just run into.

I finally broke down and called Shantell.

She flew out here a couple of days later and paid my bail. The last thing I wanted was for Shantell to see me fucking up again. She was cool about it though.

My hair has grown out to my shoulders, but I'm still wearing it natural. I'm still thugging out, but not as hard. I'm just trying to maintain, trying to stay sober.

So that I can be a good example for my nephew.

REVELATIONS
chapter 13

Seven months later...

I walk in the door from work. Shantell is feeding Raven, and Pauly is at the grocery store. The smell of baked chicken, collard greens and macaroni and cheese fills the air. We don't cook that much, so I'm a little curious as to why we're about to have a feast.

"Just be patient, London," Shantell says cunningly. "Go take a shower and change your clothes, dinner should be ready shortly."

I do as my sister requests: take a shower, put on a black sports bra, a white "wife beater", a T-shirt and a *Phat Farm* pullover sweater and jeans. I look up and see Shantell standing in the doorway like old times. I brush my wet and wavy hair back into a ponytail, and smooth out my eyebrows.

I come into the living room and start playing with Raven. Me, Raven, Shantell and Pauly moved into a house three months ago. With everyone's combined salary, we were able to pull it off.

The doorbell now rings.

I put Raven down and go see who's at the door.

"Hello," I say, but no one answers.

The doorbell rings again.

I open the door and almost thought I saw a ghost.

"Happy birthday!" wished by a very sexy Mercedes and Saiel.

"Huh? U-m-m-m, thanks," I respond, giving her and Saiel a very confused look.

"You going to invite us in, or are we going to have to barge our way in?" Mercedes playfully asks.

"Yeah, come in." I move out the way so they can enter, Saiel immediately takes a seat on the recliner. "I'm just shocked to see you, that's all. How'd you find out where I lived?"

"Your sister came to visit me at the shop a few weeks ago. We had a real long talk. Shantell helped me understand you better. I'm going to be real with you, London...I was pissed at what you did. I mean, I aingt never messed with a girl before...the whole thing blew my mind, and I was tripping for all the wrong reasons.

"I've been doing a lot of thinking, and talking to my sisters and father. The truth is...I really did love you...I still love you, and no matter how hard I try to stop loving you, I can't," Mercedes confesses. She now places her fingers on my lips to stop me from saying what I'm about to say. "Don't speak." Mercedes then pulls my face close to hers, and kisses me long and deep. When we stop kissing, me and Mercedes both have tears in our eyes. "Let's start over, London. No lies...no secrets."

With that being said, I feel like I should tell Mercedes about me and Saiel: "Mercedes...there is something you should know," I say shyly.

"What?"

"U-m-m-m...way back when, me and Saiel—"

"I already know, London; I told her to do that. I know about the last time, too, although I *didn't* tell her to do that—we talked about it all. London, squash it. I just want to start over, is that cool?"

"Yeah, it's cool."

We all then sit down to eat the birthday dinner Shantell has prepared. It's peace, yo, I'm happy again; it feels great! Me and the bunch laugh all night, and at the end of the gathering, Shantell reveals that she's pregnant again. Raven's now a little over one, and Shantell always said that she wanted her kids to be close in age; like me and her.

"London, come here," Mercedes calls.

"What's up?" I ask, concerned. Mercedes pulls me into my room, and pins me up against the door....

* * * * *

To everyone's surprise, things between Mercedes and me are going rather smoothly. It's almost this level of perfection, all over again. I'm still not quite sure what Shantell has said to her, but I appreciate it.

I have no idea if the next few months to come will actually be *fucked* up.

I don't care.

All I know is that, a chick that I tried so hard to be real with, finally understands me.

I realize that everything in life happens for a reason. And although I can't understand why Mercedes is truly digging me...

110

I don't care.

Each day that makes up this relationship we're in, seems more-and-more interesting. Jaguar is *not* happy that Mercedes decided to be with me; and he makes it be known, every chance he gets. I quickly became, one of the many people who are banned from the auto shop, and I know that Jaguar is waiting for me to *fuck* up.

"Young lady, I will tell you once, and once only. If you hurt my daughter, Mercedes as severely as you did the last time, you will forever live to *regret* it," Jaguar says calmly.

"What you mean by that?" I ask, although I really have a good idea what Jaguar means.

"Simply don't hurt her. If you do, you'll wish that you never set foot in *Detroit*. I don't feel the need to go into details, because then the threat becomes idol. Just understand me, London…and if you *don't* believe me—try me."

Jaguar now looks at me with mad intensity in his eyes…

I know what he means by the determination in his voice, but in my opinion, there's nothing that Jaguar can do to truly scare me. I've been through too much *shit* to let Jaguar scare me!

I don't care.

I'm happy.

And I'm not going to let anything change that.

Jaguar can't ever understand what I'm feeling.

I won this one!

A girl that truly knew nothing about me, has fallen head-over-heels for me, again!

CAN'T *NOTHING* STOP THIS!

"Look, Jaguar…I understand your concern, but I aingt about to do *shit* to hurt your daughter. You aingt even gotta *worry* about that, and you *really* don't have to be casting no threats on me. If this *shit* ends with me and Mercedes, it's because Mercedes ended it. Simple as that."

I give Jaguar a look that shows that he can trust me, but Jaguar stares right through me.

Whatever!

I aingt really worrying about it.

He's trying to break me…

But that *aingt* going to work.

All I know is that I got Mercedes…

That's peace!

Lexi walks up to the main door of London's parents' house, and hesitantly rings the doorbell. She hasn't been there since her two best friends, London and Shantell have left *"The Bean"*—beginning a whole new life in *Detroit.*

It takes several minutes and three doorbell rings, before Lorraine finally strolls to the door: "Lexi? What brings you by?" Lorraine asks with genuine interest.

"Well, I was in the neighborhood, and I just figured I would come by and see how you were doing."

"That's very nice of you. Please, do come in," Lorraine instructs, moving out of the way, in order for Lexi to enter the doorway. Lexi then looks 'round as if she's never set foot in the house.

Nothing has changed in appearance.

Not physically anyway.

Yet, the place had a completely different aura.

Spiritually, Lorraine's home is at ease—the energy feels good. There used to be so much tension lingering in the air. You *never* knew what to expect when you walked into this house. As a result of this, Lexi never came to visit London.

"Lexi, can I get you something to drink?" Lorraine asks, breaking Lexi's train of thought.

"Oh…sure." Lexi then smiles at Lorraine, as Lorraine heads into the kitchen to fix a drink for her. Lexi follows.

"What's on your mind, Lexi?"

"Nothing. I just wanted to say hello."

"From the look on your face, you seem as though you want to say *more* than hello," Lorraine replies, handing Lexi a glass of apple juice.

"Is it that obvious?"

"Yes, talk," Lorraine demands.

Lexi takes a deep breath before she begins: "…This is going to sound stupid but…I miss London. I miss her *so* much that it hurts! And it's obvious that London doesn't miss me, because she hasn't tried to contact me at all. London wrote me once when she first got out there in *Detroit*, and I talked to London in person seven months ago when she came back to *Boston*, but that's it.

"I don't even know why I miss London. It's *not* like she ever really cared about my feelings, or what I had to say about anything, but at the same time, I've *never* felt feelings so intensely for anyone." Lexi then looks at Lorraine with tears in her eyes.

"Lexi, it's always hard to separate yourself from the one you love the most. Take Randy for example. As *horrible* as that man is…there's not a night that goes by when I don't miss him. I find myself crying a lot at night. Lexi, I feel so *helpless* at times, but in my situation, I *needed* to let Randy go. He's not healthy for me or my kids. My problem was that I waited *too* long to realize that, and both of my kids have isolated themselves from my love."

Lorraine takes a breath, "…Lexi, my point is this, London can be a very *challenging* person to reach out to. She's been through *so* much that, London doesn't know *how* to express her love. She doesn't know how to show her appreciation, and London doesn't know how to ask for help. Her father has raised her with the mentality of a man. That's why it hurt Randy so much when London turned into this dramatic tomboy, right before his eyes; Randy *never* expected her to adopt his words as her lifestyle.

"Lexi, London does love you…I can honestly say that, because out of all the girls that has come in-and-out of this house, you have been around the longest. Lexi, if you feel as empty as you say without London, then you *need* to do something about it."

"But what if it's not healthy?"

"You won't know until you try," Lorraine says confidently.

"It's really not that simple. Me knowing London, there's probably some chick up there making her happy."

"And me, her mother knowing London, there probably isn't." Lorraine then scribbles on a piece of paper and hands it to Lexi.

"So you think that I should just write London? Even though she probably won't respond?"

"Lexi, if you want to be with my daughter, then you will do whatever it takes."

Lexi sits here for a moment, pondering the situation before her. *This is completely idiotic!* Lexi thinks. Lexi knows that she wants to be in contact with London, but she's extremely scared of the possibility of rejection.

Lexi can't believe that she's about to set herself up, for the most humiliating experience in her life. But, as Lorraine said, *"Whatever it takes."*

Lexi decides to give it a try.

Lexi now rises from the seat she's in and heads for the door. She then stops before opening it, and turns in Lorraine's direction: "Thank you. I might be back," Lexi says and laughs.

"You better."

Lorraine then gives Lexi a long hug, and closes the door behind her. Seconds later, Lorraine sits on her couch and thinks about the conversation that she had with Lexi.

She can't understand why girls fall so hard for London.

Lorraine can't count how many times, females have come crying at her doorstep, 'cause London tricked them, fooled them, loved them, then played them.

Lorraine also can't understand how these girls never knew that London was a girl. Any female that found out that London was a girl, is 'cause Lorraine told them. These girls would call-and-call-and-call over the phone, and when Lorraine got fed up, she would say, *"You do know that London is a girl, right?"*

The girl on the other end of the phone gets silent…

Silence, followed by a dial tone.

As sad as it was, Lorraine found a great amount of enjoyment out of telling them. Of course London would come in the house pissed off, but that was *her* fault.

Nobody *ever* taught London to be deceitful!

She deserved whatever she got when these girls confronted London later on. The most amusing thing about it was: Lorraine would see these same girls at her door a month later.

The girls didn't care.

And Lorraine could care less for *any* of them!

But, she had a special place in her heart for Lexi.

Lorraine knew that Lexi would be the one to set London straight. Lorraine also felt in her heart that she did the right thing by giving Lexi' the address to where London lived. For once, Lorraine wanted to do right by her kids—this can be a start.

Ten minutes later, Lorraine walks over to her entertainment center, and puts on an old *Otis Redding* album. She plays *The Dock of the Bay*, a song Lorraine listens to a lot when she's sad. The music has a way of helping Lorraine clear her thoughts, and clarity is much needed these days.

Lorraine now pours herself a glass of scotch. Although she was never a heavy drinker, Lorraine finds herself indulging more often. In all reality, she hates liquor—Randy has spoiled all that made liquor sexy.

Randy has taken something so simple, occasional and fun, turning the act of drinking into something very complex, habitual and evil.

Randy became the Devil himself!

Now, there's nothing beautiful about that, but at the same time, Lorraine satisfies her mental thirst with the regiment.

There are so many things that I need to organize...Here I am, giving Lexi advice, and I'm the one who needs to be reuniting with London and Shantell.

I don't understand myself sometimes....

It's ridiculous. I can't even begin to imagine how I would go to re-enter their lives...I suppose it's worth a try. I mean, what do I have to lose? ...No...no...it's not that simple. I have betrayed them so many times...I've let London and Shantell down in times when I was just trying to make things right. My philosophy of how I wanted things to go, backfired in my face, and now, I am here...alone...wallowing.

Lorraine sips the rest of her drink...

Puts the glass in the sink.

Turns off the radio.

Heads upstairs.

All she now wants to do is take a nap.

Depression is a strange thing...

It tends to consume your life, when nothing else does.

A sad situation.

As Lorraine stands in the doorway of London's old room, she thinks about the nights that London and Shantell left her home.

"Your daughter is a fuck up, and I want London out of my house, NOW!" Randy's voice plays over-and-over in Lorraine's her head.

"What? You kicking me out? You picking that nigga over your own flesh and blood? Your first born, ma? You just kicking me out like that?" London's voice now blares in the vessels of her brain.

"London, you are not a child anymore. Everything that you've done, you chose to do, London. You don't need to be here.... You don't hardly be here anyway, London," Lorraine then

115

hears her own words.

"N-O-O-O-O-O-O!" Lorraine now recollects Shantell's scream, one that echoed across the entire house. *"This is all your fault! It's your fault that my sister's gone! How could you do this?"* was Shantell's reaction. Lorraine, caught up in the rapture of her thoughts, ponders long and hard on Shantell's anger, pain, disappointment and exit.

Lorraine now lays on her bed, and cries the familiar tears that expresses her regrets. She isn't sure on how she will get through to her daughters. Neither London or Shantell were planning on coming back home to live. Shantell is with Pauly and Raven—her new family, and London, living under the same roof as her sister, wasn't going back to *Boston.*

Maybe I'll surprise London and Shantell.... Save some money, get a train ticket and surprise them.... No, that wouldn't work, they may be busy...or may not even let me in the door. ...But I'm their mother, of course they'll let me in their home, especially since I would've traveled all the way there.

I'll figure it out....

It really doesn't make sense to sit here and worry myself about it. I'll just sleep.

When I wake up, everything will come to me.

LEERY LEXI
chapter 15

Lexi stares at the address that Lorraine has given her. It's not like she doesn't have it already, but it's more of a confirmation that Lexi needs to use it.

Lexi now wonders what she will say to London....

How will Lexi express to London that, she needs her in her life, without sounding like some pitiful and desperate person? ...Lexi can't describe it, nor can she fully understand it, but, what Lexi does know is that, she connected with London in unimaginable ways.

"YO, WHAT ARE YOU *DOING* IN THERE?" yells a male voice from the bedroom. It's Corey, the dude that Lexi's been messing with on-and-off since London left. There isn't anything special or nice about Corey, he's just convenient. Yet, Corey knows the right things to say, and at the right time. Although he can be very aggravating, Corey also creates brief moments of sweetness.

Corey's been waiting for Lexi to fix him something to eat, but she's gotten so caught up in her thoughts that, it completely slips Lexi's mind.

"I'm coming!" Lexi yells back, as she slowly makes her way to the kitchen.

"WELL HURRY UP, YO! I GOT *SHIT* TO DO, AND *NOT* A LOT OF TIME TO DO IT!"

"What do you want?"

"A SANDWICH IS FINE—JUST FIX SOMETHING QUICK SO I CAN GET THE *HELL*-OUT OF-HERE!" Corey snaps. Lexi now looks in the opposite direction of the room, and feels bad about jumping to Corey's every whim.

What am I doing? Lexi thinks to herself, as she begins preparing Corey's sandwich. *I can't believe I'm letting this nigga run me...that's not even my style. I'm not trying to have it! If he's hungry, Corey can fix his own food!*

Lexi stops in mid preparation, throwing the knife unto the counter before she slides the plate to the left; causing it to tremble. Corey then walks into the kitchen with a shocked look on his face, as he bites his bottom lip.

"What the *hell* is your problem? If you *didn't* want to fix me something to eat, then you should have said so from the jump! Sitting up here *wasting* my *fucking* time! ...I told you I got *shit* to do!"

"Yeah, well, I do, too; so fix your food and go," Lexi demands.

"You're tripping, Lexi! You've been tripping a lot lately...if you *don't* watch out, you going to find yourself alone!" Corey threatens.

"Do what you gotta do, perhaps I *need* to be alone.... It's about time I had a little space."

"Space? ...You want space, this coming from a *bitch* who pages me every hour, asking when I'm coming over. You don't know what space is. But you got that now, I'll *give* you your space, but *don't* be calling me when you get lonely. I'm out!" Corey says and walks out the door.

Lexi has only been using Corey as a safety net, but truthfully, she's not really feeling him these days. Lexi's been spending way too much time, thinking about London, knowing that she should've been concentrating on Corey. He noticed it, too.

Corey also knows about Lexi and London, but doesn't care. He actually thought that it would've given him the opportunity to have a threesome, but Lexi shot that down *real* quick. She can't understand why *niggas* always think they can get in on the action when they find out that their female friends are bi. Straight girls don't run around trying to dip in the sex life of some bi man. It's crazy!

Everyone in the neighborhood questions Lexi's infatuation with London. All they see is London's persona, or rather, the "image" she puts on. They all are unaware of the conversations that Lexi and London have had, the looks that they'd shared, and the passion the two both have and relate to.

Lexi and London have a lot in common; at least Lexi feels like they do. She met London at a time when nothing was going right, and although London had her own agenda, she was still able to bring Lexi out of a really down period. London was the only person who showed interest in Lexi. Lexi didn't have anybody.

No one to talk to.

No one to help her when she needed it.

Then London came along.

118

London feels like family to Lexi, and that's what she needs. Lexi's been an orphan for as long as she can remember. At the tender age of two, her mother had given her up. Lexi bounced around within the system until age five. Back then, she was placed in a long-term foster home, but when Lexi was ten-years-old, she'd been removed from that home; due to her foster father molesting her.

Unfortunately, Lexi was then placed in several more group homes. At age twelve, she was placed at the *Italian Home Group Home* in *Jamaica Plain,* but ran away from there when she was fifteen. During this time, Lexi spent six months living on the streets, but couldn't deal with the lifestyle. She was placed into the *Greentree Girls Program* in *Brockton, Massachusetts* for the next two years. Yet, Lexi ran away again, spending more time living on the streets.

Three months before her sixteenth birthday, Lexi was arrested for several criminal offenses; spending the next two years in the custody of *D.Y.S.* When released, she was then placed in an independent living program, and stayed there until age nineteen. The program helped Lexi find an apartment, where's she's been residing ever since.

Lexi had met London a week after she'd moved, and although London had tried her hardest to pull off the image of a man—Lexi knew the *real* deal from-the-jump!

She didn't care that London was a chick, but Lexi allowed people to think that she didn't know about London being female.

It made it more interesting.

Lexi was intrigued by their reactions and comments.

London tried her best to pretend that Lexi was just a *fuck!*

But Lexi knew that wasn't the case.

Granted, sex was the basis of their relationship, but some way, somehow, there's more to it than just meaningless romps in the bedroom.

Lexi now stands up and shakes herself back into the real world. She just spent an hour sitting and thinking about what to do—Lexi now needs a break. She decides to clean up her house, before fixing something to eat.

Lexi's house is a *mess!*

Corey left all his *shit* everywhere.

Lexi hates this.

One great thing she can say about London is: that London's neat. London can't stand messy areas—a filthy place can put her in a bad mood.

Lexi now straightens up the entire apartment.

She then pulls out some leftover steak from last night.

Warms it up.

Sits at the table.

What am going to do? ...I need to write London. What's the worst that can happen? She won't write back...but at least if London doesn't write back, I won't have to worry about being embarrassed. Lexi ponders these questions and thoughts, over-and-over again. By the time she's finished eating, Lexi still doesn't have a clue on what to do.

She decides that a hot bath will do a little justice. Lexi now travels into the bathroom, and runs a tub full of water. The scorching water is so intense that, she can see steam rising from the faucet. Lexi then adds a very small amount of cold water, followed by pouring in two capfuls of bubble bath.

It smells like lavender.

She lights three candles.

Now a *"Vanilla"* incense.

And voluntarily seeps into the pool of relaxation...

Feels so good...

Lexi can feel every muscle in her body relaxing. Although the water is severely hot and burns her a little, Lexi needs this.

Lexi is somewhat satisfied that Corey is out of the picture for right now. She really doesn't need him confusing her mind. Hell, it's hard enough for Lexi to think even without Corey buzzing around.

Lexi now stares at the ceiling...

Sits in the tub until the water is cold...

Fingers are now wrinkled.

Her light-skinned body with golden undertones shivers, as Lexi dries off and puts her bathrobe around her. She then stands in the mirror and combs out her full, thick, black hair that frizzed up from the heat.

Lexi now smiles, but quickly wipes it away.

She stands in front of the mirror for a while longer, fighting back her tears. Lexi then turns up the heat a little higher and sits down on her couch.

Lexi doesn't feel the need to get dressed.

She stays in her robe.

Lexi eventually reaches in the drawer next to her and pulls out a stack of stationery. Lexi places a sheet of paper on a clipboard, and holds her favorite pen in her left hand. Lexi isn't sure about what to say...but two hours and four drafts later, she's finished.

Lexi now reads it over, to make sure there aren't any mistakes, and places it in an envelope. She puts a stamp on it, and quickly runs outside to insert it in the mailbox. Lexi wants it out of her possession before changing her mind on sending it.

It's done.

Now all that is left to do is wait....

THE GAME
chapter 16

"What *exactly* is your reason behind doing this?" Saiel asks Mercedes, as they stand in the break room of Jaguar's shop.

It's been three months since London and Mercedes have gotten back together. According to London, things are going rather lovely, but, Mercedes has a different point of view.

"Revenge. What else?" Mercedes replies.

"Why?"

"Why not, Saiel. You mean to *tell* me that if *you* got played like *I* got played, you wouldn't want to get back at that person?"

"Mercedes, I'm just saying it's a waste of time. It's not worth it—just drop it!" Saiel demands.

"Yeah right! You *must* be out your *fucking* mind! I…aingt…dropping…*shit!* That *bitch* is going to get what she deserves! And that's *all* it is to it! Now, you can either help me, or be a *pussy* and run scared. Regardless, Saiel, I'm doing this," Mercedes says and smiles intensely.

"I'm just saying, Mercedes, you need to watch out. London aingt no typical chick. She truly has the mentality of a dude—I just don't want you to get hurt. If you're still angry, then break up with London, but don't go doing nothing stupid," Saiel instructs, as she looks at Mercedes with pleading eyes.

"*FUCK* THAT! I'M NOT GOING OUT LIKE NO *PUNK!* London has met her match, and she's going to pay! Saiel, why you acting like you weren't there? Like you weren't the one who found out about London? Why the change of heart all-of-a-sudden? You were willing to play a-l-l the other games I played, why not this one?"

"BECAUSE IT'S GETTING OLD, MERCEDES! *I'M* GETTING TOO OLD FOR THIS *BULLSHIT,* AND SO ARE YOU! So you got played. *Everyone* gets played at some point in their life. GET OVER IT!" Saiel snaps, and gives Mercedes a look that potentially has the power to kill.

The two stand in the back room in silence for five minutes. Neither one of them knows how to process this argument.

Saiel can't believe that Mercedes is spending so much time trying to get back at London. Maybe Mercedes has every right to, considering how London deceived her, but at the same time, nothing but *drama* is going to come out of this!

Saiel now breaks the silence: "Whatever, Mercedes. Do as you will, but keep me *out* of it."

Mercedes just laughs at her request, and goes back to working on the car that Mercedes has been playing around with all day; knowing that she needs to get it fixed before Jaguar gets back. Saiel stands speechless, wondering if she should warn London.

But she doesn't want any part of it.

Not even to prevent it.

Saiel stops pondering.

Walks out the break room.

Heads toward the front door.

"You *don't* understand, Saiel. London *hurt* me! She made me believe that I was falling in love with this great guy. London didn't even *bother* to tell me the truth when we first me. That was just dirty! There isn't *anything* that can justify that. The *bitch* is to get hers!"

"But in the meantime, Mercedes, you're going to keep on *fucking* her? Making London think that you're really feeling her? That's even dirtier! You're the one who keeps saying that you aingt no dyke."

"I AINGT!"

"But, Mercedes, you keep *fucking* this chick...you're not straight. You now know she's a girl, and you're still *fucking* her. Mercedes, you're setting yourself up for something harsh," Saiel warns before she begins walking out the door. "Speaking of the devil," Saiel blurts out, as London walks in as Saiel exits.

London looks a little confused, sensing that there's some type of tension in the air. Mercedes watches London hard, as London walks toward her with a dozen of white roses in her hand. Mercedes now tries to put on a smile, one that matches the smile London's wearing. London extends her arms out, and Mercedes hugs her.

"What's up, baby?" London asks.

"Nada. Just trying to finish working on this car."

"Yo, Mercedes, what was that all about?" London asks, referring to the conversation she walked in on.

"What? Saiel? Don't worry about that. I think she's jealous or something. Saiel's been tripping lately. If she ever comes to you with some *bullshit,* remember, it's just that, *bullshit.*" Mercedes then smiles and gives London a kiss on her cheek.

"I see. Well, aiiight. Where's your father?"

"He drove to *Flint.* He had to find some parts for that 1967 *Chevy* over there. Daddy will be back in a few hours; he's been gone all day." Mercedes now walks back toward the break room. London follows. "London, what you been up to today?"

"Besides thinking about you? Nothing. You like the flowers?"

"Huh? Oh, yeah—they're beautiful. You didn't have to do that though."

"I wanted to," London states while leaning in for a kiss. She settles for grazing her tongue across Mercedes top lip. Mercedes smiles.

"You're always spending money on me, you don't have to do that. I'm really not interested in how much money you can flash, and how often you do it," Mercedes points out to London.

"It's not about that," London says, as she leans in once more for a kiss. This time, London gently bites on Mercedes' bottom lip, and sucks it into hers. Mercedes then smoothly pulls away.

"London...why do you want to be with me so bad?" Mercedes asks. London looks at her rather confused.

"Mercedes, you make it seem like I'm being extra pushy. I'm just going with the flow. But *shit,* you're beautiful, smart, funny, good with your hands—ha; in more ways than one!" London says before smiling.

"So it's about the sex."

"No!"

"That's what it sounds like, London."

"That's not the case. Of course sex plays a part, but I was just joking when I said that about the hands. Damn!"

Mercedes reads the expression upon London's face, seeing that she's insulted by Mercedes' remarks.

"I'm sorry, London. I didn't mean it like that. I was just curious," Mercedes explains, as she holds her hand out to London. London receives it. "I don't know about you, London. I really don't."

Mercedes then puts her arms around London's shoulders, before moving in closer to her—Mercedes and London are now face-to-face. Their eyes meet and their lips interact. Mercedes and London's tongues play slowly, and their hearts race quickly.

The kissing gets intense...

Mercedes now feels London's hands traveling south...

Mercedes doesn't want foreplay.

She hates London with a passion!

But finds it hard to resist the temptation...

One that comes with the sexual aspect of their relationship.

Mercedes gently pulls away, but continues to stare into London's eyes. London's big brown eyes are so pretty, that it's almost scary.

When she looks at Mercedes, Mercedes feels like London is able to see right through her. Like London is able to figure out Mercedes flaws, her new agenda...just by looking.

"We can't get into this here. I don't know exactly when my dad will be back, and I'm not *trying* to hear his mouth! You better go, London. I'll call or come by later," Mercedes assures, before giving London another passionate kiss.

And then the two go separate ways.

Mercedes really doesn't consider herself to be a *dyke*.

But she enjoys the way London turns her on.

Mercedes loves London's soft full lips...

How thick and long London's fingers are...

She finds pleasure from the warmth of London's tongue...

Especially against her lower half...

Most of all, Mercedes really likes the complete level of ecstasy that London brings her.

Mercedes now wants have her cake and eat it, too.

But Mercedes *definitely* has to be careful...

Before she fucks around and fall in love all over again.

Jaguar returns at seven o'clock this evening. He has a trailer full of car parts; Mercedes immediately begins helping her father unload and organize the parts properly. Jaguar makes his way into the break room, and takes a well-needed rest. He's exhausted from driving all day; in addition to not having much energy lately.

"You work too *hard*, daddy. You need to take a break sometimes," Mercedes indicates while rubbing her father's back.

"Where did these come from?" Jaguar asks, pointing to the flowers London had given her.

"U-m-m-m, London sent those," Mercedes replies hesitantly.

"I see. So she was here?" Jaguar asks.

Silence…

"After I distinctly *told* you not to bring London around here?" Jaguar's voice grows sternly.

"I know, daddy, but I didn't know she was going to come by. London surprised me, but don't worry, she won't be around for long."

"What does that mean?"

"Let's just say, that I am planning something. And when I'm done…London will be history."

"Mercedes, don't go *getting* yourself in trouble! Especially over this *lowlife!*"

"I won't, daddy, I promise. But, am I *wrong* for wanting to get revenge on London? I mean, what she did to me was wrong; I would *never* do anything like that to anyone!" Mercedes retorts, sounding like a little girl, pleading her case.

"Mercedes, I can't say that it is *wrong* to want to get revenge, but I didn't raise you like that. I didn't raise *you,* or *any* of your sisters to be spiteful in any way; regardless of the situation. I would prefer that you didn't go out and try to hurt London."

"But she hurt *me!* Why shouldn't I do the same to her? That's *fucked* up!"

"WATCH YOUR MOUTH!"

"Sorry, daddy, but you don't understand; no one understands."

"What I don't understand, Mercedes, is *how* you didn't know that London was a girl. How could you be intimate with someone and not know? That's my question, Mercedes.

"I find that *awfully* hard to believe. …I think that it's down right *sad,* you being naïve enough to be fooled by London. Perhaps you deserved it, Mercedes.

"…You better not do nothing *stupid,* because if you disgrace this family, then you will have *me* to answer to! Go home!" Jaguar demanded, before continuing to organize the

126

equipment.

*   *   *   *   *

EVERYONE CAN KISS MY ASS FOR ALL I CARE! They trying to make me look like I'm the one who fucked up! Whatever! ...I will get London back, if it's the last thing that I do!" Mercedes thinks while fighting back her tears, as she angrily drives down the street.

Mercedes is on her way to London's house…

She immediately regroups, wanting to appear as her "normal" self when arriving at London's place.

Mercedes quietly cruises down the street that London and Shantell's house is on, and parks two houses down the road. She doesn't want them to know that she's sitting outside of their house.

Now gathering her thoughts, Mercedes checks herself in the car mirror, making sure that there isn't any evidence of tears, or an angry expression upon her face for that matter.

Mercedes knows that if it seems like something is wrong, that London will be grilling her.

LONDON'S FOG

"Yo, Shantell, u-m-m-m, I've been thinking about getting my *GED.* ...It's about that time for me to really do something with my life. Fortunately, I found another job, but, I *don't* want to be working in *nobody's* factory all my life!"

I look at Shantell as she processes everything I just said. This school *shit* is something that I've been thinking bout doing for the longest.

It's time for me to *grow* up!

I've been through enough *bullshit* and damn, it's time for a change.

"Yeah, London, I know what you mean. I've been wanting to go to college and *shit.* I tried to get you to get your *G.E.D.* before, remember? But you weren't trying to hear it," Shantell says.

I look at Shantell again, this time, having a bashful expression on my face, while searching my brain for the right reply: "I know Shantell, I wasn't ready at the time, but *shit,* things are *finally* going right for me. I might as well make it a complete package."

I then stand up.

Stretch my body.

Go over to the playpen.

And pick up Raven.

This little nigga is getting so big!

Raven runs 'round this house like a monster truck! And when he isn't destroying shit, Raven's either yelling, crying, or trying to talk. It's cute though. That's my *nigga!* I can take him any and everywhere.

...I wonder what the new baby is going to look like. Raven's new brother or sister will be here before we know it. Shantell's six months now, and her belly is h-u-g-e! I *hope* she aingt having twins. 'Cause that *shit* can be crucial!

"Aye, you talk to Lexi lately?" I ask.

"Naw, not in a while, London. The last I talked to her was about a month ago. It's funny hearing you ask about her."

"What? Don't trip, Shantell. Lexi be on my mind all the time...but what am I suppose to do?"

"You can call Lexi, write her—something. Instead, you continue to dog her," Shantell says before rolling her eyes at me, while following Raven's every move.

"Whatever, Shantell! How am *I* dogging Lexi? She's in *Boston,* I'm in *Detroit*—how the *hell* am *I* dogging her?"

"London, Lexi has been the *o-n-l-y* one who has been real with you. You claim to have loved her, but you don't really give-a-*damn* about Lexi."

"What? That's *bullshit* and you know it! If I didn't give a *damn* about Lexi, then I wouldn't have just *asked* about her! Look, Shantell, there's only so much I can do. Lexi knows me...she knows better than to expect shit from me. Besides—"

My sentence is interrupted by a knock at the door.

I walk to the door.

Open it.

Only to find Mercedes, standing on the other side.

"What's up, baby?" I ask, before giving Mercedes a hug and a kiss.

"Nothing," Mercedes replies. I step out of the way, and watch her, as Mercedes struts into the house and sits in the chair.

I can tell something isn't right with Mercedes...

But I don't feel like being "Miss Sensitive".

It's hard as *hell* being this new person!

People expect you to be all changed and *shit* all the time.

It don't *work* like that!

Shantell gives me this weird look that leaves me confused. She picks up Raven, and swiftly heads into the other room. *Shantell's been acting mad funny for the past month....* I don't want to believe that it has to do with Mercedes, but, whenever she comes to the house, Shantell immediately goes into her bedroom.

I don't *f-e-e-l* like asking Shantell about it. So I *don't!*

I'm *really* not in the mood for the *bullshit,* and I know if Shantell comes at me with some *shit,* that I'm liable to cuss her out! That will automatically open up a can of worms.

SHIT!

Tonight is *not* the night!

Mercedes looks tired today. It looks as though she's carrying the weight of the world on her back. Yet, Mercedes has miles to go before she actually can let go.

129

Mercedes also looks really cute today. It's not like her outfit is anything spectacular, but Mercedes looks good. She's wearing some black fitted and a gray sweater, both by *Baby Phat,* and a pair of black and gray *Timberlands.*

I walk over to the living room and sit on the couch. The silence in the room is strange.... The only noise that can be heard is Raven, cooing and laughing at the show he's watching on TV.

"So," I begin with Mercedes, trying to break the now, very awkward silence, "I was just telling Shantell that I'm thinking about going back to school; you know, doing that *G.E.D.* thing."

"Really?" Mercedes replies. "That will be good, I guess. How old are you again? Eighteen, right? You can always go back to school."

"What? Yeah right! What do I look like *chilling* up in somebody's high school? Naw, if I'm going to do anything, it will be the *G.E.D.* thing."

"What does Shantell have to say about it?"

"That I should do it, that I should've done it a long time ago. By the way, Mercedes, I'm nineteen."

"Oh w-o-w! Nineteen!" Mercedes jokes.

"You act like you're much older."

"*Shit,* I'm older than your young *ass,* London."

"Whatever! I still run this shit!"

"Yeah? Keep thinking that," Mercedes retorts, as she stands up and heads towards my bedroom. "You coming?" Mercedes asks as she stops abruptly.

I follow Mercedes...

Close the door behind me.

Lock it shut.

Mercedes now stands in the middle of my floor with this very seductive look upon her face.

MERCEDES IS A TRIP!

It seems like we have *more* sex now than we did when she thought I was a dude.

I don't understand it...

Mercedes does this shit likes she a pro, but at the same time, Mercedes still has mad issues about messing with a chick.

WHATEVER!

I'm *still* getting mines!

That's all that matters.

Mercedes can have her second thoughts later.

130

I walk over to Mercedes, and move her hair off of her neck. Mercedes flinches a little, 'cause my hands are cold.

I gently kiss her neck.

Making sure that my tongue glides across Mercedes' skin, just the right way.

She takes a deep breath...

I now softly stroke Mercedes long hair while continuing to kiss her on the neck. I can feel Mercedes gripping the back of my T-shirt, as she rests her head on my shoulder.

I lift Mercedes' chin with my index finger...

Gingerly, I kiss her sweet lips...

No tongue.

Just a soft kiss on the lips.

Mercedes now quickly shakes her head in a "I don't know" fashion, and closes her eyes.

I kiss Mercedes again...

This time, slowly slipping my tongue in her mouth...

Mercedes' grip grows tighter.

Mercedes massages my tongue with hers and slides her hands underneath my T-shirt.

SHIT!

...Mercedes' hands are just as cold as mine!

But it doesn't matter.

'Cause the burning heat that's quickly rising...

Creates a comfortable mix.

Mercedes opens her eyes up and pulls away smoothly.

It's intensely interesting...

Every time we do something together.

I don't understand it.

Mercedes slowly moves her hands around the front of me, and raises my shirt over my head. Her eyes, still fixed on mine, glistens, as Mercedes curiously traces the trail on my stomach.

MERCEDES CRASHES
chapter 18

I walk up to London and Shantell's house, and find myself quite hesitant to ring the bell. I really *don't* want to be here, but for some reason, while I was driving, I couldn't help but travel in this direction.

I sit in my car for ten minutes, and I figure the neighbors will start to get a little suspicious. It takes London a long time to come to the door, but she finally answers it.

"What's up, baby?" London says, and gives me a hug. I hug her back, but I'm *not* in the mood to be affectionate!

I reply with a simple, "Nothing," and walk in, heading straight for the recliner chair that I always sit in when I come to the house. I see Shantell go into her bedroom when I walk in the door, but I *don't* feel like being social. Plus, she hasn't been trying to be too friendly with me lately anyway.

WHATEVER!

I'm not here to see that *bitch* anyway!

I'm here to see the other *bitch*—London!

London walks over, and sits down on the couch. She still has on her work clothes: blue painter pants, a blue T-shirt, and some filthy brown work boots. London's shirt is covered in dirt, like she's been doing some construction or something.

London needs to take a shower!

But whatever…

I don't really care…

It's just an observation.

Me and London sit here in silence for a grip…it doesn't bother me, but it must makes London uncomfortable, because London starts talking about how she's thinking about going to get her *G.E.D.*

I don't give a *fuck* if London gets her *G.E.D.* or not!

She can be a bum for the *rest* of her life for all I care!

But I know I need to sound a little interested.

I suggest to London that she should go back to high school, since she's only eighteen. But London quickly reminds me that high school wouldn't be the place for her.

I know that.

But that's the only response I could think of.

The lack of decent conversation is making me feel weird, so I stand up and walked toward London's room.

"You coming?" I ask her, after noticing that London's still sitting down. Like a little puppy, she comes running right behind me.

This is a *damn* shame...

I got this *bitch* wrapped around my finger!

This revenge *shit* is going to be easier than I thought.

London now closes the door behind her, and I turn to face London. We just kinda stare at each other for a while....

London's eyes always put me in a trance...

They're really pretty.

But I need to stay completely focused.

London walks closer to me, and moves the hair that's resting on the right side of my neck.

Her lips against my neck feels so good...

The way London gently touches me with her tongue...

...Incredible.

I'm truly weak when it comes to London sexually.

Perhaps we can just have a sexual relationship.

Maybe I shouldn't spend so much time, trying to get back at London. But revenge feels so good!

London now caresses my hair as she proceeds to kiss on my neck. I have a hold on the back of London's T-shirt that's maybe a little too tight, just for a peck on the neck. She notices how I'm latched on to her. This causes London to bring her body closer to mine, while lifting my chin with her finger.

London kisses me...

But we don't share any tongue.

Not yet anyway.

So many thoughts are running through my head...

I can feel myself shaking...

...I'm shaking my head.

London just stares at me.

Her facial expression is full of questions, yet, London just kisses me again. This time, she respectfully forces her tongue into my mouth, and me and London kiss like we have never shared a kiss a day in our lives!

I grip London's shirt even tighter, and I begin to feel my

hormones intensifying. I gracefully pull away from her, just to gaze into London's beautiful eyes.

If she o-n-l-y knew...

If London only knew how *fucked* up this whole thing is going to become.

London looks so sweet...

...Taste sweet.

But, I *can't* forgive her for turning me out like that!

I can't forgive London for not even *giving* me a chance to decide if I *wanted* to be in this type of situation!

...It's a shame.

At this point, I'm no longer thinking for myself.

I don't want to sleep with London!

But I don't have any willpower.

I lift up London's dirty-*ass* T-shirt over her head, and trace the dark line on her stomach with my eyes. She just looks at me, and as always, proceeds to take my sweater off.

My pretty purple laced bra exposes my desperately hard nipples, and London doesn't waste any time taking it off. Once again, her tongue sends chills through me. London has this seductive way of looking at me when she's doing things...

It makes me feel really weird.

Like I'm doing something completely wrong...

It makes me feel bad.

London now guides my body to the bed, and begins to take off my boots...pants...and matching panties.

At this time, I'm so hot, that I *can't* think about much of anything!

London now enters me with her three fingers...

I let out a soft moan...

...One that even surprises me.

For London to be the older sister, it sure seems like I'm *always* taking on her role instead.

London is *so* dependent on me!

Sometimes I wish that she will get the confidence to do things on her own; without *my* approval! I mean, London's nineteen now, and she *still* hasn't done anything really productive.

London does have a job, which is good, but if it wasn't for Pauly, she wouldn't even have that! I guess that we should be grateful that London hasn't quit, or gotten fired.

But *damn!*

Let me not *sit* up here and *act* like my life is all perfect and *shit,* because I know it's not. I'm barely eighteen with a child who will be two in the next few months; and another on the way. I graduated from school, but I finished late because of the baby, and because of constantly worrying about London. That's when Pauly and I decided to move out here to *Detroit* to be closer to her.

I'm now taking classes at *Michigan State*—but I could've done more with my life…just like London can be doing much more with *hers!*

She's so wrapped up into this *damn* girl, Mercedes!

There's just something about Mercedes that I *don't* like.

She seems sneaky…

And if anything happens to London, it will be all my fault, because I'm the one who brought this chick back into London's life.

London walks into the room that I'm in, and begins playing with Raven. London loves him like he's her own. I wonder how she will be when the new baby gets here.

Everyone's so excited.

I can't *believe* that I'm already six months pregnant; I'm having another boy. I was kinda hoping for a girl, but based on the sonogram, it's clearly a boy. Pauly and I are going with the name Israel Rahiem. There isn't any significant meaning or story behind this name, like with Raven, we just liked the way it flowed.

London begins talking about how she's thinking about

taking the *G.E.D.* exam. It's like London read my mind or something. I tell her that it's a good idea to do so, but London should've done it when I first suggested it a little while ago.

London now looks at me with her usual smile, and begins playing with Raven again.

"Aye, you talk to Lexi lately?" London asks.

"Naw, not in a while, London. The last I talked to her was about a month ago," I answer. It's kinda funny to hear London ask about Lexi.

This is something that she's *never* done before.

London and Lexi have a weird thing going on. As hard as London tries to pretend that she doesn't care, I *know* she still has feelings for Lexi.

It's obvious.

If I had it my way, Lexi would be out here with us, too. Then we would truly be living happily ever after. But this aingt no *damn* fantasy, and those two aren't going to get back together just like that.

London be fronting when it comes to Lexi.

London will do *everything* possible to make you believe that she isn't still digging Lexi. London dogs her in the process, but I know it's *bullshit*.

I tell London all the time that she needs to write Lexi, or call her or something. Lexi calls me a lot, but she's always scared to talk to London. Half the time, London isn't home anyway, always "busy" outside doing something. London and Lexi need to stop acting like kids! They're like little kids, playing the "do you like me?" game.

Lexi's a grown-ass woman, she's twenty-two-years-old now. I don't know what it is about my sister…but Lexi is forever whipped. Actually, I have to say that London is whipped, too. Although London goes through girls like drawers, Lexi always makes her way back into the picture.

At one point, London did admit that Lexi could be her "wifey", but that shit went down back home in *Boston,* and the two never committed to each other. Now, London thinks it's too late for them to get together, but it's never too late for love. Lexi isn't married to anybody, neither is London. So it's *not* too late.

London hates it when I say that she dogged Lexi.

But she did. And still does.

London has a bad habit of treating women like shit! In a

way, it's not her fault though—London is truly my father's child. I just hope that she never adopts *all* of his behaviors.

A knock at the door interrupts my conversation with London about Lexi. It's…Mercedes…. She and London exchange their hellos, and I pick up Raven and go into my bedroom. Like I said…there's something about Mercedes that I *don't* like! She rubs me the wrong way.

Pauly thinks it's just because I'm stuck on London and Lexi being together. But really, it's not even about that. This chick Mercedes is *shiesty!* The *only* reason I'd put my two cents in about her and London was because, London kept *begging* me to go talk to her. I would've *never* done that at my own free will, but, of course I'm always trying to help London out.

Sometimes I feel like I owe her…

It if wasn't for me, Scottie would've never been killed… If I hadn't had London fight with Ryan, he would've never taken revenge out on her; and Scottie wouldn't have gotten caught in the middle.

I place Raven in the center of the bed, and put on a *Barney* videotape for him. I don't want to go back out there, because I'm really *not* in the mood to be walking into anything.

London is truly blinded….

I'm not sure why London would fall for a chick that would send her sister to seduce her!

That *shit* is *fucked* up!

I want to believe that London is just in for the sex. But some things that she says to me, leads me to believe that London is falling hard for this *trifling* chick!

I know I need to keep my eyes open.

This *bitch,* Mercedes is up to something…

And I need to be able to put a stop to it before it starts.

I'd been asleep for twenty minutes when the phone rang.

"Hello," I greet in a very tired voice.

"Hey, sweetie, how are you?" It's my mother. She doesn't call that often, but when my mother does, it's usually an intense conversation.

"Hey, ma. I'm fine. How are you today?"

"Oh, I could be better, but I shouldn't complain. Is everything okay, Shantell?"

"Yes, I', good. Tired, but good."

"And London, how is she?"

"London's doing alright. She's here, but has company now...they're are a little bit preoccupied."

"Sounds like London. Please tell her I send my love, and I would really like for her to call me. London and I really need to talk," my mother indicates before pausing. "...How is Raven? I know he's probably getting so big. When are you going to send me some pictures of him?"

"When I get a chance, ma. Things around here are so busy. With Raven, and the new baby on the way, I-I just haven't had time; but I promise to send some soon."

My mother is now on the other end of the phone in complete silence.... She wants to say something, but my mother is trying to find the confidence to say it.

"Ma, what?"

"...Huh?"

"Ma, you seem as if you have something on your mind. Um, have you talked to daddy? He's been on mind lately. I heard that daddy got out of jail, but might have to go back. Is this true?"

"Well, Shantell. I honestly don't know. I haven't spoken with your father since he left. He doesn't try to contact me...and I don't need to try to contact to him. If you want to find your father, call his sister."

"I don't know if I want to do all that. I was just curious; just wanted to know if you heard from him, I guess."

We both now are silent...

I wonder what my mom has to say...

London hasn't been back to *Boston* since Scottie died, and I haven't been there since Pauly and I moved out here to Detroit.

I miss being at home....

I miss being with my mom, and *shit,* I even miss my dad. I miss Camille and Ariel.

I want to go home.

Granted, there isn't much going on in *"The Bean"*, but I need to be there.

"Shantell...I...u-m-m-m...Shantell, I want you to come home for a while, you know, just for a visit," my mom says, as if it has taken everything in her to state.

"Really?"

"Yes. I want both you and London to come home. I *need*

you two to come around. It's been *really* lonely without you all, and I just want you all to come home. Thanksgiving, ...how does that sound?"

"U-m-m-m, I have to talk it over with Pauly, and it might take some extra convincing on London's end. But, yeah, Thanksgiving sounds good."

"Great! I'll start planning the menu. Shantell...I have to go, but give Raven a kiss for me, and tell London to call."

"I will, ma...I love you."

"You, too, sweetie," my mother says, before we hang up the phone. I then lay in the bed, staring at Raven, as his little body moves in a steady pattern.

I loved to watch Raven sleep...

He looks so peaceful...

Amazing.

It's so amazing that Pauly and I have created a boy so beautiful. To think I'll have two little ones laying beside me.

I'm so scared...

I'll be *eighteen* with two kids!

That's crazy!

But it's my reality...

I *have* to make the best of it.

I wouldn't mind moving back to Boston. I can be closer to my mom, and Pauly would be closer to his family.

It would be nice to have the help.

It would also be nice to be back to what I know. Anyway, I'm tired. I really need to get some rest, because Pauly is going to have to get his rest later. Now that he's working two jobs, we have to take turns on the sleeping thing.

London's real good about watching Raven, but...

You know...

She's "busy"!

WRECKED MERCEDES
chapter 20

I slip from under the covers quietly and quickly retrieve my clothes. London is sound asleep. *She looks so sweet...*

BUT I *CAN'T* PRETEND!

I can't go on *pretending* that everything is perfect between the two of us. London *fucked* up my pride!

The only thing left to do is to *fuck* up hers!

I swiftly throw my clothes on and creep out the door. Before completely leaving, I take London's wallet out of her jeans. Without any hesitation, I help myself to twenty of the forty dollars that's in there. *She won't miss it.* If London does ask about it, she won't really care that I took it; not after I "explain" that I had no money for gas, and that I didn't want to wake her asking for some.

I also help myself to one of London's blank checks. She doesn't have to know that I took it, besides, London's not that responsible to even keep track like that. The things I have in store will be evidence enough, then again, London probably still won't realize I'm the villain.

I peek out the door before I step out.

I don't want to run into Shantell or Pauly.

Fortunately, neither one of them are in sight.

I walk outside and stand here for a moment, allowing the night air to hit me. I then get halfway to my car, before I decide to turn back. London's new *Toyota Camry* sits in a parking space adjacent to the house. It's a tight little ride; London has it all hooked up, and the cherry-red color sets it off. It has five stars on it, and is trimmed in chrome.

Oh well, I think to myself, as I kneel down beside London's car and pull out my razorblade. I look around to make sure there aren't any peeping Toms lurking, before I slash all four tires. I then key the word "BITCH" on each side of the car.

I would do more...

But anything else will cause a lot of noise.

And it's too late for all that *shit!*

So I run to my car and quickly drove off.

I then stop about a mile up the road in a vacant parking

lot. *I need to get myself together.* London will sleep through the rest of the night. She won't notice the damage to her car, until London gets ready to leave for work tomorrow morning.

I have to admit, this is kinda childish.

But I have to start somewhere.

* * * * *

I wake up this morning to find my cell phone beeping at me, alerting that I have voice messages. *Who the hell is leaving me messages at eight o'clock in the morning?"* I don't bother to look through the 'missed calls' list, I just dial my number and password to check my voice mail.

"You have three new messages. To check your messages press 'one'."

I press "one", and position myself more comfortably.

"Message one. Received at 6:52 AM: 'Mercedes, it's London! I'M HEATED, YO! SOMEBODY FUCKED UP MY CAR! Call me back!'"

I laugh and delete the message.

"Message two. Received at 7:01 AM: 'Mercedes, It's London again! I was wondering if you saw anything when you left. Did you notice that it was messed up? Did you see anyone 'round here?"

"Naw, *bitch!*" I say to the recording. I delete that message and listen to the last one.

"Message three. Received at 7:15 AM: 'Mercedes...it's London...yo, come over here as soon as you get this message.'"

I look at my phone, and dial London's number. After three rings, she answers.

"Mercedes."

"London, you know I can't come over there, I have to go to work. I'm sorry to hear about your car, that *shit* is *fucked* up! You have any idea who did it?" I ask, trying to sound concerned.

"Naw...not at all. I don't even have *beef* with nobody like that. I can see if this was *Boston*—I can easily point out mad heads who would be *hating* on me like that. But not here."

"Did you call the police?"

"Yeah, but they couldn't get nothing. Po-Po didn't get so much as a fingerprint. I got a *fucking* estimate of the damage, and *Maaco* said this *shit* is going to cost like four hundred dollars; not to mention what's going to cost to get all new tires," London says,

141

sounding stressed.

"By the way, London, I borrowed twenty dollars. I'll give it back to you ASAP."

"Don't sweat that *shit.*"

"But from the sound of things, you could use it."

"Perhaps. But twenty dollars aingt going to do *shit* for me, Mercedes. Keep it!"

"So what are you going to do?"

"I don't know. I can't worry about my car right now. I got other *shit* to take care of. Rent is coming, and I got some other things to take care of, too."

"Like what?" I ask, wondering what the *hell* London had to do. *What is this bitch keeping secret?*

London sits on the other end of the phone in silence....

I can tell that she's really pissed about her car. London has put so much effort into it. *That's what the bitch gets!*

The car is like a leg for London. *Shit,* this chick sounds like she wants to cry or something. All London needs is a little paint job and some tires. She can even get one of those ghetto-ass *niggas* to take care of that. But no, London has to be all big and go to damn *Maaco*! That's why her *ass* never has any money!

"Look, I hate to sound insensitive, but I gotta get ready to go. My father has been trippin lately, and I can't afford to lose my job."

"Oh *shit!* I'm about to be late myself. Can you give me a ride?"

"London, I have to be at work in twenty minutes."

"Just tell your dad that you're running a little late. Please, Mercedes, I can't *afford* to be late," London begs and pleads.

I sit here on the phone...

I really don't want to do this.

But *shit,* it's the least I can do: "I'll be there in ten minutes, London. You *better* be ready!"

We both hang up the phone. I proceed to get dressed.

When I arrive at London's house, I can see how good of a job I did on her car. *Funny...it looks even more fucked in daylight.* London walks towards my car, and I quickly switch from having a devious smile, to a friendly one. She gets into my car and barely says a word.

Damn, this bitch is heated, for real! I would hate to think what London would do to me, if she ever found out that I'm behind

all of this....
WHATEVER!
This chick is crazy.
But not that crazy!
I d-a-r-e her ass to pull some shit with me!
My father will put his foot, so far up London's ass...
That she'd be wishing she was a faggot.
Because a dick would feel a w-h-o-l-e lot better!

"Have a good day," I say as London gets out the car.

"Don't worry about it, London...it will all work out."

I smile and drive away.

It's time to start putting together my next course of action.

"Crystal, it's Mercedes. Meet me at the spot, I need a little help with something."

LONDON'S BRIDGE IS...

chapter 21

I don't know if my day can get any more *fucked* up than it is! I wake up this morning, get dressed, and thought I was on my way to work. Instead, I find not one, not two, not three, but *all* four of my *fucking* tires slashed!

WHAT KINDA SHIT IS THAT?

Then, to top it off, someone keys my car, too! They put "BITCH" on both sides of my car!

I'M HEATED!

I WANT TO SCREAM!

CURSE!

CRY...

...WHO THE *HELL* GOT BEEF WITH ME?

And furthermore, who's going to be *childish* enough to pull some *shit* like this?

I call Mercedes to see if she saw anything when she left. Mercedes' now not answering her phone. She's either still sleep or in the shower. Mercedes has to be at work in a little while herself.

I don't know *what* I'm going to do!

I *can't* be late to work!

We got a major shipment to move, and heads be acting lazy on my job. It seems like I'm the only one who really does something at my unit. Those other *bitches* be sitting 'round talking and smoking. The manager of my section stay having to redirect people.

It's *bullshit!*

Pauly hasn't gotten home yet from his night job, and Shantell woke up when I came back in the house, *bitching* about my car. She's trying her best to calm me down, but Shantell knows that it's going to take more than a few *"Chill, London's."*

An hour later, Mercedes finally calls back. Says that she didn't notice anything when she left, but it was mad dark outside, too. Mercedes then agrees to give me a ride to work, and tells me to be ready.

That's set. I'm ready.

All I have to do is wait on her.

I go outside and light myself a *Newport* cigarette. It does the job temporarily, but what I *really* want is some trees. I haven't been this angry in a while. Granted, it's just a car, but I did a lot to get this car. I saved up mad loot, just to get the rims for this *shit!* So you can image what I had to do to get the total package.

Mercedes now pulls up and I jump in the car. She tries her best to give a comforting smile, but it doesn't work. The car ride is beyond silent, but I guess that doesn't bother neither one of us, because me and Mercedes don't try to break the silence.

When I walk into the building where I work at, I immediately go to my manager's office, explaining to Mr. Jenkins what happened. He doesn't care about my reason, but Mr. Jenkins accepts it. I then leave his office to perform my duties.

I thought that the rest of my day today would be pleasant, and it was…at least up until three o'clock this afternoon.

Check this. Here I am, just getting off of a break, when this chick comes struting into the building. Now, don't get me wrong, this *bitch* was fine-as-hell! Kinda ghetto, but fine! Every man and woman had stopped what they were doing to see what this chick had wanted. She began to cause a scene.

"LONDON! LONDON WALTERS!" the girl yells, "BRING-YO'-*ASS*-OUT-HERE-RIGHT-NOW!"

I lean up against a wall, therefore, she can't see me.

"LONDON! LONDON! BITCH, I *KNOW* YOU HEAR ME! BRING-YO'-ASS-OUT-HERE-RIGHT-NOW!" the girl exclaims again. Everyone now looks at me as if to say "you better go out there".

"Who are you?" I ask, 'cause honestly, I don't know this *bitch* from a hole in the wall.

"Oh, so you want to *pretend* like you don't know me? Yeah right!"

"You know what, I don't have time for this. Take your stank *ass,* and your games, and get the *fuck* out my face!" I say, and attempt to walk away. She then flips on me.

"WHATEVER, *BITCH!* IT'S NOT *EVEN* GOING *DOWN* LIKE THAT! YOU THINK YO' ASS CAN JUST *FUCK* ME ONE DAY, AND TRY TO BE ALL UP IN SOME OTHER *BITCH'S* PUSSY THE NEXT? *FUCK* THAT! DID YOU THINK I WOULDN'T FIND OUT? YOU THINK THAT JUST BECAUSE YOUR A BIG-ASS *DYKE*, YOU AINGT GOTTA BE FAITHFUL?" the girl blurts out.

I laugh.

I have to, 'cause I want to slap the *shit* out of this *bitch!*

"You wasn't laughing when we was *fucking* in that back room," she says and points to a storage room in the building.

"Oh shit!" and laughs escape from my co-workers.

"What are you *talking* about? I don't even *know* you."

"Hmmmph! You wasn't saying that when we also *fucked* on your boss' desk!" the girl then says and smiles, as Mr. Jenkins walks out of his office to see what the commotion is.

I'm really getting *HEATED* at this point!

"What is going on here?" Mr. Jenkins asks, as everyone now scurries back to work.

"I don't know. I don't even know this girl."

"Like hell you don't!"

"Mr. Jenkins, I *swear* I don't know her."

"Mr. Jenkins, that's your name right?" the girl now asks.

"Yes," he replies curiously.

"Don't let this girl, London fool you; she knows me *very* well."

"WHAT?" I scream.

"London knows me well enough to *fuck* me on your desk! That is your office over there, right?" she asks and points to Mr. Jenkins' office. My manager now looks towards his office and then at me, angrily.

"She's lying, Mr. Jenkins! For real, yo, she's lying!" I plead. "I have *no* idea who this girl is. She's obviously some *bitch* who's stalking me!"

The girl then laughs.

She then opens a "Sour Apple" *Blow Pop,* and begins sucking on it, like it's a *dick!*

"Miss, I'm going to have to ask you to leave. London, my office—now!"

The girl smiles at me, and flickers her tongue seductively while walking away. I don't understand what just happened here. For all know, this can be the same person who *fucked* up my car.

It has to be…

But why?

I enter Mr. Jenkins' office, and his facial expression is a cross between the principal calling your parents, and getting caught stealin from the petty cash drawer. I begin explaining again.

"Mr. Jenkins, I swear I don't know her. I don't have anything to do with what she did or said. I swear," I explain, but my manager holds his hand up, signaling me to stop talkin. I then exhale and lean back in the chair.

"London, I have been getting a lot of phone calls for you, and about you lately! I didn't say anything about them, because I figured it was just someone playing a bad joke on you. But this has gone *too* far! I *can't* allow this type of behavior to happen here!"

"What you do on your own time is none of my business, but when it starts to interfere with your work, that's when I get upset! I don't *care* if you know that girl or not—she knows you. She was bold enough to come into your place of business, and put your business out in the street; that makes this place look bad. I *can't* have that!"

I just sit here...

Staring at my manager...

Waiting for him to tell me that I'm fired.

"What were these phone calls about?" I ask dryly.

"I would rather not go into the details."

"FUCK THAT!" I scream while slamming my hands on Mr. Jenkins' desk. "That's bull; I have the right to know what people are saying! People who are obviously trying *fuck* up my life! Tell me!" I demand.

"You need to calm down, London."

"TELL ME, *DAMMIT!* WHAT ARE THEY SAYING?" I shout, as my mood worsens.

My manager just stands here calmly and says, "If you don't remove yourself from my office, I will have security escort you out."

So I left.

I guess that's his way of firing me, because Mr. Jenkins told me not to bother returning tomorrow.

What the fuck just happened here?

What did I get myself into?

Who's trying to fuck me over?

Who called my job, hating on me?

Where I worked is public access. Anyone can come in-or-out of that place. Anyone could've seen how the site is set up.

I'M FIRED UP!

I WANT TO HIT SOMETHING!

SOMEONE!

...There isn't *shit* I can do.
'Cause I don't know who's behind this.
But trust, when I find out...
IT'S ON!

* * * * *

"What are you doing home so early?" Shantell asks, as I walk into the house 'round 4 PM.

"Long story. I don't even want to get into it."

I pick up the pile of mail with my name on it and start sifting through it: "Bills, bills, bills, Lexi?"

I got a letter from Lexi? At first, I just stared at her name in the top left hand corner of the envelope.

For once in my life, I'm scared.

"So, you're going to open it or not?" Shantell asks.

"U-m-m-m...yeah. Yeah."

I walk into my room and close the door behind me.

I'm so nervous...

I haven't talked to Lexi in what feels like forever.

The envelope smells good...

Victoria's Secret's "Endless Love".

A scent that has the power to make me weak in the knees.

I take a deep breath...

And begin reading:

Dear London,

I really don't know why I'm writing you. Many might say that I am so stupid for even trying to connect with you, but I find it harder to just act like you no longer exist. I don't have it in me...I don't have it in me to just let you go, at least not without a fight. When I first met you, I knew that you would be the one to take my heart, and then turn around and break it. I knew that you would turn me out beyond measure, but I was cool with that. I even knew that you wouldn't appreciate me, or what I would try to do for you. But at the same time, I felt like I could change all that.

London, you have no idea what you mean to me. These past two years or so that you've been gone has been the hardest thing for me to go through, and I feel like it's been just as hard for you. I understand why you had to leave, but I don't understand how you could just vanish and not give a damn about what

148

happens to me. You said that you loved me...and I wanted so badly to believe that, but it's hard to believe something when there isn't any proof to back it up.

I think that I am the best thing that has ever happened to you. I think that I make you feel good—I challenge you. I make you understand that there is more to life than playing bitches. On a deeper level, I feel like I am the only person who has the capability to bring you to an indescribable level of ecstasy. If I had it my way, you would be here, laying in my arms right now. I would be teasing you...with a melting ice cube...and we would wake up with each other, day-after-day.

London, I need you. This is not a statement of desperation, but more so an act of reality, because the truth is, you need me, too. You want to be with me just as bad as I want to be with you. You left because you were scared. You were too afraid to commit, and that's okay. At the time, you were young, but your mentality has always been advanced—one of the things that I like the most about you.

I'm trying to keep this letter real basic—you need to bring your ass home! You need to come back to me, because I am the only one who is going to love you the way you need to be loved. I am a stronger person than what I was when we first started to kick it, and if you do come back to me, shit is going to change. But I think we can both handle it, if we try. London it's on you. This is my only attempt at making things right. Let me know.

I love you as many times as the rain hits the earth.

Always,
Lexi Davenport

I fold the letter back up and sit on the edge of my bed sniffing the papers.

I'm confused...

I never expected Lexi to be so forward.

I mean, she can be aggressive.

But more weak than anything.

That was the thing that I *didn't* like about Lexi.

I didn't like the fact that she let me treat her any ole kinda way. But this letter...Lexi's been thinking about this shit for a minute. I have to admit, I did run away. I could've easily stayed in *Boston* and lived with Scottie; and worked *shit* out with Lexi. I could've easily done everything differently, but, I don't know…

I don't know…

And I don't really want to think about it right now.

I lay on the bed, and stick the letter under my pillow.

The dream I'm having is a trip! …Lexi and Mercedes are both in it. They're fighting over me! And I can't decide which one I want. When I suggest that we should all become this one, big, happy trio, Lexi and Mercedes both jump me….

I wake up when "dream girl" Mercedes slaps me!

…I sit up in my bed.

Look to the left-and-right.

I quickly remember the details of today.

Even more so, the details of Lexi's letter.

I need to get my car fixed.

I need to find a new job!

I need to think…

Mercedes will probably be here in a little while. I decide to take a shower and get something to eat…*I…AM…SO BROKE!*

LOVE YOU TO THE LETTER
chapter 22

It's been three weeks since I wrote my letter to London.
I haven't heard back from her.

Shantell called me the other day, but said that London wasn't home. London probably was home, but didn't want to talk to me. That's cool though....

I'm not going to *sweat* her.

If London doesn't want me then, she just doesn't want me.

I've done *all* that I can to make this *shit* work!

London knows where I stand. I can only plead my case for so long, without feeling like an *idiot* myself.

From what Shantell told me, London's been struggling out there in *Detroit.* Someone is *hating* on London hard, and she doesn't know who it is. Shantell's convinced that London's girlfriend, Mercedes has something to do with this, but she doesn't have any proof.

Whoever is behind this, caused London to lose her job—and they *fucked* up her car. London got it fixed recently, and someone *fucked* it up again, this time, the person stole the *shit* and stripped it. London found the frame three blocks away.

Shantell says London has nothing but *evil* written all over her face. I kinda wish I was there...I'm sure I would be able to keep London calm. Then again, who knows...no one can really calm London down, once she reaches what I call "blackout mode".

I have to hurry up and get ready! Me and Lorraine have a lunch date. We've been hanging out a lot lately over the past few weeks. *Shit,* me and Lorraine both share the same emotion—we both miss Shantell and London.

Lorraine is starting to get really depressed, so I now check on her everyday. Lorraine is kinda like family, it's cool. It feels good to have someone to talk when I need to. Someone who can truly understand where I'm coming from.

Corey popped up a couple of times last week, but that *shit* aingt the same. I guess I was just using him to fill the emptiness I felt when London left. Until I hear otherwise, there's still hope that London will come back to me. I guess I have a one track mind.

I meet Lorraine at *The Middle East* in *Central Square*. I like getting away from our neighborhood. *Central Square* is filled with international restaurants, old school record stores, Goth costume stores and shops. There isn't *shit* happening where I live but the same ole-same ole: *niggas* fighting, chicks getting pregnant—chicks fighting.

It's getting old.

Honestly, I don't blame London for getting away from here, but unfortunately, drama seems to follow her wherever London goes. Luckily, I haven't heard her name come up in a while around here, heads are mainly wondering where London is.

Half of London's people are either dead now, or on lock. Maverick's in prison, and I haven't seen Shawn in a grip. Last I heard he was down South somewhere—Shawn's mom sent him to live with his grandmother, because Shawn was getting into too much *shit* up here.

"Hey," I greet Lorraine, as I walk up to the table where she's sitting at.

"How are you, Lexi?" Lorraine asks with a warm smile.

"I'm doing good. You?"

"I've seen better days, Lexi, but it's cool. I talked to Shantell. They're thinking about coming home for Thanksgiving. You should come over as well."

"Really? That would be nice. I have to see."

"Now, Lexi, where else are you going to go? I *refuse* to let you sit in your apartment alone. My parents are coming over—so is my sister. Hopefully London, Shantell, Pauly and Raven will definitely be there. Lexi, you have to come; I won't take no for an answer," Lorraine says and smiles.

"Thanksgiving is *such* a long way from now."

"*Only* two months, dear. Don't try to talk me out of it…. Is it London? Are you afraid to see her, Lexi? You and I both know that it's a possibility that London might not even come. Please don't base your decision on her."

"Alright, I'll be there. I promise."

"Thank you. Now, let's order; I'm starving!" Lorraine demands playfully.

We finish our lunch and decide to walk around *Central Square* for a while. Lorraine wants me to help her pick out some things for everyone, knowing that she always has a hard time buying gifts for them. I don't think it really matters what Lorraine got them, she just wanted to get her family something. It's a nice afternoon, and I think we both needed it.

At least I know I did.

* * * * *

"WHERE YOU BEEN?" Corey rudely asks, while sitting on the steps of my building as I walk up.

"I was out. Since when you start *questioning* me about *shit?*"

"I'm saying, Lexi, you been *tripping* lately. I be trying to spend time with you, and you keep *blowing* me off."

"Corey, I told you I just needed a little space. Why are you acting like you're all attached and *shit?* Because I know that's *not* the case."

"A *nigga* can't be concerned? *Fuck* you then! Stupid *bitch!*" Corey says and walks away. Some of my neighbors were watching our little spat, but turned in the other direction once Corey walked away.

Drama!

Shit I don't need!

I go in the house and *slam* the door!

The light on my answering machine is flashing, so I press the bottom to retrieve the message: *"Lexi, it's London. I sent you a letter—be on the lookout for it."*

Short but sweet.

London sounds so sexy.

I can't *wait* until I receive her letter!

My level of excitement hits the roof.

I need to take a shower.

* * * * *

One Week Later...

Lexi,

What's up? Yo, I was kinda surprised to get your letter. You were the last person I expected to write me. It seems like you always know when to pop in my life. I don't know what to say...and I don't know what you want me to say. I would be lying if I said that I don't think about you. I do...I think about you a lot

153

actually, but things don't always go the way we want it to. I miss you, too.

And shit out here is getting hot. Did Shantell tell you that someone stole my car and made me lose my job? All kinds of shit has been going on up here over the past month. I'm trying to be cool, but if one more thing happens, I swear I'ma flip!

Lexi, I don't know what you want me to say about your letter—I'm still processing it. I mean, I have a girlfriend now...more importantly, I'm in Detroit. We can't make nothing pop off with this distance.

Honestly, you're making shit hard right now. I am really digging my girl, Mercedes, and she's really digging me. Have you ever thought about the fact that, maybe our time is up? Maybe me and you need to move on. You've spent so much time waiting on me, and I don't understand that shit. I don't....

I also don't have an answer for you right now, and it may take a while, too. Maybe I'm scared. Maybe I'm too afraid to see what it would be like, being in a serious set-up with you.

Anyway, Shantell is trying to get me to go home to see my moms for Thanksgiving. I'll be there. You should come over to the house. But, Mercedes is suppose to be coming with me, so it might make things awkward. I don't know...but I am glad that you wrote me, and you better write back.

Lexi, I do agree that we need to be in contact, and you're right, you are the best thing that's ever happen to me. But sometimes we have to settle for less than best.

> *Peace,*
> *London*

P.S., I'm digging the scent...but you know that.

London ends the letter with a "happy face" drawing. I smile at the last line, and put the letter in a shoe box. I'm more surprised that she wrote me back than I am about the contents of the letter. *So London' planning on coming home for Thanksgiving. That will be nice, even if she is bringing this Mercedes chick with her. Hmmmph! ...Shit, I was here first...and I will get London back!*

My excitement is completely overwhelming, I have to tell someone!

"Hello," Lorraine answers her phone.

"Hey. It's me, Lexi."

"Hey. What's up?" she asks pleasantly.

"London wrote me back, she really wrote me," I state, sounding like I was about to start crying. I'm too happy! "London said that she was glad to receive my letter, and that she's been thinking about me a lot. But—"

"But?"

"...But she's feeling this girl, Mercedes. Shantell feels like the girl is bad news though, but London is wrapped up in Mercedes. London's even thinking about bringing Mercedes when they come home for Thanksgiving. I don't know, but the letter was pleasant. I'm about to write her back."

"That's good, just be careful. Don't get too excited too soon, we both know how London can be. Lexi, you don't deserve to go through another broken heart. Keep me posted. So, they are coming home for Thanksgiving?"

"Yeah, that's what London said in the letter."

"Great. That's really wonderful!" Lorraine blurts out, now sounding like she wants to cry.

"U-m-m-m, yeah...I just wanted to share this moment with you. I will give you a call back later, okay?"

"Alright, sweetie. Take care," Lorraine says, and we both hang up the phone. I take the letter back out and read it once more.

I had to make sure that it was real.

That may sound absolutely silly but...

I had to.

PAYBACK'S A BITCH
chapter 23

"Saiel, you should see London, she's *so* paranoid that this 'mystery person' is going to do something else. First it was her car, then her job, London credit cards have now been maxed, and, her bank account is *fucked!* It's amazing what you can do when you have a person's social security number—it's great!

"London's now *pissed,* and what does she keep doing when *shit* gets even crazier? Run to me like a little puppy, wanting to be pet!" I say, before cracking this rather evil smile in my sister's direction.

Saiel just looks at me.

I don't know what's happening to her these days. It's like Saiel has a conscious all of a sudden. She didn't have one when she was trying to *fuck* London! *Shit,* for all I know, London and Saiel did *fuck*, although they both say nothing happened.

Whatever!

I *don't* care!

I need to do something big, something that would top off all of these other things that I've been doing.

"Saiel, I could use a little input here!"

"About what, Mercedes?"

"London! Who else? I need something, something major. Something that will send London running with her tail between her legs! Something that London will never forget, or forgive."

"As if everything that you have already done, *isn't* enough?"

"*Bitch,* please! That stuff was child's play, she'll get over that. London will get a new job, buy a new car, and the credit card people will erase all that credit *shit!* I want something that will *truly* affect London."

"I don't know, Mercedes, you sound obsessed. This is getting way out-of-hand, and I would prefer that you didn't even tell me about it," Saiel says and walks away, and I stand here, still trying to figure out what to do.

I wish that Shantell wasn't pregnant, because I would just do something to her! That would really set London off, but London might try to kill my ass if she ever found out. I suppose that would be a tad bit extreme, but who cares.

The bitch, Shantell has said one too many smart-ass comments to me. She thinks she knows me. For example, the other day I'm chilling at her and London's house, minding my own business when, this bitch, Shantell comes out of nowhere with:

"Mercedes, what do you want from my sister? Why are you even with London? It's obvious that you don't love her, or whatever the hell you claim to feel, why don't you just save yourself the time and effort and step!"

I replied: *"Why the fuck are you so concerned about how I feel about London? How do you know how I feel? If I didn't like her, love her, whatever, I wouldn't be here. Bitch, you tracked me down! Begged me to give your sister another chance!"*

Shantell answers: *"Yes, and it was a mistake! You're not shit, and you don't deserve my sister!"*

I then hit Shantell with: *"Hmmmph! London seems to feel otherwise, you need to mind your business. Tend to your little nappy-headed child and that fat belly of yours! Shantell, you also need to be figuring out a way to please your man, with your pregnant ass! He's probably out creeping!"*

Shantell immediately tried to get at me: *"Bitch, don't even bring Pauly or my child in this! The point is, something aingt right about you. Your little ass is up to something, and if you fucking hurt my sister, that will be the last thing you ever do!"*

Then, the bitch, Shantell just walks away.

Like nothing was ever said.

I *should* do something to her...

Just to show Shantell she's *fucking* with the wrong person!

I shake these thoughts out of my head, and continue working on the car. I have to have three cars finished by four o'clock, and it's already two. I just completed the first car. I've been spending so much time daydreaming about my plot against London, that I completely forgot about work.

Three o'clock strikes, and it's almost as if a light bulb turns on in my head! *I have the perfect finale to my plan.* I look around the shop to make sure there isn't any wandering eyes or ears, and head into the office.

My hands are filled with grease, so I wash them before I sit down. I feel kinda nervous...almost as if I shouldn't do this. Out of everything I have done to London, this is going to be the most intense.

Do I really want to do this?

...I'm not quite sure, but for whatever reason, I pick up the phone and dial the number anyway: *5-5-5-6-3-6-8.*

It begins to ring...

When the voice answers on the other end, I know I have to either do it, or hang up.

I don't hang up.

CORRESPONDENCES
chapter 24

Sept 23, 2002

London,

 It was really good to receive your letter; I honestly didn't expect you to write me back. But I'm glad you did. What do you mean you don't know what to say? How can you be confused? I don't even see where there's a comparison between me and that chick Mercedes. Me and you have been through everything, she don't know shit about you. And the things that Mercedes does know, she probably don't respect.

 Anyway, I talked to your mom the other day, she's really excited that you all are coming home for Thanksgiving. She reminds me of the dinner everyday.... Shit, it's two months away, and your mother wants to know if I'm really going to come.

 London, Why are you going to bring Mercedes with you? Doesn't she have her own family to spend it with. It's like you don't even want to give me and you a chance to talk or whatever. You know if you bring that girl with you, she will probably be all in your shit, leaving us no time to be alone.

 Well, you do what you want, London, you know where I stand, and what I want to come out of it. I gotta go.

   Love,
   Lexi

   *   *   *   *   *

Sept 30, 2002

Lexi, Lexi, Lexi,

Don't even act like that. Don't start tripping on me about bullshit! I do want to talk to you, and spend some time with you, but you have to understand and respect the fact that, I got a girl. A girl that I'm really feeling...one that's also feeling me. Shit! I am so confused. If everything had played out differently, you would've been wifey.

You had the power to make me feel things that I didn't think I could feel, and fuck, I don't know.... Perhaps you still do have those powers, but I can't let myself get all wrapped up in you, Lexi, especially since I'm all the way here in Detroit. It aingt that simple just move back home. Yeah, I'll be there for Thanksgiving, but don't count on me staying any longer than that.

If we did try again, Lexi, what would you do to make sure that everything works out the way you want it to? How do I know that shit isn't going to fall apart? Do you really expect me to just drop my girl and get with you? That's kinda shady don't you think? Anyway, we'll talk about it. I have to go for now, I got shit to handle.

Peace,
London

*   *   *   *   *

October 3, 2002

My sweet London,

You are so fucking blinded at times. Since when do you worry about being shady toward some bitch? That aingt even like you. Your way of thinking is usually: London first, then everyone else. I don't give a fuck about this chick, Mercedes. I'm out to get mines, which is you. Besides, she aingt even good enough for you. Shantell even said there is something up with her. Hasn't Shantell told you that, or are you so wrapped up in Mercedes that you don't even take your own sister's advice anymore?

I can tell you what I want, and what I want to do. I can beg you, plead, but I'm tired of making myself look desperate. And shit, that aingt even the case. The point is, if you wanted me as bad

160

as I want you, London, you would do whatever it takes to make me and you a complete unit.

It's funny, two years have gone by, and I swear I'm in love with you, even more now than I was back then. I think that I might be in love with the fantasy of loving you, and being with you. It's kinda stupid for me to still be feeling you...and I've barely heard from you. I'm trying not to hold my breath on these letters. I feel like you're going to get tired of writing back as well. But until then, take care.

> Love always,
> Lexi

*   *   *   *   *

October 11, 2002

Lexi,

You underestimate me sometimes. Lexi, you really think that I don't give a fuck about you? That aingt even true. I care about you more than you know, and more than you can even imagine. But, this shit is fucking hard. It's like you got a spell on me, making me love you when I try not to. I still do.... It was easier for me not to be in contact with you, but now that I'm getting letters from you regularly, I'm going crazy!

Lexi, I've changed in a lot of ways. Yes, I'm still a total fuck up, but my respect level for women has improved. If it was really that easy, I would drop everything, and live happily ever after. But shit don't work like that. Life isn't that picture perfect....

You said a while back that I turned you out, shit, Lexi, you turned my ass out! For once in my life, I can honestly say that, I was pussy-whipped when I was with you. I aingt even like that with Mercedes. I mean, she's good...but Mercedes don't compare to you.... If me and you were together, had the chance to explore once again, now in our mature lives, what would you do?

> Holla back,
> London

*   *   *   *   *

October 20, 2002

London,

    You really expect me to write you a detailed letter of what I would do if we were together? I could say a lot, but it would be better if I showed you. Shit, what haven't we done? I hope you don't think that you going to come home for Thanksgiving, fuck me, and be on your merry way. It aingt even going to happen like that! Regardless of how bad I want you.

    You need to be coming home with some decisions and choices made. I'm getting too old for the bullshit and games! I'm not feeling that anymore.

    I will say this though, London, you know how you like it when my tongue slides across your happy trail? Or when my tongue ring connects to, well...you know where? Or when my fingers start walking and exploring? Getting you to the point when you're creaming...steaming...gleaming...

    Redeeming your composure?

    How I expose your insecurities, and baby-sit all of your needs? Feed you whip cream, and have you dreaming? Set high expectations in the beginning, forgetting about our past, as you, London, gently touch my ass.

    I want to make you cum...

    I want to make you scream my name...

    Day-after-day...

    I want to look in your eyes when you try to resist the urge. I want you completely, submerged in my deepest ocean. Focused, on nothing but my satisfaction. I want to define all your weaknesses, and turn them into strengths. I want to fuck you one night, and make love to you the next. I want to make sure you remember that, I will forever be the best, leaving all these other hoes oppressed! I want our sun and moon to combine, leaving an undefined eclipse.

    I want us to be one...

    Can you handle that? Are you ready to meet my needs?

                Always,
                 Lexi

*   *   *   *

October 27, 2002

Lexi,

    D-A-M-N!

    ...Did you really have to get poetic on me? You caught me off-guard with that shit! I didn't even know you could write like that! Maybe that's one of the things that's changed about you. I'm digging it though...and I'm digging your words.

    Shit, you had my ass at a loss for words! I was sitting here like: "Damn, nigga!" I had to let Shantell read it. She just smiled-and-smiled-and-smiled! Shantell was like, "Yo, London, you need to do something about that; you know you want to." All I could do is smile, too!

    I don't know, Lexi...you got me thinking...you got me considering shit. I don't know what to do about Mercedes though. I mean, our shit is going good.

    Yo, I might not be able to write you for a while...I have to take care of something, and I don't know how it's going to play out. But, understand this: I do love you! As much as I don't want to, I do. I'm glad that we had this chance to write and shit.

    As soon as I handle shit, I'll send you another letter. But trust, I'll see you on Thanksgiving! So, if I try to kiss you or something, will you let me? Or will you diss me?

    Just wondering....

        Love,
        London Walters

ROLES
chapter 25

November 3, 2002

    Lexi puts the last letter she received from London in the drawer with all the rest. She feels bittersweet since they've been writing back-and-forth. It almost feels like a fairytale to Lexi—she never imagined that things would workout so smoothly. She's now sitting on her couch, but is interrupted by the heavy banging on her door.

Who can this be at this time of night?

Reluctant to open the door, Lexi sits for a while longer, but the pounding continues.

"Damn!" Lexi says as she heads for the door. "Who?"

"Corey. Let me in, Lexi, we need to talk."

"Do you know what *time* it is? It's almost midnight—banging on my door like you're crazy and *shit.* Come back tomorrow."

"Lexi, come on. Please, I need to talk to you. Please…it will only take a few minutes, then I'll leave."

Lexi stands at the door for a moment, soon deciding to opening it. Corey stumbles into the apartment, and falls onto the couch in the living room. He reeks of liquor and weed, looking totally exhausted.

"Corey, you're *fucked* up. Why don't you go home? We'll talk in the morning."

"Naw, baby. I'm here. I want to talk *now!* Shit! …I aingt going *nowhere.* Shit! …Come here," Corey instructs and pats the seat next to him. Lexi obeys. "Why don't you call me anymore, Lexi?"

"I've been busy. Corey, I told you a while ago that I just needed some space."

"Yeah, but you aingt come to me with no decision. You just leave a *nigga* hanging—that *aingt* cool, Lexi!" Corey replies, looking at Lexi with bloodshot eyes; waiting for a response.

"My bad…I didn't think you cared like that. I just figured that you had some other *bitch* to take my place."

"Well, you thought wrong, Lexi. I've been waiting for

you," Corey answers softly in a low, sweet voice.

His response scares Lexi.

"Look, Corey. I didn't mean to keep you waiting for me, I just don't think me and you need to kick it anymore. We're not right for each other."

"...What yo mean we aingt *right* for each other? We're *everything* for each other! What? What you got someone else? Some other *nigga?* 'Cause can't no other *nigga* compare to me, not while I got this big ole *dick!*" Corey rudely snaps while grabbing his genitals.

"It aingt that, Corey, I just can't be with you. It's not going to work," Lexi responds and stands up, signaling Corey that it's time for him to leave. Corey then forcefully grabs her by the arm, and yanks Lexi back onto the couch.

"I'M NOT DONE *TALKING!*" Corey states angrily.

"Corey, let go of me; you're scaring me," Lexi squeals, as she tries to pry her arm away from Corey. His grip gets tighter. "Corey, chill, for real! You need to get out of my house, *now!*"

Corey now astonished, looks at Lexi, then at her arm. Noticing the tight hold he has on Lexi, he now lets go.

"Yo, baby, I'm sorry about that. must be the combo," Corey indicates, referring to the blend of "Hershey" weed and *Bacardi* rum he heavily consumed.

"Which is more the reason why you need to leave. I'm not *playing,* please, get out!" Lexi insists, as she stands up again and walks toward the apartment door, now opening it. This time, Corey follows behind Lexi, and proceeds to walk out the door.

All of a sudden, Corey stops abruptly in the living room and turns to face Lexi. The deranged look in his eyes startles Lexi. A demented expression, one she'll never forget.

"COREY NO!" Lexi yells, as Corey pushes her across the living room. He then swiftly closed and locked the door. Lexi falls to the floor, and tries to get up quickly before Corey comes near her. She now runs to the other side of the living room and picks up a vase. Lexi throws it at Corey, but misses. This only pisses him off more, causing Corey's anger to grow.

"Corey! Corey, please, please, chill!" Lexi begs. Corey reaches out for her and Lexi slaps his hand away. Corey's reflex instantly causes him to punch her—Lexi hits the floor once again.

Corey then pulls Lexi up by her shirt, and she tries to kick him in the testicles. Corey moves to the side, dodging Lexi's kick.

She then attempts to run away again, but Corey grabs Lexi and lifts her off her feet, Lexi now having her back against his stomach. Corey, with a tight hold, now carries Lexi to her bedroom, as she's manically kicking and screaming like a crazed woman.

"You done *fucked* up now *bitch!*" Corey states while throwing Lexi on the bed. She tries hard to escape, but Corey forcefully holds Lexi down.

Although he's a lot bigger and stronger than Lexi, she's trying her best to fight back; but Corey's strength is much more powerful. He now pins Lexi down with half of his body, Corey fiercely rips her lace panties off with his free hand before pulling down his sweatpants.

"Corey, please don't do this—*P-L-E-A-S-E!*" Lexi pleads, crying uncontrollably. Corey ignores her and continues imposing.

I can't believe this is happening to me....

The reality of Lexi being raped, by Corey, in her own place, devastates her. In awe, Lexi desperately tries to keep her legs closed, but Corey pries them open, violently forcing himself inside of her; being turned on by Lexi's resistance. Raging, Corey thrusts as hard as he can inside of Lexi, whispering and panting in her ear the whole time, as Corey increases the pace of penetrating Lexi.

"You like this, don't you, Lexi? You love this big *fucking* dick inside you, right? Huh? ...Stupid *bitch!* ...You think you going to diss a *nigga* like me and get away with it? *Fuck* that!"

Corey now pumps Lexi even harder!

...Faster!

Going deeper-and deeper each time.

Lexi has never felt agonizing pain or force this intense— she now wants to roll over and die. Corey continues his plunging .

FASTER!

HARDER!

FASTER!

HARDER!

Involuntarily, Corey lets out a deep and low groan, as his body jerks—Corey now splashing his semen inside of Lexi. She just lays here...shocked...crying...looking dazed. It's all surreal to Lexi, like she's havin an outer body experience.

Oh my God, I'm bleeding....

Lexi slowly gazes down at her vagina as Corey carelessly

pulls his penis out of her. Lexi notices the blood and semen dripping from Corey's testicles, as she now examines the blood-soaked sheet. Corey's forceful penetration made Lexi vaginal walls tear, causing her to bleed while he ripped deep into Lexi.

So much blood....

Still in disbelief of what just happened, Lexi stares down momentarily at the bloodied bedding, before looking confused into Corey's shifty eyes. He then pulled up his sweatpants and looked away, acting as if nothing wrong occurred before leaving Lexi's bedroom.

Stunned, Lexi looks around the room, now back at her lap. The pain and sight of the blood flowing, now causes Lexi to shake hysterically: "OH GOD! OH GOD, NO!" She then jumps out of the bed and falls upon the floor. At this point, Lexi's legs are very weak, feeling as heavy as a ton of lead.

She manages to pull herself up and walks toward her closet; reaching up to the shelf. Way in the back on the shelf, Lexi retrieves a small box, pulling it out and quickly unlocking the box.

She then stares at the nine millimeter pistol London had given her some time ago. Lexi never used it, never had to.

But today is different....

She loads the gun with bullets, and walks into the living room where Corey is. Corey, who's now helped himself to a sandwich, sits comfortably on Lexi's couch, eating and watching TV.

I know this fool isn't chilling on my couch!

As Lexi gets closer up on Corey, he feels her presence behind him. Corey quickly turns around and immediately stands up.

"What the *fuck* are doing with that?" Corey asks confidently. Lexi doesn't respond, instead, she closes her eyes and pulls the trigger—sending three bullets into Corey's chest.

Lexi fades to black.

Passes out.

Hits the floor....

Ten minutes later, Lexi opens her eyes, finding herself laying on the floor with policemen standing over her. Lexi looks around the blurry room within her home, noticing a white sheet covering up something she can't quite recognize from a distance...

...Corey's dead body.

"Ma'am, can you tell me what happened here?" one of the officers asks. Lexi just looks at him confused. "Ma'am, I really need you to tell me what happened. Please, I know you're scared, but I need to know."

Again, Lexi looks at the officer in a dazed manner.

She then begins to shake uncontrollably, shaking as if having a seizure. Lexi now closes her eyes, and scenes from the rape incident flashes before them.

"I-I killed him...Corey, he raped me. ...He wouldn't leave, Corey just...he-he just...oh my God...just kept forcing himself on me. Corey *raped* me...I got scared, I, I got the gun, and I don't know, I just wanted him to *leave* me alone. He wouldn't stop! He wouldn't stop!" Lexi confesses while crying, as one of the female cops come over to comfort her.

The paramedics now arrive.

Lexi's rushed to *Boston Medical Center*.

A nurse administers a rape kit on her.

Confirm Lexi's accusations.

*   *   *   *   *

Three hours later, detectives appear at Lexi's hospital room to speak with her. After reviewing the case, examining Lexi's bed sheets, and receiving the diagnosis from the rape kit the nurse administered on Lexi, the cops inform Lexi that they're going to write the report up as a self-defense incident.

They ask her a few questions, hand Lexi cards with contact numbers, reassure her that everything will be okay, and explain that if they need anymore information regarding the case, that they will be in touch. The detectives leave the scene, and Lexi is somewhat more at ease.

"Excuse me, Lexi. Is there anyone you want me to call for you?" The nurse asks Lexi.

"Um...I don't know.... I don't really have anyone. Wait, call 442-7765, ask for Lorraine. She's like family," Lexi states, before she sips on her water and pulls the covers up over her.

"Are you interested in taking 'the morning after pill'? It's a pill that will end a potential pregnancy after conception. If so, Lexi, you will need to let me know shortly," the nurse explains to Lexi before leaving the hospital room.

Lexi lays in bed...

The last thing she wants to think about is a "morning-after pill".

* * * * *

Lorraine gets a call that Lexi's in the hospital, and immediately rushes out the door. Over the past few months, Lexi has become like one of her own.

Lorraine is so scared...

She doesn't know what to think, or what to expect.

Lorraine arrives at *Boston Medical Center* at 3:30 AM. The nurse's station directs her to Lexi's room. Lorraine quietly walks into the room. Lexi turns in her direction, and cracks a faint smile.

"Hey you. Are you okay?" Lorraine asks.

"I could be better."

"What happened, Lexi?"

"You remember Corey?"

"Yeah."

"Well...he came to my house drunk and high-as-hell, and...raped me."

"Oh my God, Lexi. Did they catch him? Is Corey in jail?"

"The bastard is dead," Lexi confirms with tears in her eyes. Lorraine wipes the tears from Lexi's face, and observes the bruise on Lexi's left side.

Lorraine then decides not to make Lexi talk about the rape scenario anymore, instead, she tucks Lexi in, and lays herself on the empty bed next to Lexi.

At eight in the morning, Lexi is discharged. Soon after, she rests in London's old bed, as Lorraine lounges on the couch.

I have to get everyone back together. Too many things are beginning to happen, Lorraine now thinks to herself.

* * * * *

When London walks into the doorway of Jaguar's auto shop, the last person she expects to see is Saul, chatting it away with Mercedes.

How does these two know each other?

London quickly slips back out the door, and watches their every move. She looks on as Mercedes and Saul hug as if they're long lost friends. London also observes Jaguar, as he soon comes

169

over and gives Saul a hearty hug as well.

What the fuck is going on here? London also ponders. She can't hear any of the conversation, but now has a bad feeling. London then hides in the alley, next to the auto shop, when she sees Saul and Mercedes making their way to the door.

"So you're going to do that for me, right?" Mercedes asks Saul, once outside.

"Of course, I got you, baby. That dyke-*bitch,* London is broke-as-*shit* right now! Even asked me to hook her up with work recently, 'cause her ass aingt got no nine-to-five no more. Don't worry, when I make London go make this run for me tonight, I'll take care of it then."

"Good, Saul. 'Cause I'm tired of pretending to be feeling this chick. London don't catch a *fucking* hint. You would think that she was smart enough to put two-and-two together—I guess not."

"Well, like I said, when London comes to make this run for me, I'll handle it. That's my word."

"Saul, don't hurt her. Just teach London a lesson—a good one."

"Whatever! I got this!" Saul replies and hugs Mercedes, before the two parted ways.

London can't believe what she just heard.

Fuck Mercedes mean I can't take a hint?

Yo, I'm heated!

REAL HEATED!

And I'm not about to go out like no *sucker!*

* * * * *

London runs into her house and changes her clothes. London puts on her usual rugged outfit that she wears when making runs for Saul: a thermal hoodie, a long John shirt, baggie corduroy cargo pants, and a pair of Timberlands—all in black.

London's not sure what's going to happen, but figures that Saul might think something is up if she doesn't show up.

What the fuck is going on? What's all this shit about?

After pondering for a few seconds, London instantly calls the one person who just might be able to help her.

Saiel.

* * * * *

"I'm glad you could meet me—we need to talk," London says to Saiel, as the two sit inside of *Burger King* on *Renaissance*.

"I shouldn't be here, London, so *whatever* you have to say, say it."

"Yo, Saiel, since when did Saul and Mercedes start chilling?"

Saiel lets out a deep breath and shakes her head.

"London, you're putting me in a tough place; you really are."

"Saiel, please, what's going on? I overheard them talking earlier, and it sounded like Mercedes is setting me up. What the *fuck*, yo?"

"London. Damn! ...Do you *really* not realize what's happening? Are you *really* that oblivious to shit? I find that hard to believe—really, I do."

"What the *fuck* are you talking about?"

"London, Mercedes *hates* you!"

"What? No she doesn't!"

"London, yes she does. Mercedes is still *pissed* that you tricked her. The *o-n-l-y* reason she even got back with you, was to get back at you. It's all been a game, London—your car, your job, your credit cards, bank account; all that shit. A game. Mercedes has been behind it all. It's like she's obsessed with getting back at you. Mercedes said that you *fucked* up her ego, and she doesn't like that."

"What? ...Are you serious? All that *shit?* Mercedes was the one behind it? ...You've *got* to be joking! ALL THAT *FUCKING* SHIT? MERCEDES WAS THE ONE DOING IT? ...HA! ...And you let her, Saiel, you didn't even have the *decency* to warn me!"

"What was I suppose to say London? That's my sister. When you're long, gone away, I will still have to see Mercedes' face every day. How did you *expect* me to make a decision like that?"

"I'm saying, Saiel, you could've told me. You could've sent an anonymous letter or something!"

"Nigga, this *aingt* the movies, shit don't happen like that. I'm putting myself at risk talking to you right now. I don't know what the *fuck* she got going on with Saul, but if I were you, I wouldn't make that run tonight. I don't trust it. Saul is bad news, for real. The fact that Mercedes even called him, scares the *shit* out of me."

"How do y'all even know him?"

"...He's our brother."

"WHAT? Wait a minute, what the *fuck?* How the *hell* is that nigga your brother?"

"Before my mom left, my dad was creeping with this chick named Lordes. They had Saul. When my mom left, my dad kicked it with Saul's mother for a minute—but *shit* didn't work out. Saul doesn't come around unless we really need something, because he knows everything and everyone out here. London be careful, please. Look, I got to go," Saiel says before leaving the restaurant hurriedly.

London is in a state-of-shock!

She doesn't know what to do.

London doesn't want to punk out.

She doesn't want to set herself up either.

London doesn't want to lose this battle.

She doesn't know how to handle this...

If London doesn't show up tonight...

Saul will just come to her house.

He's done it before.

Saul made his promise to Mercedes.

He's going to keep it!

London heads up to Pauly's day job. She now explains everything to him.

"Yo, is there anyway you can take Shantell and Raven and leave for *Boston* tonight?"

"I don't know, man, it was hard enough getting the days off that I got before."

"Pauly, please! If you *love* my sister like you *say-you-do*, you'll bounce! Stay with my moms, or with yours—just get Shantell and Raven out of *Detroit* this evening. Please!" London begs.

London's never been this scared in her life!

She knows about all the rumors of Saul beating the shit out of people, never giving a damn. London's even aware that he's killed many.... She doesn't know how to handle this!

"Look, I'll pay the difference on the train tickets, just go!" London pleads, as Pauly sees the seriousness in her eyes.

* * * * *

London goes to the train station and upgrades tickets for Pauly, Shantell and Raven. Tonight, she puts them on the ten o'clock train to Boston.

"London, what are you going to do?" Shantell asks.

"I don't know. It depends on what Saul does."

"Don't do nothing *stupid*. London, you really need to be on this train with us."

"I aingt running, Shantell. That's all I ever do is run. I'm tired of that. I'm going to handle this, and whatever happens, happens."

London then looks at Pauly, before Shantell kisses her goodbye. London also gives Raven a kiss, too. He just laughs. So innocent, Raven has no idea of what's going on.

And that's a good thing.

* * * * *

November 5, 2002

Pauly and Shantell arrives at Lorraine's house in the wee hours of the morning. Shantell feels weird, she hasn't stepped foot in this house since she left two years ago. Mostly everything looks the same, yet, some new furniture here and there. The place is peaceful—everything is good.

Shantell walks into her old room and places Raven in the middle of the bed. Lorraine soon joins, and tells Shantell about the *shit* that went down with Lexi.

Shantell then peeks in London's old room where Lexi is sound asleep. She doesn't want to wake Lexi, but Shantell is so excited to see her, she can't help not to: "Lexi...Lexi...wake up," Shantell whispers while shaking Lexi.

"Huh? ...What?" Lexi responds in a tired voice.

"Aye you. What's up?"

"Oh *shit!* Look what the wind blew in," Lexi replies while sitting up in the bed. "When did you get in?"

"We just got here."

"Really?" Lexi's excitement peers through.

"Yeah, but before you get *too* excited, London isn't here."

"Oh? ...Why not?"

"Drama. I told you that *bitch,* Mercedes was up to no good. She was scheming on London the whole time. Now London

173

is caught up in some serious *shit*. Mercedes now has the roughest *nigga* in town after her. She begged us to leave town and come back here to *Boston* last night. Lexi, I don't know what the *fuck* is going on."

"Damn," Lexi replies, as she exhales and readjusts herself. She's still in pain from the incident with Corey; he'd broken one of her ribs, and she has bruises on her back and shoulder area.

"Lexi, how are you?" Shantell asks, being concerned.

"It looks worst than it really is…. Scary though, I keep having flashbacks, like Corey's going to come back or something; like something is going to get me."

"You know that's not true though, you're safe."

"Yeah, I hope so," Lexi says without confidence. "Where's my little man?"

"Girl, Raven's asleep. He's getting so big."

"I got to see him," Lexi says, as she attempts to get out of bed.

"Should you be getting up?"

"I got to pee, don't I?"

"Ha-ha-ha. Look, bitch, don't get smart!" Shantell says and smiles. The two then walks to Shantell's old room, and watches as he sleeps.

"So cute," Lexi admits. "Shantell, I can't believe you and Pauly made such a beautiful child, *and* have another one on the way."

"I know, but it's cool. Pauly and I have a plan. I'm taking classes in *Michigan*, but who knows. If we stay here, I might end up at *Boston University*. I always wanted to go there." Shantell states.

"I need to go to school, too. I've been slipping on the college thing."

"Yeah. Lexi, maybe when London gets back, we'll all go to college, live that fairytale life for once."

"That would be peace."

Lexi and Shantell spends the rest of the early morning talking. Later that morning, Pauly heads over with Raven to his family's house.

This is the start of a well-needed visit.

I meet Saul at the usual spot 'round midnight like he told me to. I'm not sure what Saul's going to do but, I'm prepared.

I'm strapped.

Packing a glock.

Saul soon appears out of nowhere, like a vampire or something. The first thing he does is punch me dead in my stomach. Saul then takes my gun, and pushes me up against the wall.

I can take it though.

I can take whatever he dishes out.

I now swing on Saul and tag him right in his eye.

This causes Saul to pound on my ass even harder!

"That's all you got?" I ask. "A big-ass *nigga* like you, and that's *all* you got!"

We fight like two little kids, rolling 'round in the yard. I can tell that Saul wants to hold back, but I guess he underestimated my strength, and grows angrier with each punch I plant.

I don't care though.

I gave Saul everything I have!

I don't trust him...

I don't know if Saul's going to take out anything...

He's already starting to forget that he's fighting a chick.

After a while, we both get tired and Saul gets pissed!

When he puts the glock to my head...I know this is it.

I know all I've worked for will never be seen.

"Saul, you don't want to kill me—you aingt got a reason to."

"Since when the *fuck* did I need a reason to *kill* someone? ...I aingt sensitive, I don't give a *fuck!* You *fucked* over my sister, and Mercedes wants you to pay."

"She said not to hurt me though. I heard her, I was there."

"I do *shit* my way! MY WAY! London, you played Mercedes, you even played me, do you play *everyone* you come across? That aingt cool, kid. If I let you live, I'm going to look like a punk," Saul states, as he takes the gun from my head, and starts walking around like he completely lost his mind. "You see, London, you don't understand, Mercedes *needs* me to teach you a lesson. How will I know if you truly learned your lesson if I—"

"I did Saul! I learned it! I won't trick another female, I promise!" I plead.

"I don't know that! You really *fucked* Mercedes' head up, for real, dog. It's sad...are you *that* insecure about being a *dyke* that you go 'round pretending to be a dude? *Nigga,* I must admit, you play this *shit* off well though. Hell, you even had me convinced. London, I *have* to teach you a lesson, you *have* to pay," Saul continues, as he walks 'round pondering, trying to figure on what to do next.

I want to run.

But I'm frozen...

I just stand up against the wall.

Waiting....

It seems like forever.

It takes Saul a long while to finally make a decision. When he whips the glock back 'round in my direction, I *KNOW MY LIFE IS OVER!* ...Saul then cocks back the chamber of the glock.

"S-A-U-L!"

A voice rang out.

Me and Saul both turn 'round and see Mercedes stepping out of a dark corner. The only light shining comes from a street light, attached to the top of the red-brick building.

I swallow hard.

"What are you *doing* here, yo? Let me *handle* this!" Saul insists to Mercedes. He looks at Mercedes who's now step into the light. She wear a black fitted, one-piece *Dickies* jumpsuit. Mercedes' hair is pulled back into a tight bun, and black leather gloves conceal her hands. A silver twenty-two caliber pistol rests in Mercedes' right hand, now aimed at Saul.

"You're not handling it the way I said to, Saul," Mercedes says in a calm tone. She slowly walks toward us. Although Saul is looking at Mercedes, his gun remains on me.

I now stand in a straight line of fire.

If Mercedes shoots Saul, then the force will probably cause him to shoot me. I'm stuck against this wall, wanting to move. But I'm uncertain about Mercedes motives, so I wait....

"WHAT THE *FUCK*, MERCEDES? YOU COME TO ME about THIS PROBLEM, SO LET ME HANDLE THE *SHIT*—DAMN!"

Mercedes walks closer to Saul. They're only inches apart from each other, and although Saul's tall body towers over Mercedes, she faces him, as the two meet, eye-to-eye.

"*Nigga,* I'm trying to make sure your dumb *ass* don't do nothing *stupid*. If you off her, *nigga* I'm going to be the one caught up!" Mercedes says with attitude. Saul still hasn't turned back to face me, so I begin to slowly inch my way to the left; out of the direct range of both guns. I will have to run 'round both Saul and Mercedes to reach the only opening to the alley.

It's a chance worth taking.

While Saul and Mercedes continue to debate over how I should be "handled", I quickly search the ground with my eyes for any type of weapon I can find.

There isn't anything in sight!

And even if I get past Saul, it doesn't mean that I will get past Mercedes. She's unpredictable. I take a deep breath, and determine that I can try to knock the gun out of Saul's hand. If it goes off at this point, I won't be in direct risk of getting shot.

The uneven lighting in the alley causes me to overlook a metal pipe lying by my foot. I take six steps...before almost tripping over it.

Saul and Mercedes continue to argue with each other. They don't notice me bending down—I grip the metal pipe with my left hand. I then arched my back a little bit, slipping the pipe behind me, while placing it in my right hand.

When Saul turns to look back at me, I *crack* him in the head with the pipe! Saul stumbles, hits the ground really hard— he's now out for the count.

The glock falls to the ground.

Me and Mercedes both scramble to get to the gun first.

We're face-to-face.

Both pointing guns at each other.

"Mercedes, I don't want to shoot you, but if that's what I have to do to get out this alley then," I say and shrug my shoulders to imply the rest.

"You wouldn't shoot me, London. You love me! Remember?" Mercedes states sarcastically.

"Just let it go, Mercedes. It's over, You've made your

point." I slowly begin to move in the direction of the entrance to the alley. Mercedes follows my every move, keeping her steel pointed at me.

Mercedes says nothing.

I now have a clear path out of the alley. I keep Saul's gun aimed at Mercedes, as I back out of the alley. Saul's body lays still on the ground from the blow to the head.

As I now reach the corner of the street, I tuck the gun in my waist; Mercedes stops and looks on in the darkness, shadowed silhouette fades out from a distance.

"IT'S NOT OVER, LONDON! I PROMISE, THIS SHIT IS NOT OVER!" Mercedes yells as I begin to run.

I run for eight blocks.

Then I stop.

Look from left-to-right to see if anyone's watching.

The coast is clear.

I remove the gun from my waist.

Wipe off my fingerprints with my hoodie.

Wrap the glock in several sheets of newspaper.

Toss it in the middle of a nearby dumpster.

There are also cardboard boxes laying along the side of the street, I break them down and throw them in the dumpster as well.

Just to be on the safe side.

My bus for *Boston* leaves at 10:30 AM. I decide to walk a few blocks more, before taking a cab the rest of the way.

It'll be safer to wait in the station 'til morning.

THANKSGIVING
chapter 27

I take a deep breath before ringing my mom's doorbell.

I want this to be perfect.

I want to be able to walk in this house and everything falls into place. The past two weeks has been crazy.

When I finally got to the station from havin that scuffle with Saul and Mercedes, it was 2 AM. My bag was already packed hours before in a locker waiting for me; 'cause I knew something was going to jump off.

I now keep having flashbacks of Saul's gun in my face.

If I would've made the wrong decision, this whole situation could've gone a different way. I decided that night that, the person I needed to be with was Lexi.

She's right, Lexi's the only person who truly feels me.

I need love...

I need her.

When I got into to *Boston* two weeks ago that night, I called Nature, Scottie's baby's mother, and crashed at his old crib. I needed to clear my head, and make sure that everything was truly peace. I don't put anything past Mercedes, after everything that has happened, so I chilled at Nature's until today.

I now stand at my mother's door, trying to get the nerve to ring the bell...yet, the only thing I can really think about is Lexi. Shantell opens the door, and gives me a big hug upon first sight.

"So I guess everything worked out?" Shantell asks.

"For now," I nervously answer. I walk in and look around...amazed at how many people are in my mother's house. All of Pauly's family is here playing with Raven, my grandparents, Camille, Ariel, and my baby, Lexi.

When my moms sees me, her eyes fill up with tears. To my surprise, so does mine.

"I'm glad you came, London," My mom says while hugging me long and hard. She looks me over and tells me that I look great. If my moms *o-n-l-y* knew what I've gone through! She loves my hair, and thinks that I look really healthy.

I go 'round the room and said "hello" to everyone. My

grandparents are so happy, it feels really good. Out of the corner of my eye, I can see Lexi going upstairs. As soon as I get a chance, I follow behind her.

"Hey, where are you going?" I ask Lexi in a soft voice.

"I have to take my meds."

"Meds? ...For what?" I ask, concerned. Lexi still has some minor bruises from the rape incident, and when she tells me what happened between her and Corey, all I want to do is hold Lexi.

"Lexi, I am *so* sorry. I'm sorry that I wasn't there to protect you. I promise I will *never* leave again."

Lexi now wipes the tears from my eyes and gently kisses me.

I feel it....

I feel that feeling that everyone is always talking about. You know, that sensation you experience when you know that person you're with is the one.

I feel it.

I feel it now when Lexi kisses me, and I realize that, I've felt it all along.

I was just fighting it.

Perhaps everything does happen for a reason. I guess good things *do* come to those who wait. I don't know...what I do know is that, I now want to spend as much time as possible with Lexi, my moms...and maybe even one day, with my pops. He's still locked up unfortunately, and will probably stay in prison for about a year or so, but who knows.

After an hour, Lexi and I join the rest of the people downstairs. Camille and Ariel has Shantell cornered, catching up on all the gossip. Lexi and my moms stand across the room from me. Pauly and his family are enjoying time with Raven. Although I'm happy here...I feel responsible for Lexi getting raped....

Lexi trusted that I would always be here for her, that I would never let her down this way. I'm just glad that I'm here now, yet, this rape shit is heavily on my mind....

I now walk over to my where Lexi and my moms are standing, as I stand to the right of my moms. My moms senses something is bothering me.

"London, I'm sorry," my mom begins, "If I could change everything I would. I never thought things would have gotten to this point."

"Don't worry about it, ma; it's in the past," I assure her.

I just want to have my family back.

There *aingt* no point in dwelling on the past!

Can't change it.

We can only learn from it.

I put my left arm 'round my mom's waist, and pull her into a hug. She holds me tight and kisses my forehead, like I'm five-years-old again. Lexi stands next to us with her head lowered. She smiles at me and my mom's reunion.

"I aingt going nowhere, I aingt going nowhere, ma," I confirm. I then get Lexi's attention and stare into her eyes; eyes telling Lexi that I'm here to stay.

Uncertain of what the future holds....

Yet, very clear that Mercedes isn't done with me.

"What you going to do about pops?" I ask my mother after releasing her from the hug. She gives me a look of defeat and says, "I filed for a divorce yesterday.... London, your father and I have had our time. He's no longer the guy I fell in love with twenty years ago. Your father needs a lot of help, and has yet to accept the fact that, it was his drinking that really tore this family apart. Not you, London, nor the way you choose to express yourself.

"I can't be with a man who would rather place blame elsewhere. I'm okay though...I think I'm going to get back into consulting, maybe even go back to school. I haven't decided yet, but I have everyone, and everything I need right here."

At this time, Shantell and Pauly joins in on our moment. Raven now plays with Ariel and Camille. I look at Camille.

W-o-w...I remember the first day Camille met me, trying to figure out if I was a boy or a girl. Camille was shocked when Ariel told her that I was Shantell's sister.

Hours later, I update Pauly, Shantell and Lexi with everything that happened between me, Saul and Mercedes that night in Detroit, once all the guest have left. Lexi leans against me as I tell the whole story. Knowing that Shantell and Pauly have to go back to *Detroit* eventually is unsettling, but I have to trust that they will be okay when they return.

* * * * *

At the end of the night, I crawl into my old bed next to Lexi, and hold her in the spooning position as tight as I can.

I want Lexi to know that she's safe now.

"Lexi," I whisper.

"Yeah?" Lexi responds softly, turning her head just enough to make eye contact with me.

"I'm sorry for everything."

Lexi doesn't say anything in return, but she smiles. Lexi now snuggles her body deeper into mine, which fully lets me know that she's my ride-or-die chick. After all these years, Lexi's *still* willing to hold me down!

"Lexi," I whisper again.

"Yes, London."

"I-I love you!"

I then sigh and close my eyes, not really expecting Lexi to respond. She turns her body 'round so that we're face-to-face. Lexi then grazes her thumb across my lips, kisses me passionately, before rolling over back into the spooning position.

"I love you, too, London. I love you, too."

GLOSSARY

AA – Alcoholics Anonymous
AG/Aggressor – Hardcore lesbian
Aiiight – Alright
Banger – Gang member
Banging/Off-da-chain – Hot/Fly
Blunt/Tees/Weed – Marijuana
Bubble Gut – Gas inside of stomach
Burbs – Suburbs
But-on-the-real – Seriously
Cum – To have an orgasm
Daps – Informal handshake
Dip – To run fast
Dogging – Taking advantage of
Drops – Making drug deliveries
DSS – Department of Social Services
DYS – Department of Youth Services
Dyke – lesbian
'Fro – Afro
Gas – To make someone believe something that's false
GED – General Educational Development
Ghetto – A way of thinking/behavior evolved from poor areas
Grand – A thousand dollars
Grilling – To badger with questions
Grip – A long period of time
Hit – To have sex
Key – To scratch car's exterior with a sharp object
Kicking it – Dating/Enjoying one's company
Knocked up – Pregnant
Mad – Many
My Bad – One's fault/mistake
Nada – No
Na-Na's - Breasts
Off – To kill/murder
On Lock – Arrested
Paper – Cash
Peace – Okay/Cool
Peeps/Heads – People
Piece – Gun
Po-Po – Police

Pop Off/Popping – Happening
Pulling – Getting/Attracting
Pushin'/Hustlin'/Flippin' – Selling drugs
Pussy-Whipped – Being controlled by a female
Right-quick – Fast
Rocks – Crack/cocaine
'Round – Around
Seeds – Kids
Shiesty – Crooked
Shook – Scared/Nervous
Sprung – Overly infatuated with
Spoonin' – To intimately lay behind someone in bed
Straight – Okay/Fine
'Sup? – What's up
Tape – A faded haircut
The Bean – Slang term for Boston
The Bird – To rudely stick middle finger up at someone
Thugging Out – Acting overly masculine
Tight – Nice
Whachu – What you
Wife Beater – Tank top
Wifey – Main girlfriend
Y – YMCA

An excerpt from *PARIS SKY* by
A. C. BRITT
A GHETTOHEAT® PRODUCTION

It was a windy Monday afternoon when Ella Braden, *MSW,* arrived to pick up Paris Jacobs, one of her most delinquent clients, from the *Edgemont Home for Girls* around 3 PM. She'd been prepping Paris for this transition into foster placement for about a month, but determining who was more nervous, Paris or Ms. Braden, was a different question.

Paris, slightly thuggish, stands at 5'8" tall, and weighed 160 pounds. Her skin is a smooth, butterscotch complexion, which changes to more of an almond shade during the summer. Paris' eyes are hazel colored, and her long eyelashes cause Paris to constantly wipe at her eyes.

Paris' hair is a reddish-brown color that hangs to the middle of her back when she wears it out, which is rarely. Paris prefers to keep her hair braided in either cornrows or box braids—It's easier to manage. Paris' full, pink lips with darker edges, show proof of her years of weed smoking. She has what some might call a "unique" personality, and a reputation that over exceeds most people's level of tolerance; it's often hard to see the potential.

Paris took one last look around her room to make sure she hadn't forgotten anything. Once she left this program, Paris never wanted to set foot back here again.

"I'm ready," Paris said, as she peeked into the office that her social worker was standing in.

"Good, I'll be just a moment; you can start putting your belongings in the car," Ms. Braden replied. Paris gave her a nonverbal look of understanding and headed outside. Paris didn't really care about much, she just wanted to get out of the direct watch of *DSS* and *DYS;* needing a break from the whole system. Paris understood that it was solely up to her to make this placement a successful one, after all, her cousin, Ashley didn't have to take her in; in which Paris was truly grateful.

Paris sat in the front passenger seat of Ms. Braden's 2002 *Honda Protégé'.* The car was pretty fly, and Paris was always impressed with the details of the car. Given the type of personality that Ms. Braden has, Paris would have never imagined the woman even hooking her car up.

By the time Ms. Braden arrived at the car, Paris had already made herself very comfortable, fiddling with the radio stations.

"Paris! Don't *make* me have to pull you from this placement!" Ms. Braden demanded.

"I'm not going to mess this up," Paris replied.

"You better not, because this is the *last* time, Paris. If you even *think* about getting into trouble, I'm pulling you out and placing you back into a residential until your eighteenth birthday—it's that's simple."

Paris just looked at Ms. Braden, knowing that the woman was serious.

After twenty minutes of driving, the two arrived in front of a small white house in a very quiet neighborhood in *Quincy*. Ms. Braden then shut off the car and popped the trunk. Paris just sat there for a while, wondering what this experience would be like; wondering if she even had it in her to totally enter back into society.

Paris was scared, but at seventeen, she knew that she needed family in her life right now. Paris had no idea what she was going to do once she turned eighteen, therefore, it was comforting to have a little bit of stability.

Thoughts of how Paris' mother gave up on her, ran through her head, and the feeling of someday being alone penetrated her mind. Paris' mother's decision to relinquish all rights had nothing to do with her inability to handle Paris' delinquent behavior. It was an effort to prevent family embarrassment, to prevent disgrace.

She simply didn't want to deal. Painful thoughts haunted Paris on a daily basis, and it had been a year since she'd spoken with her mother. If it wasn't for Paris' sister Payton, she'd have no contact at all.

"Paris, ...let's go," Ms. Braden said, interrupting Paris' thought. Paris then took a deep breath and lifted herself out of the car. She brushed the lint off her navy-colored pants, and adjusted the orange hoodie she wore. Ms. Braden had already taken Paris' things out of the car, and was beginning to place them on the stairs that led to the house.

"It will be alright, Paris, you're going to be just fine," said Ms. Braden.

"Yeah...I guess."

Ms. Braden rang the bell and a short, thick woman answered the door. She was dark brown, with even darker hair that hung to her shoulders. The woman had it cut in layers, and the way her hair shaped her face, made her look like a natural beauty.

"Ashley Jacobs?" Ms. Braden inquired.

"Yes, come in," Ashley said while stepping to the side, allowing Paris and Ms. Braden to enter.

An excerpt from ***GHETTOHEAT*®** by
HICKSON
A GHETTOHEAT® PRODUCTION

GHETTOHEAT®

S-S-S-S-S-S-S!
Can you feel it? Scaldin' breath of frisky spirits
Surroundin' you in the streets
The intensity
S-S-S-S-S-S-S!
That's GHETTOHEAT®!
The energy – Electric sparks
Better watch ya back after dark!
Dogs bark – Cats hiss
Rank smells of trash and piss
Internalize – Realize
No surprise – Naughty spirits frolic in disguise
S-S-S-S-S-S-S!
INTENSITY: CLIMBIN'! CLIMBIN'! CLIMBIN'! CLIMBIN'!
GHETTOHEAT®: RISIN'! RISIN'! RISIN'! RISIN'!

Streets is watchin'
      Hoes talkin' – Thugs stalkin'
POW! POW! POW!
Start speed-walkin'!
Heggies down – Rob that clown
Snatch his stash – Jet downtown
El Barrio – Spanish Harlem:

"MIRA, NO! WE DON'T WANNO PROBLEM!"

Bullets graze – I'm not amazed
GHETTOHEAT®!
Niggas start blazin'
Air's scathin' – Gangs blood-bathin'
Five-O's misbehavin' – Wifey's rantin'-n-ravin'!
My left: The Bloods – My right: The Crips
Niggas start prayin' – Murk-out in ya whip!

Internalize – Realize
No surprise – Naughty spirits frolic in disguise
S-S-S-S-S-S-S!
INTENSITY: CLIMBIN'! CLIMBIN'! CLIMBIN'! CLIMBIN'!
GHETTOHEAT®: RISIN'! RISIN'! RISIN'! RISIN'!

Mean hoodlums – Plottin' schemes
A swoop-down – 'Bout to rob me – Seems like a bad dream
Thugs around – It's goin' down
'BOUT TO BE SOME SHIT!
But I'm ghetto – Know how to spit
Gully mentality – Thinkin' of reality of planned-out casualty
I fake wit' the trickery:
"ASS-ALAMUALAIKUM"

"STICK 'EM UP!"

"YO, DON'T FUCK WIT' HIM – HE'S MUSLIM!"

Flipped script wit' quickness
Changed demeanor – The swiftness
Not dimwitted – Felt the flames of evil spirits!
Hid chain in shirt – I don't catch pain – Don't get hurt
No desire gettin' burnt by the fire
Thermometer soars, yo, higher-and-higher
In the PRO-JECTS – Fightin' to protect ya neck
Gotta earn respect – Defend ya rep
Or BEAT-DOWNS you'll collect
The furor – The fever – My gun – My cleaver
Bitches brewin' – Slits a-stewin'
Sheets roastin' – Champagne toastin' – Gangstas boastin':

"The ghetto – Nuthin's mellow
The ghetto – Cries in falsetto
The ghetto – A dream bordello
The ghetto – Hotter than Soweto"

Internalize – Realize
No surprise – Naughty spirits frolic in disguise
S-S-S-S-S-S-S!
INTENSITY: CLIMBIN'! CLIMBIN'! CLIMBIN'! CLIMBIN'!
GHETTOHEAT®: RISIN'! RISIN'! RISIN'! RISIN'!

Red-hot hustlers – Broilin' at the spot
Boilin' alcohol – The lucky crackpot
Streets a-scorchin' – Crackheads torchin'
Stems ignited – Junkies delighted
Money's flowin' – Pusherman's excited
The first and fifteenth: BLOCK-HUGGERS' JUNETEENTH!
Comin' ya way – Take ya benefits today
Intoxication – Self-medication – The air's dense
Ghetto-suffocation – Volcanic maniacs attackin'
Cash stackin' – Niggas packin' – Daddy Rock's mackin':

"The ghetto – Nuthin's mellow
The ghetto – Cries in falsetto
The ghetto – A dream bordello
The ghetto – Hotter than Soweto"

BedStuy – Do or die: *BUCK! BUCK! BUCK! BUCK!*

They don't give a FUCK!
In The Bronx – You'll fry – Tossin' lye – WATCH YA EYES!

Walk straight – Tunnel vision – False move – Bad decision
So hot – Starts to drizzle – Steamy sidewalks – Begin to sizzle
HOT-TO-DEF! Intense GHETTOHEAT®

"DO YOU FEEL IT? DO YOU FEEL IT?"
"THE HOTNESS IN THE STREETS!!!™"

So hot – Got ya mase?
Too hot – PEPPER SPRAYIN' IN A NIGGA'S FACE!
The Madness – Sadness: Don't you know the flare of street-glow?
OH! Meltingly – Swelteringly: *S-S-S-S-S-S-S!*
HOOD IN-FER-NO!
Internalize – Realize
No surprise – Naughty spirits frolic in disguise
S-S-S-S-S-S-S!
INTENSITY: CLIMBIN'! CLIMBIN'! CLIMBIN'! CLIMBIN'!
GHETTOHEAT®: RISIN'! RISIN'! RISIN'! RISIN'!
INTENSITY: CLIMBIN'! CLIMBIN'! CLIMBIN'! CLIMBIN'!
GHETTOHEAT®: RISIN'! RISIN'! RISIN'! RISIN'!
S-S-S-S-S-S-S!

190

"Sweets, you're in cell 1325; upper bunk," the Correctional Officer had indicated, as he instructed Candy on which cell to report to. When she heard 'upper bunk', Candy had wondered who would be occupying the cell with her. As Candy had grabbed her bedroll and headed towards the cell, located near the far end of the tier and away from the officer's desk and sight, butterflies had grown deep inside of Candy's stomach, as she'd become overwhelmed with nervousness; Candy tried hard to camouflage her fear.

This was Candy's first time in prison and she'd been frightened, forcefully trapped in terror against her will. Candy had become extremely horrified, especially when her eyes met directly with Trigger's, the young, hostile thug she'd accidentally bumped into as she'd been placed inside the holding cell. Trigger had rudely shoved Candy when she first arrived to the facility.

"THE *FUCK* YOU LOOKIN' AT, HOMO?" Trigger had spat; embarrassed that Candy had looked at him. Trigger immediately wondered if she was able to detect that something was different about him and his masculinity; Trigger had hoped that Candy hadn't gotten any ideas that he might've been attracted to her, since Candy had caught him staring hard at her.

She'd quickly turned her face in the opposite direction, Candy wanted desperately not to provoke Trigger, as the thought of getting beat down by him instantly had come to Candy's mind. She couldn't exactly figure out the young thug, although Candy thought she might've had a clue as to why he'd displayed so much anger and hatred towards her. Yet, this hadn't been the time to come to any conclusions, as Candy was more concerned with whom she'd be sharing the cell with.

When Candy had reached cell 1325, she glanced twice at the number printed above on the door, and had made sure that she was at the right cell before she'd entered. Candy then peeped inside the window to see if anyone had been there. Seeing that it was empty, she'd stepped inside of the cell that would serve as her new home for the next five-and-a-half years.

Candy was overwhelmed with joy when she found the cell

had been perfectly neat and clean; and for a moment, Candy had sensed that it had a woman's touch. The room smelled like sweet perfume, instead of the strong musk oil that was sold on commissary.

Right away, Candy had dropped her bedroll and raced towards the picture board that had hung on the wall and analyzed every photo; she'd become curious to know who occupied the cell and how they'd lived. Candy believed that a photo was like a thousand words; she'd felt that people told a lot about themselves by the way they'd posed in photographs, including how they displayed their own pictures.

Candy then smiled as her eyes perused over photos of gorgeous models, both male and female, and had become happy when she'd found the huge portrait of her new cellmate. Judging by his long, jet-black wavy hair, facial features and large green eyes, Candy had assumed that he was Hispanic.

Now that she'd known the identity of her cellmate, Candy then decided that it would be best to go find him and introduce herself; she'd hoped that he would fully accept her into the room.

As Candy had turned around and headed out the door, she'd abruptly been stopped by a hard, powerful right-handed fist to her chiseled jaw, followed by the tight grip of a person's left hand hooking around her throat; her vocal cords were being crushed so she couldn't scream.

Candy had haphazardly fallen back into a corner and hit the back of her head against the wall, before she'd become unconscious momentarily. Within the first five seconds of gaining back her conscious, Candy had pondered who'd bashed her so hard in her face.

The first person that had come to mind was Trigger. Secondly, Candy also had thought it might've been her new cellmate who obviously hadn't wanted Candy in his cell, she'd assumed by the blow that Candy had taken to her flawless face.

Struggling her way back from darkness, Candy's eyes had widened wide, at that point, being terribly frightened, as she was face-to-face with two unknown convicts who'd worn white pillow cases over their heads; mean eyes had peeked from the two holes that was cut out from the cloth. The two attackers had resembled members of the Ku Klux Klan bandits as they'd hid their faces; both had been armed with sharp, ten-inch knives.

Overcome with panic, there was no doubt in Candy's

mind that she was about to be brutally raped, as there was no way out. Candy then quickly prayed to herself and had hoped that they wouldn't take her life as well. Yet, being raped no longer was an important factor to Candy, as they could've had their way with her. All Candy had been concerned with at that moment was continuing to live.

An excerpt from *HARDER* by
SHA
A GHETTOHEAT® PRODUCTION

When I finally arrived back home, Tony was heated. I didn't even realize I was out that long.

"Where the *fuck* you been, Kai?!" he yelled as I walked through the door.

"I went to the range and then shopping. I had a lot on my mind to clear and I just needed to get away. Damn, is there a law against that?"

"Nah, ain't no law, shorty! Just watch yaself, cuz if I finds out different, we gonna have major problems."

Tony was taking on a "Rico" tone with me that I did not like whatsoever.

"Who the *fuck* is you talking to, Tony? I *know* it ain't me. Ya better keep that *shit* in ya back pocket before you come at me with it."

I had never seen Tony like this before, and it made me very upset. I knew I had to calm down, before I said something that I would live to regret.

"Oh word? It's like that, Kai? Fuck you forget or something? This here is *my* house! *I'm* the star, baby girl! You *used* to be the co-star, but now you just another *fucking* spectator! Show over, get the *fuck* out!"

Just when I thought things couldn't get any worse!

"Get the fuck out? You get mad over some *bullshit* and now it's 'get the fuck out'? Tony, think about that shit for a minute." I started talking slowly and softly. "I'm ya 'co-star' alright, but do you *know* what that means? ...It means, everything you own, *I* own. All the work you put in, I put in, too.

"You forget who sees over the cooks and make sure ya deliveries are made on time? That's me, *motherfucker*. You *sure* you wanna have me running the street with all ya info, baby boy?"

That weird laugh echoed out of me again. This time, it set Tony off. He grabbed me by my throat, and *threw* me into the hard brick wall! When I hit the floor, Tony started to strangle me as he screamed, "BABY BOY?! BABY BOY? HUH? YOU FUCK THAT NIGGA?! HUH?! DON'T YOU *EVA* IN YA LIFE CALL ME 'BABY BOY' AGAIN, YOU FUCKING SLUT!"

194

Tony let go, and I hit the floor again. It took all the air I had in me, but I managed.

"Tony-I-ain't-fuckin'-nobody!"

"Oh word? You come in here acting brand-new, and you ain't *fucking* nobody? We'll see!"

Tony then picked me up by my waist and ripped my jeans off. He proceeded to remove my panties. I didn't know what Tony was up to, until he threw me onto the couch. Tony then spread my legs wide-open, as he stuck three fingers in me at the same time.

I screamed in pain...

Tony bowed his head in regret.

"I'm sorry, Kai," was all that he said, before Tony left the house for the night. I laid there until he came back early the next day. When Tony walked in the house, I'd pretended to be asleep, as he started to play with my hair.

"Kai, I hope you're listening to me. You know shit's been kinda hard since *Five Points*. You know it's hard knowing that I can't make love to you. I be seeing how dudes look at you and shit. I know your type, ma, you got the sex drive of a 18-year-old man."

I stifled a giggle.

"I just be thinking when you're gone, you out there getting the only thing I *can't* give you. I know you've been on my side since I came back home, but I still be bugging. You're a trooper, baby and that's why I love you. Please don't leave me—I need you. All this shit, is 'cause of you. I know that, ma-ma; I love you."

That became my driving force. The man that ran Queens *needed* me. It's true that behind every great man, was a great woman. I wanted to go down in history as being the greatest.

Tony would be my link to the city. I already had him in my back pocket, so that meant I had Queens in my back pocket! All I needed was the other four boroughs to fall in line.

Sure, I would step on some toes, but I would stand to be retired at twenty-five—with enough money to finance my life, for the rest of my life. AJ was right, but I had a point to prove, and money to make! After that was done, I would be game to anything else.

I started stashing away as much money as I could. I told Tony that I would no longer sleep at his house, since he put his hands on me.

Tony begged for me not to.

Instead, we came to the "agreement" that, I would *only* sleep over two or three nights out of the week, and I *had* to be on his payroll.

Tony agreed.

Every Friday morning, I got five thousand in cash.

I *never* put it in the bank.

I used some of it as pocket money, and had my checks from work directly deposited in my bank account every Thursday. I used my work money to pay my bills and other expenses. I didn't want to give "Uncle Sam" a reason to start sniffing up my ass! Instead, I hid the money that Tony gave me in my bedroom closet at my father's house.

My game plan was clear: I would be the Queen-of-the-NYC drug empire.

I had Tony do all of the dirty work, and I stopped managing the cooks. I became his silent partner, so to speak. With a little coaching from me, and a lot of strong-arming, Tony could definitely have a heavy hand in the other boroughs.

In case the Feds were watching, I had a sound-proof alibi:

I was a student…

I worked full-time, and I lived at home with my pops.

Technically.

The only way I would be fucked was if they ever wanted to search my father's crib. Tony *never* came to my house, so I doubt that would ever happen.

An excerpt from *SONZ OF DARKNESS* by
DRU NOBLE
A GHETTOHEAT® PRODUCTION

"They *won't* wake up! What did you let that woman do to our children, Wilfred?" Marilyn nervously asked.

"GET IN THE CAR!" Wilfred shouted. The expression on her husband's face told Marilyn that he was somewhat scared. She hurried into the passenger's seat, halting her frustration for the moment. Wilfred didn't bother to glance at his wife, as he started the vehicle's ignition and drove off at rapid speed.

Marilyn stared silently at the right side of Wilfred's face for ten minutes. She wanted to strike her husband so badly, for putting not only her, but their two children through the eerie circumstances.

"I know you're upset, Marilyn, but to *my* people this is sacred; it's normal," Wilfred stated, while his eyes were locked on the little bit of road the headlights revealed. Marilyn instantly frowned at his remark.

"Andrew and Gary were *screaming* inside that hut, and now they're sound asleep. This is *not* normal, I don't care *what* you say, this is wrong, Wilfred. That *bitch* did something to our kids, it's like they're drugged! Why the *hell* did you bring us out here? WHAT DID SHE DO TO THEM?" Marilyn loudly screamed, budding tears then began to run down the young, ebony mother's face.

Wilfred then took a deep breath, trying his best to maintain his composure.

"Take us to the hospital!" Marilyn demanded.

"They don't need a doctor, they're perfectly healthy."

"How can you say that? Just look at them," Marilyn argued.

"Listen to me."

"I don't want to—"

"LISTEN TO ME!" Wilfred roared over his wife's voice. Marilyn paused, glaring fiercely toward her husband as he spoke. "The Vowdun has done something to them, she's given them gifts we don't yet know. Marilyn, the Vowdun has helped many people with her magic, she once healed my broken leg in a matter of seconds. The Vowdun has brought men and women fame, wealth, and cured those stricken with deadly diseases. It was even told that she made a man immortal, who now lives in the shadows."

"I'm a Christian, and what you're talking about is satanic. You *tricked* me into coming out here to get Andrew and Gary blessed—you're a liar!" Marilyn interjected.

"That is why we came to Haiti, and it has been done—the worst is now over."

As the couple argued, Gary Romulus eyes opened. He remained silent and unknown to his parents. The infant was in a trance, detached from his surroundings. Wilfred wasn't paying attention to the road ahead, his vision was locked on his wife as they feuded. Gary was however. The newborn saw what his mother and father didn't see, way ahead in the black night.

Two huge glowing crimson eyes stared back at the baby. They were serpentine, eyes Gary would never forget. They were the same eyes he and his brother, Andrew had seen in the hut; the Vowdun's eyes. Gary reached across and gently touched his older brother's shoulder, strangely Andrew awoke in the same catatonic state as his sibling.

"Everything is going to be okay, Marilyn. I tried to pay the Vowdun her price, but she refused," Wilfred said. Marilyn gasped.

"A price?" Marilyn replied annoyingly, refusing to hear her husband's explanation.

Andrew and Gary glared at the large red eyes, which were accompanied by an ever growing shadow that seemed to make the oncoming road darker. Lashing shadows awaited the vehicle.

"WHAT PRICE?" Marilyn then retorted, consumed with anger; she could easily detect the blankness of her husband's mind. Wilfred now was at a loss of words, even he had no knowledge of what the Vowdun expected from him, that was the very thought that frightened the man to the core.

The car was moving at seventy miles per hour. The saddened mother of two turned away from Wilfred's stare, at that moment, Marilyn couldn't even bare his presence. When her sight fell on the oncoming road, Marilyn frantically screamed out in terror. Wilfred instinctively turned forward to see what frightened his wife. His mouth fell ajar at the sight of the nightmarish form ahead of them. Filled with panic, Wilfred quickly tried to turn the steering wheel to avoid crashing.

It was too late.

The sudden impact of the collision caused the speeding car to explode into immense flames that roared to the night sky. The creature that had caused it suddenly disappeared, leaving behind its chaotic destruction and the reason for it.

Out of the flickering flames and screeching metal came young Andrew, who held his baby brother carefully in his fragile arms. An illuminating blue sphere then surrounded their forms, which kept Andrew and Gary unscathed from the fires and jagged metal of the wreckage; incredibly, the two brothers were physically unharmed.

Andrew walked away from the crash feeling melancholy. In the middle of his forehead was a newly formed third eye, which stared out bizarrely. Not until he and Gary were far enough away from the accident did Andrew sit down, and the blue orb vanished.

Gary then looked up at his older brother and cooed to get his attention. Andrew ignored him, he was staring at the flaming vehicle as their parents' flesh burned horridly, causing a horrible stench to pollute the air. Through glassy eyes, Andrew's vision didn't waver, the child was beyond mourning.

Finally, Andrew gazed down at his precious baby brother before he embraced Gary. Gary smiled assured, unfazed by the tragic event. With his tiny arms, Gary then tried to reach upwards, to touch the strange silver eye on his brother's forehead, playfully. Gary was as amused by the new organ as he would've been about a brand new toy.

"Mommy and daddy are gone now," Andrew then sobbed, as streams of tears rolled down his young face. He was trying his best to explain his sorrow. "I will *never* leave you, Gary—I promise," The young boy cried. Gary giggled, still trying to reach Andrew's third eye as best he could.

For the price of the Vowdun to bestow her gifts from her dark powers to the children, Wilfred Romulus had paid the ultimate price—he and his wife's lives. Their children were given gifts far beyond their father's imagination, and for this, they were also cursed with fates not of their choosing. The future held in store untold suffering.

Andrew and Gary were no longer innocent, no longer children of Wilfred and Marilyn Romulus—they were now *Sonz of Darkness*.

An excerpt from **AND GOD CREATED WOMAN** by
MIKA MILLER
A GHETTOHEAT® PRODUCTION

Some people call me a *hoe* because I strip for niggas and hustle for cash.

Yeah, I turn tricks.

I tell niggas, "If the price is right, then the deal is real." My momma used to say, *"As long as you got a pussy, you sittin' on a goldmine. Never give your shit away for free."*

If that means I'm a hoe, so be it!

None of these *bitches* pays my bills or puts food on my mutha...fuckin' table, so fuck 'em!

God didn't give me the type of brains where I can understand all that "technical" book shit. In elementary school, I was never good at math and, to tell the truth, I was never that good at readin' either.

It's not like I didn't try.

It's just that, when it came to school, nothin' really registered. In high school, I tried to learn the secretarial trade. I figured that if I had some sort of technical skill, that I could at least get a halfway decent gig after I graduated. Well, it turns out that typin' and shorthand was just another thing that I failed at.

So bein' somebody's secretary was out of the question.

With no real education or skill, I had to settle for minimum wage jobs. My first job was workin' as a maid at a five-star hotel. After about two weeks, I got tired of cleanin' after rich bitches that shitted all over the toilet seats, and hid bloody tampons all over the *goddamn* place!

And I wasn't 'bout to work in *nobody's* fast-food restaurant. So I had to come up with a new plan. And that's when I met this f-i-n-e-ass, Puerto Rican *muthafucka* by the name of Ricky.

Ricky was a straight-up thug. He had tattoos all across his chest and stomach like *Tupac* and shit. When I met Ricky, I had two kids. I was single, workin' my ass off as a hostess in a restaurant and braidin' hair on the side.

I was finally maintainin', you know, gettin' money. But I was always workin', so I didn't have no time to enjoy my kids or my money.

Ricky came on the scene and promised me all kinds of shit. He was like, *"Baby, you ain't gotta work that hard, why don't you lemme take care o' you and nem kids."*

Ricky had my head gassed up, for real!

Plus he was layin' the pipe on the regular. Fuckin' me *real* good wit' his fine ass. So one night, after Ricky got finished eatin' my cooch, he was like, *"Baby, I'ma take you to Philadelphia wit' me. You an' the kids can come wit' me, and I'll hook ya'll up wit' errythang."*

Me, bein' naive, I followed his fine ass all the way to Philly and shit, and the nigga started trippin'! Beatin' me up, knockin' me all upside my head, accusin' me of cheatin'...which I wasn't. Ricky started kickin' my ass to the point that I was too ashamed to go to work with black eyes and busted lips, and I eventually got fired.

Long story short. After a while, I finally had enough. I packed me and my kids up and went to a shelter. I didn't know no fuckin' body, I didn't know shit about Philadelphia—all I knew that I was broke and I needed a place to stay for me and my kids.

So I went to the welfare office....

I tried to work within the system. Well, welfare was draggin' they feet, and in the meantime, I needed to make some cash, fast.

That's when Marilyn popped up on the scene. Marilyn was basically a po' white trash version of myself. She was stayin' wit' me at the shelter.

Marilyn told me between puffs of her *Marlboro* cigarette: *"Mekka why don't you strip? You got a beautiful body, and I know you would make plenty of money 'cause you tall, you got them big, perky titties, and you high yellow. You could make some good money and be outta here in no time; you perky titty bitch!"*

I figured what I lacked in the brains department I'd make up for with the "gifts" that God did give me: my pretty face, this small waist and these big ole titties!

So I took Marilyn's advice. I rolled around wit' her, and she took me to some strip clubs. That's how I got this gig where I'm at now. Strippin' at a hole-in-the-wall called *Dutch Gardens*. *Dutch Gardens* is where "Mekka" was born, but I gotta finish this story another time, I think I hear them callin' my name.

"Hey Mekka, you go on in five," Trish hollers from the entrance of the locker room. Trish is a white bitch who *swears* she's black!

Only fucks Black men....

And she can get away wit' it 'cause, Trish got a ghetto-booty and a body like a sista. And some niggas think that "white is right", but they'll be alright. Trish is kinda cool though, as far as white girls go.

"Hey hoe; Mekka, you hear me?" Trish calls again.

"Bitch wait! I heard your *muthafuckin'* ass!"

I check my face in my magnetic mirror hung on the inside of my locker, spray on a hint of *Bulgari* "Omnia Eau de Toilette" body mist, adjust my g-string and tighten the laces on my thigh-high boots. Other bitches wear them tall shoes, but I'm gettin' old, and my old-ass feet and ankles need a lil' mo' support.

Plus, it's easier to slide them dollar bills in your boots and keep it movin'.

I slam my locker shut and take inventory of my surroundings. There's a room full of beautiful bitches all *hatin'* on me!

They wanna know how I make it-do-what-it-do! How I make all dat dough in the course of three hours, and they been in here all night lettin' niggas suck on they titties and finger their coochies...and still comin' up broke?

FUCK BITCHES!

Like I always say: "Money over niggas; bitches, stick to the script!"

An excerpt from **GHOST TOWN HUSTLERS** by
CARTEL: CASTILLO
A GHETTOHEAT® PRODUCTION

It was early in the morning when I heard someone knock on the door, calling my name. I sat up and reached for my watch that I'd placed on top of the nightstand.

It was seventy-thirty.

"WHO IS IT?"

"Senor! Lo estan esperando pa desallunar! (Sir! They're waiting for you to come have breakfast!) I hear the voice of Maria yell from behind the door.

"Dame unos cuanto minutos!" (Give me a couple of minutes!"

I hear footsteps going away. I get out of bed, walk over to a table on the far left corner of the room, where a vase full of fresh water has been set. Once downstairs, I see the boys sitting down at the table along with Emilio. I sit next to Pedrito.

"Where's Martha?" I ask.

"She didn't want to eat," Pedrito says while shrugging his shoulders.

Minutes later after we'd eaten, Pedrito and I got up and walked out onto the porch, sat down and lit up our cigarettes. Emilio lit up a cigar, like the one Don Avila used to smoke.

Pedrito then said he wanted to show me something, so we stood up and walked away from the house. He explained to me that the two men that were sent to pick Don Avila up from the airport had betrayed them, and that Emilio had all of his men looking throughout Medellin; having his connections search the rest of Colombia for any signs of them. So far, no one was able to find anything.

We notice that the house was barely visible, so we decide to go back. When we reach the house, the boys were inside, and Emilio was waiting for Pedrito with three men by his side.

"Come," Emilio says, gesturing with his hand to Pedrito. "I want to show you something I found." Emilio had a smile on his face, but I noticed that it was very different than any other smiles he'd given before. It was as if Emilio was smiling to himself and not at Pedrito.

"Can Raul come, too?" I heard Pedrito ask. I stop midway up the stairs, proceeding to go into the house. I look back and see Emilio staring at me, almost as if he was thinking about what to answer.

"Sure," Emilio replied shortly. "He can come." Emilio began walking towards the back of the house, where there were three smaller houses that weren't visible from the front of the main house. One of the smaller houses were guarded by two men. One was holding a rifle, the other had a gun tucked inside the waist of his pants.

"Donde estan esos hijo-eh-putas?" (Where are those sons-of-bitches?) Emilio asked once he, Pedrito and I were before the guards.

"Hai dentro patron!" the guardsman with the gun at his waist answered, as he opened the door for us.

We walked into an unfurnished room, yet, it was well lit. In the center of the room, there were two men on the floor on their knees, with their arms raised above their heads; tied up with rope that had been thrown over a beam and secured to a pole. They're shirtless, and it seems as if someone has been beating them badly with a whip—the two men having cuts on their chest and faces. They were bleeding profusely from their wounds.

"These are the ones that sold out your father," Emilio said, pointing to the two men who are still on their knees. "They're responsible for the death of your father. That's Angel, and that's Miguel.

"Pedrito walked up to the two badly beaten men: "Who killed my father?" Neither of the two men answered. Pedrito then forcefully kicked Angel in his stomach. "QUIEN?" (WHO?) Pedrito shouts.

"Pedrito—" I say while taking a step forward. I immediately stopped when I felt a hand rest upon my shoulder firmly. I look back to see that it's Emilio.

"Leave him," Emilio commands. I turn to look at Pedrito, who's now violently shaking Miguel's head, grabbing him by his hair as he continues to yell loudly.

"QUIEN FUE? DIME!" (WHO WAS IT? TELL ME) Pedrito asks and shouts. Moments later, Pedrito looks around, still holding Miguel by his hair. He then let's go of Miguel and walks toward Emilio and I.

The guardsman who let us inside is now standing next to Emilio. Pedrito walks up to him, snatches the gun from his waist, cocks it, and runs back to where Angel and Miguel is. I see that Angel and Miguel's eyes are dilated before Pedrito blocks my view of the two men, now standing in front of them.

"Por f-f-f-avor no-no-no-no me maates!" (P-l-e-a-s-e don't kill me!) Angel begs for his life. "Yo no fui quien le mato." (It wasn't me who killed him."

"Entonce fuiste tu, eh?" Pedrito says, turning the gun to Miguel.

"N-O-O-O-O-O-O-O!" Miguel screams.

An excerpt from **GAMES WOMEN PLAY** by
TONY COLLINS
A GHETTOHEAT® PRODUCTION

A woman always sees a man before he sees her. Then, in a blink of an eye, she completely checks out everything him about him from head-to-toe—without him even knowing what the woman is doing. Even faster than her lightening quick assessment of him, she studies very swiftly, all of his surroundings; including any other woman who is interested in him.

Yes, a woman notices every little personal detail about a man. That's right, not one thing about him escapes her laser-like focus. So, as she studies him, at the same time, the woman makes a complete mental list of the number of turn-ons and turn-offs regarding any or all of his personal details. These turn-ons or turn-off may include: details about his personality, his looks, a man's level of personal grooming and cleanliness, body type, clothing, shoes and accessories, financial status, a man's relationship status, and so on.

However, a woman doesn't just stop at this point, the level of merely making a "check list" of superficial observations about a man. She doesn't stop her analysis of a man at the point that most men would end their analysis of a woman. A woman looks beyond the surface of a man's visible details, when she considers whether or not to pursue him. A woman analysis of a man is more complex.

Not only does a woman make a mental check list of all the personal details that a man possess, but also, she notices how well he maintains his personal details. Yet, a woman doesn't stop even at this point in her study of him. She is still not done putting him under her mental microscope. She takes her analysis of him to an even deeper level.

A woman notices if any of his personal details lacking, and she observes which personal details a man should have, but are completely missing. Why does a woman go through all these levels of observation regarding a man's personal details? Well, a woman makes such an in depth study, because she knows that by analyzing the presence, and/or the absence, and/or the condition of a man's personal details, that these three factors raises questions in her mind about him, making the woman go "Hmmm, I wonder

206

why that is?"

Once she begins to ponder, then her naturally-analytical mind, kicks right into high gear. Instantly, a woman starts trying to figure out what's the most probable answer to each of the questions raised in her mind—from studying a man's personal details; putting two-and-two together.

By taking this approach, and backed by a lifetime of observing men, combined with her training from the "Female Mafia", a woman knows that what she can come up with quite a lot of accurate information about a man. Although she may not always be exactly correct with all of her on-the-spot analysis, and "guesstimates" about him, usually a woman is very accurate with most of her breakdown regarding him.

Even more amazing, and usually to a man's complete bewilderment, a woman's reading of him, using his personal details, can be so on point, that she even figures out things about a man that he was purposely trying to conceal.

So, from studying the presence, the absence, or the condition of a man's personal details, and then "guesstimating" the most probable answers to the questions raised by studying them, a woman gets not only a superficial understanding of him, but also, she gets a deeper insight into who this man really is, and what he is really about; at the core of his being, beyond the image that he is presenting to the world.

Therefore, given this scenario, let's follow along as she studies, analyzes, questions, and then figures out, everything about a man without him even knowing what she is doing; all of this taking place in a blink of an eye.

An excerpt from *TANTRUM* by
CHARLES D. ELLISON
A GHETTOHEAT® PRODUCTION

Walking past *Broad Street,* delusions is the anonymous, homeless and dirty dread-headed dark man of no darkness, but the blackness of bad happenings consuming him. It's not time that weathers the man as much as the distance of many endless avenues, nameless streets and missed beats thrown off by skips and fits of gambled fate.

Owns little beyond an empty wallet and a ripped backpack that survives the dogged survivalist terrain of his depressing urban adventure. This is what he does, how he exists, the day-in and day-out of a vagabond walk that never ends. And so, on this day, the man tackles a long stretch of *Broad Street,* tripping over buckled sidewalk when—for no reason because, his life has no reason; worn sneakers from the local shelter suddenly spring a right turn into a gas station.

There's nothing unique about this particular gas station because, it resembles every other gas station in the city that has pumps, broken car vacuums and dingy mini-marts selling junk food, expired condoms and cigarettes behind bulletproof windows.

He then attempts to add a little personality to it, adjusting into street-beggar mode while sticking his hands out: "Excuse me—do you have a *dollar* for a bite to eat?" He poses a very strategic question, because it somehow cracks the irritated faces and gritty *Nicetown* dispositions of people passing him by. A polite question, but it's also fast and pointed enough, yet touching in his acclaimed search for food: *Which is bullshit,* he's thinks, *because there's a methadone clinic only blocks away where I might be able to grip a bottle of Oxycontin to wash the day's sins away.*

Most ignore his requests for random charity; a few are pretty damn nasty about it. But, a good number offer loose change and crumpled dollar bills—a rare few out of compassion; the rest out of guilt or something like that. The man despises the occasional smart-ass who will test his *"bite to eat"* by offering to buy the food instead. Those walks to the carryout across the street waste time, and he gets vicious heartburn from the MSG. But he has little choice but to play it off.

We will call him "Dread". His identity is unknown because it is filed away in abandoned houses, train yards, warehouses and cardboard boxes under bridges. There are the humiliations, of course: the muggings at night; drunken kids looking for a bum fight; he might score nauseating sex from an infected crack-head who requires his scarce dollar for the next fix.

At some point, Dread figured *he* was all worth forgetting. Driver's license; Social Security card; an old photo of a daughter Dread thinks is his—all of that is at the bottom of a brown, polluted *Schuylkill River*. Strangely enough, though, he possesses a library card. The books keep a fraction of sanity maintained and he always brings them back on time.

While at the gas station, Dread stops for a moment to case the scene. It's morning, and the stress of stressed out people are moving about their business quickly, moving briskly in an effort to end the day as soon as they humanly can. They all shower him with petty looks and pitiless stares, as a frigid fall wind blows through *Broad Street.*

The ominous, refitted brick and metal frame of an abandoned clothing factory, rises above the corner of *Broad* and *Lehigh* like a haunted Scottish castle on an urban landscape. Within two years, Dread expects a multi-million dollar condominium park to replace the old factory halls across the street from the gas station. If he doesn't get harassed by the impending police presence in the wake of yuppie emergence on his corner, Dread anticipates new revenue streams from wealthier individuals. He argues this point just yesterday with another lost, dingy soul under the *Ben Franklin Bridge*, while on an extended evening drink binge.

"Them yuppies movin' in? That's loot, son. That's guilty modern professionals tryin' to get a conscience, so they throw money at you." Dread was loquacious that night, lit and limed on a killer pint of rum he snatched from the corner liquor store. All Dread could see was a blurred crescendo of *Camden's* skyline lights dimpling the *Jersey* side of *Delaware,* and the distorted, hamburger meat face of his other homeless friend— who was just as hopeless as Dread was.

"Dread—what you talkin' 'bout? That's called gentrification, my friend. And I will bet that it's not as progressive as you make it sound. It's overpriced condos, rising property taxes and poor folks getting pushed out of homes because of unfair

property assessments," his friend piped on about the evils of outsiders moving into blighted neighborhoods, as if he had personal knowledge about it. Perhaps it was the reason behind his present misfortune.

Dread snorted. Speech slurred. Back slumped. Genitals burning from some unknown STD: *"Seems like people livin' there should've been takin' better care of the hood,"* laughing and spitting spittle of rum. *"Now they want to get vexed because the man then moved in and figured how to make profit and high life off rundown homes."* With an unorganized band of raggedy vagrants and addicts crowding around them to listen in, that evening's conversation carried a political talk show quality to it.

And so, in the meantime, Dread watches his progress arrive: the construction crews banging away, nails hammered, wood split, massive cranes slowly moving unidentifiable objects in mid-air. The noise scrambles the concrete serenity of a *Northtown* morning, transforming it into a cluttered neo-ghetto symphony. Contractors and day laborers with scarred fingers and aging faces, bleed the filth of work that flows into puddles of caked drudgery on stubbed chins. They are like a battalion of ants building out a mound of dirt, but it's a louder, stronger, defiant intensity that rocks cold metallic atmosphere, and stirs stained pigeons into wing-flapping fury.

Angry birds looking for breadcrumbs and cigarette buds flutter about the building's noise in aimless drift. Dread sees glimpses of opportunity in this, but his sanity is long consumed by a defeated soul worn rough. Dread's life's file is heavy from the weight of unkempt locks bearing on the skull. Pacing asphalt amid the alcoholic ads, lottery billboards, and scent of price-gouging fuel, Dread pokes his soul for new answers.

"How can I find work with the hard hats banging away up there," he asks while scanning the organized chaos of construction. *My situation*, Dread continues, *is as dry as that salty stretch of burning funk I can't seem to shake. Damn!* he curses. *That funk of no direction. That funk of regression. That odor of no hope, broken promises and exhausted salutations.*

It is here where the *BANG! CLANK! BANG! CLANK!* of a ground excavator is overheard, blasting the bitter silence of the begging man's introspections.

I am in need of a much-needed break from misery, Dread cries. *I am misery. ...A job sure could reverse it*, he screams back at the excavator, and the God he thinks will hear him.

An excerpt from ***BOY-TOY*** by
DAMON "AMIN" MEADOWS
A GHETTOHEAT® PRODUCTION

Demetrius had just finished watching *Idlewild,* thinking to himself that *Outkast* needed to go back to their original style. "Me and you, yo momma and yo cousin, too," Demetrius then sang the lyrics to *Outkast's* hit single, *"Elevators",* as he made his way to the bathroom to take a shower.

The warm water sprinkling from the multifunctional shower head began to sooth Demetrius' body. He took a quick moment to wash his hair. The *Aveda "Rosemary Mint"* shampoo tingled Demetrius' scalp, as he allowed his fingers to work up a good lather. Demetrius' eyes were closed as he was enjoying the tingly sensation.

Soon after, Demetrius then became suddenly startled by a finger, gently stroking down the center of his muscular back. Demetrius' slightly flinched at the light touch.

Vellicia, he thought, smiling, as Demetrius put his head under the running shower head. He then turned around to face Vellicia. However, when Demetrius opened his eyes, he found Rose, his best friend's mother standing before him; glistening, as the water splashed over her curvaceous nakedness.

"See no evil, hear no evil speak no evil," lightly escaped Rose's lips, before she kissed Demetrius passionately, making it evident that she'd longed for the awaited moment.

Demetrius was blown away. He tried hard to resist but, Rose's soft, manicured hands had began stroking his thick manhood. Within seconds, Demetrius was erect—hard as a rock. He then wrapped his strong arms around the seductress, grabbing Rose's soft, plump ass with both hands, before lifting Rose off of her feet, placing her back against the smooth marble tiles.

Demetrius became stunned when Rose instinctively grabbed his right hand, and guided him to her throbbing pussy to finger Rose from behind; as Rose then wrapped her long legs around Demetrius' waist. He couldn't believe what was happening, but its inconceivability only added to Demetrius' desire, as he then slowly buried his big dick deep into the depths of Rose's wetness.

"A-h-h-h," Rose moaned lightly under her breath, trying

not to awaken the rest of the house with her lustful cries. The warm water streaming from the shower head had intensified Rose and Demetrius' pleasures, as the water massaged their naked bodies.

Rose's hands playfully trickled up-and-down Demetrius' muscular back, as he pumped his massive penis inside of her tight soaking slit. Rose then threw her legs around Demetrius' back, waving them about, loving the way his meat rubbed against her throbbing clit, each time Demetrius had thrust himself inside Rose's hot canal.

"M-m-m-m-m-m," Rose murmured, biting her bottom lip while tightening her vaginal walls; Rose contracted her inner muscles, as she steadily squeezed Demetrius' dick inside of her pleasurable pink passage.

Seeing Rose's body quiver, Demetrius then realized that she was about to reached her peak, as Rose's body language spoke directly to him. Demetrius then began to thrust harder and faster inside of her, powerfully pounding his pipe inside of Rose.

Momentarily changing the pace and rhythm, Demetrius rested the side of his face against her soft, silky shoulder, as he then gyrated inside of Rose in a slow, circular motion. Demetrius flexed his ass cheeks, as he throbbed and rotated his huge penis inside of her wet pussy.

The pleasure alone of Demetrius' lovemaking had sent Rose to ecstasy, a feeling that Rose didn't want to end. The passionate sensation felt so great to her, that Rose couldn't believe what she was experiencing. But, instead of not believing what was happening, the realization of how well her young son's best friend was fucking her had immediately set in.

Holding on tightly to Demetrius, as Rose tossed her head back, allowing the water to mix with the joyful tears that streamed down her face, Rose gyrated her hips faster on top of Demetrius, as she felt his body begin to jerk uncontrollably, as Demetrius spewed his hot semen into Rose's love tunnel.

An excerpt from *SKATE ON!* by
HICKSON
A GHETTOHEAT® PRODUCTION

Quickly exiting the 155th Street train station on *Eighth Avenue,* Shani, walking with her head held down low, decided to cross the street and walk parallel to the *Polo Grounds;* not chancing bumping into her parents. As she approached the corner, Shani contemplated crossing over to *Blimpie's* before walking down the block to the skating rink. She craved for a *Blimpie Burger* with cheese hero, but immediately changed her mind; fearing of ruining the outfit Keisha gave her.

Shani then headed towards *The Rooftop*, feeling overly anxious to meet with her two friends. As she walked down the dark and eerie block, Mo-Mo crept up behind Shani and proceeded to put her in a headlock; throwing Shani off-guard.

"GET OFF OF ME!" Shani pleaded as she squirmed, trying to break free. Already holding Shani with a firm grip, Mo-Mo applied more pressure around her neck.

Trying to defend herself the best way she knew how, Shani reached behind for Mo-Mo's eyes and attempted to scratch her face. Mo-Mo pushed her forward and laughed.

"Yeah, *bitch,* whachu gon' do?" Mo-Mo teased. "SIKE!" Startled, Shani turned around with a surprised expression on her face.

"Mo-Mo, why are you always *playing* so much? You almost scared me half-to-death!" Shani said while panting heavily, trying hard to catch her breath.

Mo-Mo continued to laugh, "Yo, I had ya heart! You almost *shitted* on yaself! I could've put ya ass to sleep, Bee!"

"Mo-Mo, please stop swearing so much," Shani replied, as she smiled and reached out to hug Mo-Mo. Mo-Mo then teasingly tugged at the plunging neckline of Shani's leotard, pulling it down to reveal more of Shani's cleavage.

"Since when you started dressin' like a lil' hoe?"

Shani, quickly removing Mo-Mo's hand from her breasts, became self-conscious of what she was wearing.

"I knew I shouldn't have put this on. Keisha made me wear this. Do I *really* look sleazy?"

Mo-Mo frowned. "Whah? Shani, stop *buggin'!* You look

aiiight. I'm just not used to seein' you dressin' all *sexy* and shit."

Shani then looked towards *Eighth Avenue* to see if Keisha was nearby.

"Mo-Mo, where's Keisha? I thought you two were coming to *The Rooftop* together."

Mo-Mo then pointed across the street, as she loudly chewed and popped on her apple flavored *Super Bubble* gum.

"Yo, see that black *Toyota Corolla* double-parked by *The Rucker?* She in there talkin' to some Dominican *nigga* named, Diego we met earlier. We made that *fool* take us to *Ling Fung Chinese Restaurant* on Broadway. Keisha jerked him for a plate of Lobster Cantonese—I got chicken wings and pork-fried rice."

Shani shook her head and chuckled, "You two are always scheming on some guy."

"And you *know* it! A *bitch* gotta eat, right?!" Mo-Mo asked, before blowing a huge bubble with her gum, playfully plucking Shani on her forehead.

Mo-Mo was a belligerent, lowly-educated, hardcore ghetto-girl who was extremely violent and wild. Known for her southpaw boxing skill and powerful knockout punches, she'd often amused herself by fighting other peoples' battles on the block for sport. That's how Mo-Mo met Shani.

Last January, Sheneeda and Jaiwockateema tried to rob Shani of her *Bonsoir* "B" bag near Building 1. Mo-Mo observed what has happening and had rescued Shani, feverishly pounding both girls over their heads with her glass *Kabangers*.

She didn't even know Shani at the time, but fought for her as if they were childhood cronies. Since then, the two have become close friends—Mo-Mo admiring Shani's intelligence, innocence and sincerity.

In addition to her volatile temper, ill manners and street-bitch antics, Mo-Mo was rough around the edges—literally and figuratively. Eighteen-years-old and having dark, rich, coffee-colored skin, Mo-Mo's complexion was beautiful, even with suffering from the mild case of eczema on her hands—and with her face, full of blemishes and bumps from the excessive fighting, junk food and sodas she'd habitually drank.

Bearing a small scar on her left cheek from being sliced with a box cutter, Mo-Mo proudly endured her battle mark. *"The Deceptinettes"*, a female gang who jumped Mo-Mo inside of *Park West High School's* girls' locker room last year, physically attacked her. Mo-Mo took on the dangerous crew of girls all by herself, winning the brutal brawl, due to her knowing how to fight hard and dirty.

With deep brown eyes, full lips and high cheekbones, she highly resembled an African queen. Mo-Mo wasn't bad looking, she just didn't take care of herself; nor was she ever taught how. Because of this, Mo-Mo was often forsaken for her ignorance by most.

Awkwardly standing knock-kneed and pigeon-toed at five-foot-seven, big boned with an hourglass figure, Mo-Mo was a brick house! Thick and curvaceous with a body that wouldn't quit, she had ample sized forty-two D breasts, shifting wide hips, big legs, with well-toned thighs. Having the largest ass in Harlem, Mo-Mo's behind was humongous—nicely rounded and firm. It automatically became a sideshow attraction whenever she appeared, as everyone, young and old stared in disbelief; amazed at the shape, fullness and size of Mo-Mo's butt. A man once joked about "spanking" Mo-Mo's rear, claiming that when he'd knocked it…her ass knocked him back!

Her hair length was short, in which Mo-Mo wore individual box braids, braiding it herself; having real, human hair extensions. Often, her braids were sloppy and unkempt, having naps and a fuzzy hairline. Mo-Mo's coarse, natural hair grain never matched the soft and silky texture of her extensions, but she always soaked the ends in a pot of scalding, hot water to achieve a wet-and-wavy look.

Mo-Mo never polished her nails or kept them clean, having dirt underneath them regularly. Rarely shaving the hair from under her armpits or bikini line caused Mo-Mo to have a rank, body odor. Someone even left a package at her apartment door one day, filled with a large can of *Right Guard, Nair* and a bottle of *FDS Feminine Deodorant Spray* with a typewritten note attached. It read: *"Aye, Funkbox, clean ya stank pussy and stop puttin' Buckwheat in a headlock—you nasty bitch!"* Mo-Mo assumed it was either a prank from Sheneeda and Jaiwockateema, or Oscardo—still sulking over Mo-Mo kicking his ass six years ago.

She'd now lived alone in the *Polo Grounds,* due to her mother's untimely death six months ago—dying of sclerosis of the liver from her excessive drinking of hard alcohol. Just days after Mo-Mo's mother's death, she'd received a letter from *Social*

Services, stating that they were aware of her mother's passing, her only legal guardian, and that she would receive a visit from a social worker; one who would be instructed to place Mo-Mo in an all-girls group home in East Harlem.

Mo-Mo had begged her other family members to allow her to live with them, but they refused, not wanting to deal with her nasty disposition, constant fighting and barbaric lifestyle. Nor did they wish to support Mo-Mo emotionally or financially, resulting her to rely on public assistance from the welfare office. At that point, Mo-Mo hadn't any relatives whom she can depend upon—she was on her own and had to grow up fast.

Luckily Mo-Mo's eighteenth birthday had arrived a day before she was accosted in the lobby of her building by a male social worker, having the rude investigator from *Social Services* antagonize her with legal documents; indicating that she was to temporarily be in his custody and taken immediately to the group home.

"SUCK A FAT BABY'S ASS!" was what Mo-Mo yelled at the social worker before defiantly slamming the door in his face.

Failing most of her classes, Mo-Mo barely attended school. She was in the tenth grade, but had belonged in the twelfth. Mo-Mo was still a special education student, now having a six-grader's reading and writing level. Her former teachers passed her in school, being totally unconcerned with Mo-Mo's learning disability. Their goal was to pass as many students as possible, in order to avoid being reprimanded by superiors for failing a large number of students. The school system had quotas to meet and didn't receive the needed funds from the government for the following term—if a large amount of students were held back.

Along with other personal issues, Mo-Mo was hot-in-the-ass, fast and promiscuous, having the temperament of a low-class whore. She was a big-time freak, a sex fiend with an insatiable appetite for men with huge dicks—becoming weak at the knees at the sight of a protruding bulge.

Mo-Mo's self esteem and subsidized income was low, but her sex drive was extremely high, having sex with men for cash while soothing her inner pain. She didn't sell her body for money due to desperation and destitute—Mo-Mo did it for the fun of it.

An excerpt from ***SOME SEXY, ORGASM 1*** by
DRU NOBLE
A GHETTOHEAT® PRODUCTION

BIG BONED

"I need you, Melissa; oh I *love* your body! Let me taste
you, mmmph, let me *love* you—just give me some sexy!" Jezebel
begged while still squeezing the woman's luscious crescents.
Melissa had no hope of resisting this sudden passionate impulse
that flooded her.

She felt Jezebel's grip tighten on her, then a finger slowly
traced between her curvaceous legs. The unexpected jolt of
excitable pleasure caused Melissa to rise on her side, throwing
Jezebel off of her. She palmed between her own thighs, trying to
silence the rest of the roaring waves threatening to overcome her
preciousness.

Jezebel couldn't take her eyes off of Melissa, as she
breathed erratically, while Melissa couldn't help but to stare back
with conflicting desperation. Melissa's hand reached out and
grasped the back of the Native-American woman's neck, as she
pulled Jezebel towards her forcefully.

Their lips touch, melded, then opened. Jezebel's tongue
dove into Melissa's mouth, finding the versatile muscle was eager
to wrestle her own. A groan vibrated down Melissa's throat. Her
hand came up, and two fingers strung like guitar strings on
Jezebel's upturned beady nipple—first playing with it, then
catching Jezebel's hardened nipple between her index and middle
fingers; closing it within tight confines.

Jezebel then straddled Melissa, the two women's hands
meeting, immediately intertwining before their kissing ended.

"I wanted you since I *first* saw you; I've been wet ever
since that moment. You're so *fucking* sexy, Melissa. I *need* you,
can I have some sexy? Give it to me," Jezebel said in a low,
hushed voice.

The twinkle in her beautiful brown eyes affected Melissa
like an intoxicating elixir. Melissa watched on, as Jezebel took her
captured hand and began to suck on two fingers with her hot,
steamy mouth. Jezebel's checked hollowed, as she continued to

218

close in on Melissa's dainty fingers.

Melissa, voluptuous and womanly, petals became slick, and damp—natural juices now running down towards her rounded rear end.

"I want you, too Jezebel, come get some sexy!" she pledged. Jezebel smiled as Melissa's fingers slid from her mouth, leading them down her body. With her lead, Melissa allowed her hand to enter into Jezebel's bikini. A glimpse of her fine, black pubic hair came into view, as Melissa then felt the lovely grace of Jezebel's vagina.

A soothing hiss breathed out of Jezebel. The moistness of her internal lake coated the fingers that ventures to its intimate space. Melissa then bent her hand so the bikini could come down, and she was grand the delightful vision of where her fingers ventured.

Jezebel's outer labia had opened, as Melissa's fingers split between her middle, like tickling a blooming rose. She tipped her hand up, and used her thumb to peel back the protective skin over Jezebel's engorged clitoris. The pink button revealed itself exclusively, and Melissa used her thumb to caress it; stirring up Jezebel's burning desire.

Melissa had never seen or touched another woman's pearl, but found that she'd loved it completely. Two of her fingers then slipped within Jezebel's hot, oily insides, and the Native-American woman had thrust her hips forward to take all Melissa had to offer.

"You're so *hot* inside; burning up my fingers, baby."

"Just don't stop; *please* don't stop what you're doing," Jezebel instructed. Her hips began to undulate, rocking herself to a sweet bliss. Jezebel rode Melissa's fingers like she would her fiancé's long, pleasure-inducing dick.

Melissa then curled her wet fingers back slightly, as she would if she were touching herself, searching inside for that magical area most women long to discover—the G-spot.

Melissa felt Jezebel's tunnel pulsate, and a shock ran through the humping woman, giving Melissa total satisfaction that she'd found Jezebel's spot; now also realizing that, by her being a woman, she had full advantage to knowing another woman's body, better than any man could.

An excerpt from ***SOME SEXY, ORGASM 2*** by
MIKA MILLER
A GHETTOHEAT® PRODUCTION

Oh God, I think I broke my clitoris...or at least fractured it. After eight months of non-stop intense and dedicated masturbation, my fingers have grown tired, my wrist threatens me with the dull twangs of carpal tunnel and, as of lately, there is no climax in sight. It's as if over the last eight months during my lack of satisfying dick, and therefore, subsequent mounting sexual frustration, I have *masturbated* myself into a physical catastrophe. My clitoris just...died. There's no longer a satisfying crescendo of orgasmic waves rushing through my pelvis. Nothing's happening South of the border. Nothing. Nada. Zilch. Not a *fucking* thing!

I flop my head back into the plushness of my Versailles jacquard-woven comforter with golden hues, and bury my head beneath the 1200 thread count, matte-satin finish bed sheets, and pray to *God* that I haven't destroyed the most powerful sexual organ on my body. I should have seen this coming.

Over the past four weeks, it's become increasingly harder-and-harder for me to reach the point of orgasm. I have *exhausted* my stash of pornographic movies, and just about bored myself to death, trying to rely on the secret sexual fantasies that I keep imbedded in the "freak" quadrant of my brain. My pornographic movies and imaginative sexual illusions, have all become doldrum. I mean, who can get off to the same *shit* night-after-night? Certainly not me.

When those efforts failed, I resorted to mechanical assistance. One evening, like a sex-addicted junkie, and in a complete state-of-desperation, I hopped in my silver, convertible *BMW Z4 Roadster*, drove forty-five minutes down Highway 35, until I saw the three, brightly-beaming red, neon letters that I sought, peering at me from the exit near the movie theater in Pluergerville: "XXX".

I parked my "Beamer" in the back of the ex-rated, adult video store, and in an attempt to be "incog-negro", I flipped the hood of my *Azzuré* tracksuit over my head, hid behind my *Oliver Peoples* "Harlot" sunglasses, and tried to nonchalantly mosey my way inside.

An hour later, after consulting with the bubblegum-popping female sales clerk; dressed in a tartan plaid, pleated ultra-mini skirt, and red, thigh-high patent leather, platform lace-up boots, I left the store with a plethora of sex-toy treasures and erotic devices: personal lubricants, battery vibrators, electric vibrators, G spot stimulators and orgasm books.

I even bought the infamous two-hundred dollar vibrator called *The Rabbit,* that I heard mentioned on *Sex in the City.* I had just partakened in an erotic shopping spree, one that would even cause *Kirk Franklin* to blush.

Needless to say that, after I tried all of my treasures (and sometimes even twice) I was still no closer to an orgasmic experience than before. So, when my orgasms began to steadily decline and weaken, and when it seemed that I had to *work* harder to implode, I blamed it on a lack of…"inspiration".

The "clitoral" truth is that, I had become a woman obsessed. What I needed to do was pump my brakes. I needed to take a sebaticle from my not-so-good vibrations. My "pussy problem" was fast becoming a perplexing conundrum.

TATTOOED TEARS by
BLUE
A GHETTOHEAT® PRODUCTION

COMING SOON